Can't Keep a Bad Bride Down

Also by Miranda Parker

A Good Excuse to Be Bad

Someone Bad and Something Blue

Published by Kensington Publishing Corp.

Can't Keep a Bad Bride Down

MIRANDA PARKER

Kensington Publishing Corp.

http://www.kensingtonbooks.com

DAFINA BOOKS are published by

Kensington Publishing Corp.
119 West 40th Street
New York, NY 10018

All Kensington Titles, Imprints, and Distributed Lines are available at special quantity discounts for bulk purchases for sales promotions, premiums, fund-raising, and educational or institutional use. Special book excerpts or customized printings can also be created to fit specific needs. For details, write or phone the office of the Kensington special sales manager: Kensington Publishing Corp., 119 West 40th Street, New York, NY 10018, attn: Special Sales Department, Phone: 1-800-221-2647.

Dafina and the Dafina logo Reg. U.S. Pat. & TM Off.

ISBN-13: 978-0-7582-5954-7
ISBN-10: 0-7582-5954-9
First Kensington Trade Paperback Edition: July 2013

eISBN-13: 978-0-7582-8919-3
eISBN-10: 0-7582-8919-7
First Kensington Electronic Edition: July 2013

10 9 8 7 6 5 4 3 2

Printed in the United States of America

To Maggie and Suzette—your lives are inspiration infinity, rest in peace.
To my mom, Dorothy, for taking cancer down by the throat
To my dad, David, for teaching me willpower.
And to Selah for all the good in my life.

When lovers pace timidly down through the green colonnades
Of the dim sweet woods, of the dear dark woods,
Of the heavenly woods and glades,
That run to the radiant marginal sand-beach within
The wide sea-marshes of Glynn.

—Sidney Lanier, "The Marshes of Glynn"

Acknowledgments

If this is your first time reading Angel's story, let me first tell you that I'm not as smart/dumb (circle best answer) as you may think. If it weren't for the village that is Miranda Parker, *Can't Keep a Bad Bride Down* would not be in your hands.

So let me acknowledge the truth of what went down getting this book published and those who really help make this work:

Kensington/Dafina Books:
To my editor, Selena James: If there was an award for Most Dedicated Editor, Selena should get it. There were so many challenges going on in my personal life I didn't have the time or energy to get back on track. Thank God for Selena. She emailed me her thoughts on my manuscript and help me to remain focused on the completion of *Can't Keep a Bad Bride Down*. I am very, very grateful to her, and thank her for being so patient with me.

To my book cover designer, Kristine Mills Noble and my book cover photographer, George Kerrigan, thank you for your great work.

Now that I've gotten that out of the way, I need to acknowledge a few people who sacrificed themselves for me while I wrote this novel.

Selah: My lovely daughter, who somehow grew up, while I was writing. I love your sweetness and sass. You teach me more than I teach you.

Mom: This has been a whirlwind year. I thank God you are here with me. When I was exhausted and wanted to ditch Angel and her crazy manhunt, you inspired me. If you could grin and bear it through radiation treatments and biopsies, I could dig in and stop whining. You're also the best direct seller on my planet and keep me on my toes about monthly sales goals. I pray for your continued health and love you!

MeLana: My inspiration for Whitney and my real little sister. You are my ride-or-die chick. When I thought no one would show up to my book signing, not only did you come, but you made my signings look fabulous. Thanks for watching our girl for me.

David: My twin. Ava is definitely not you. LOL. Thank you for getting male readers behind my book. I think I have more men fans than women. You are the best brother.

Eric and Derrick Phillips: Thanks for making my books a hit with firemen. Wonder Twins definitely united. I love you, brothers.

Daddy: Thank you for making sure Angel held her gun properly and planted her feet. It's indeed a blessing to have a former U.S. Marine sharpshooter help me write these books. I love you.

To my Ace: Dr. Natasha B: Thank you for encouraging me to move forward with this writing thing when I was still stuck in who I used to be. Love you and Aria.

To Cathy Blair: Although you're Angel's nonexistent personal assistant, you're my good friend, book buddy, prayer pal, and movie maven. Thanks for watching Selah for me when I had to do a book event, needed to write in peace, needed to know someone cared.

To Daren Gayle: My brother in Spirit. Thank you for being the best booking agent on the planet and treating Selah like the princess she is.

Now this part gets tricky, because if I miss someone, someone may get offended. I tried to name most of you in *Someone Bad and Something Blue* so double check that. However, I want to give special pen up to some people who stood out on helping me through this book:

Rhonda McKnight for being excited and supportive about my books.

Chrystal Dorsey for helping with the manuscript read-through and page proof edits. And for not only being a big fan, but for being a friend.

Tiffany Warren for all things books, comedy, and side eye.

To my International Thriller Writer Family: Jenny Milchman, Allan Leverone, Gary Kriss, and Ethan Cross. Thanks again for adding me to the family.

To my sisters in The Atlanta Georgia Peach Authors: Marissa Monteilh, Dwan Abrams, Electa Rome Parks, Gail McFarland, Jean Holloway, and D.L. Sparks. I'm Peachy and Proud.

To the Literati:

Ella Curry for calling me when I was not well, for telling everyone she knows about Miranda Parker, and for sharing your world with me.

Tashmir Parks for supporting me when only a few people knew my name.

Martin Pratt for calling me late at night and smiling through the phone. My friend.

Tasha Martin and Tee C. Royal for your support.

Myguail Chappel—DeKalb County Public Library, Nyisha Ferguson—Houston Public Library, Linda Jordan—Atlanta Fulton, South Georgia Regional Library, and everyone who provided library system support.

Apologies to those not mentioned.

To the Readers: I sincerely thank you for your continued support.

1

Saturday, 9:00 PM
Tybee Island Wedding Chapel, Tybee Island, Georgia

While at Lana Turner's wedding reception, after the most handsome man in my universe placed the prettiest ring ever seen on my finger, I decided to do something very uncharacteristic of me. I squealed in the octave of a high school cheerleader and said, "Yes."

Justus Morgan lifted me off the floor with his strong arms and then kissed me so sweetly, I almost forgot that the U.S. marshal I had recently kissed was also in the chapel and could very well ruin all this yummy goodness. Although the manhunt was over and I had killed our man, not everything had been resolved. There was still a leak in the marshal's office. But now was not the time to be in bail recovery agent Evangeline Crawford mode.

Now we were on Tybee Island for Lana's wedding at a chapel appropriately called "Tybee Island Wedding Chapel." The chapel looked like something you'd see in a Nicholas Sparks movie. It was nestled between magnolias, oak trees, and other Georgian greenery only seen in this part of the state. The chapel was white, and tonight every post and window was decorated with a deep purple satin ribbon, white lace, and a single magnolia stem. Inside the chapel a lavender color-wash illuminated every dahlia, hydrangea, and mini calla lily and rose centerpiece with just enough sparkle to melt a cold heart. It was elegant, romantic, simple, and breathtaking. I almost felt blessed to be there.

To perform my bridesmaid's duties, I looked like my Southern belle identical twin, the evangelist Ava: caramel skin accented with a rose blush, feline-shaped eyes done up nice, but instead of a sophisticated coif, I sported a pixie haircut. I was a bridesmaid by default (long story) and my younger sister/housemate Whitney was Lana's maid of honor. Mom had been here earlier with my seven-year-old daughter, Bella, but without my not-so-new, yet-absent-lots-lately stepfather. By the end of the ceremony, Bella had been tired, so my mother had taken her back to the cottage. Ava, was back home in Atlanta, more than likely secretly dating my only client, Big Tiger Jones of BT Trusted Bail Bonds. A lot of foolery was going on between them, but none of their issues were as messy as the one lurking in my periphery.

Marshal Maxim West stood inside the chancel of the chapel between the black baby grand piano and the all-male jazz singer quartet. He didn't stand out to the wedding party, because he wore a black tuxedo and matching bow-tie, which was similar to the quartet's uniform. But to me he looked out of place and more handsome than the last time I'd seen him. Although I didn't know him well, save for a stolen kiss, I knew enough to know that dressing like a penguin was not the marshal/my teacher's thing. He was the black-Stetson-hat-blue-jean-cowboy-boots-wearing type. Tonight he looked like a jilted boyfriend, lurking in the shadows.

Justus, my new fiancé, placed me back onto the floor, but I didn't want to come down. It was safer in his arms, because we were immediately mobbed by well-wishers once he let me go.

"You've made me the happiest man in this room tonight—except the groom," he said.

I heard a round of applause from everyone watching except Maxim. He hadn't moved. He didn't clap. I gulped.

Justus lifted my chin up with his hands and surveyed my eyes. "Is everything okay?"

My new fiancé shouldn't have done that. I wasn't any good when he looked me in the eye and in that way. Justus was so handsome, the kind of handsome that girls like me only saw in movies or in men's health magazines. He had this golden brown–colored skin that glowed when he was happy and blazed when he was angry. His bright smile teased my lips. His lips were perfect for smooches and long kisses, and his sultry deep voice calmed me when I had the urge to do something stupid. He had long lashes that made it incredibly hard for me to think about God when he closed his eyes to pray.

Justus prayed often. He was my pastor, and until today that fact didn't bother me at all. The only thing that bothered me was now walking toward us. I had to set things straight with Maxim and assure him that what happened after I shot Biloxi "The Knocker" James was a mistake.

A big, stupid, good-woman-trying-to-let-go-of-her-bad-girl-tendencies kind of mistake.

I turned my attention back to Justus and shook my head. "I'm in shock. That's all."

"I am, too. I didn't think you would say 'yes.' " He smiled.

"I'll say yes every day if you like. . . ." I held his face with both of my hands and leaned forward to try to kiss him.

Then I heard a shriek. I turned toward the sound's direction. It was Whitney running toward us, screaming my name. Her maid of honor dress's train was hoisted over her head, as if it were the Olympic torch. Everyone—even Mom—parted to let her through. I stepped back into Justus. She almost took my breath away when she buried her big head into my chest. I almost toppled over, but Justus kept me steady.

"You two owe your first-born's first name to me," she said, while squeezing me tighter.

I peeled her off of me and pushed her toward Maxim. "And what if he's a boy?"

"Hmm." She scrunched her nose, tightened her lips, and squinted. " 'Whitman' will do."

"Not in this lifetime," I said as I scanned the room. Maxim had disappeared.

"What about 'Whitmore Morgan'? It's my uncle's name. Would you be fine with that, Evangeline?" He nudged me.

I looked at him and blushed. I liked the way he said my name. The thought of having a child with him—coupled with his eyes wandering over my dress—made me feel warm all over. I ran my hand down my nape, to calm my hormones. I didn't think this would be a long engagement.

"Can we talk about babies after we've been married for a while? Thank you," I said and then sat down in the nearest dinner-table chair I saw. The conversation was making my ovaries ache.

"Whatever," Whitney scoffed. "But don't forget. If it wasn't for me, you two wouldn't be a couple."

I nodded. "You wouldn't let me forget it if I tried."

"True. True." She giggled. "Well, at least make me maid of honor."

"Honey, you're maid of honor by default, because Ava is a widow." I chuckled. "She's matron of honor."

"You know what I mean, so stop playing. . . ." Whitney pursed her lips and threw her hands on her hips, then paused. Our little sister was a spitfire unlike Ava and me. "I've had your back since Charlie went overseas, and when Ava wouldn't answer your calls. Just because y'all are back to yin and yang, don't mean throw me to the curb. I earned maid of honor."

Charlie was my best friend. The last time we'd talked, she was planning on coming home soon.

I looked at Justus. "Are you sure you want to be a part of this family?"

He nodded and grinned. "The sooner the better."

I blushed.

"So am I your girl?" Whitney asked.

I winced at her for interrupting us. "Depends on whether or not you complete your maid-of-honor duties for Lana."

She fanned me off with her hand. "The reception is almost over."

"And so that means you need to be helping your bride gather her things for the honeymoon, especially the honeymoon gift from the bridesmaids."

"You got that right. That poor child will leave all our hard work behind and have a sucky honeymoon. She has to blow her new hubby's mind. . . ." Whitney scurried off, although I could still hear her telling us Lana's business.

Justus and I both watched her leave and then laughed. She was a hot, funny mess.

He stepped closer toward me and extended his hand. "Since this is more than likely the last dance of the night, will you do me the honor?"

I laid my hand inside his and allowed him to scoop me up. "With pleasure."

Justus placed his hand in the small of my back and then leaned me down into a slow dip. I giggled, but he didn't laugh. He was observing my lips, then my eyes, waiting for me to say yes to his kiss. I relaxed in his arms, moaned in anticipation of his kiss, and closed my eyes.

He cleared his throat. "I hate to cut in, but . . ."

My nose crinkled. That didn't sound like Justus, but it did sound familiar. I opened one eye. It was Maxim. He had returned from wherever he had run off to. I hissed at him.

2

Saturday, 9:30 PM
Tybee Island Wedding Chapel, Tybee Island, Georgia

"Marshal West, what a surprise," Justus said as he pulled me back up onto my feet.

I was pissed.

Justus let go of me to shake Maxim's hand, while I straightened my dress and asked God to not let him ruin this good thing between me and Justus. Then I repented and prayed the truth. *God, forgive me for putting myself in another jacked-up situation.*

"It's good to see you, Marshal. You look well," Justus said.

"And you look like a man on top of the world. Congratulations to you and your beautiful bride to be." Maxim took Justus's hand into one of those manly man's handshakes. I pursed my lips at *bride to be.* "Now that's the kind of dress you should wear at a party."

Oh no he didn't. Thank goodness my mom had retired for the night—she'd be appalled by this exchange. I tried not to roll my eyes at Maxim, as he referred to that time he'd made me play the decoy for an illegal moonshine distributor. I had worn a metallic blue dress that was short enough to get us in and out of there in record time. I'd thought it was hot; he'd thought it would get me killed. I'm a bail recovery agent. The risk is part of the trade.

"We got our man with that dress, didn't I?" I asked. Sarcasm dripped all over my usually honeyed voice.

He scoffed and turned away.

Last month, Maxim had asked me to be a part of the U.S. Marshals Southeast Regional Fugitive Task Force (SERFTF). My job was to serve as a private investigator, to help them find a wanted hired hit man contracted by heavyweights in the underground moonshine distilling community. During that manhunt, Maxim had gotten shot and I'd kissed him.

I'd thought he was dying. It was a "farewell to heaven" smooch. Nothing personal, but it seemed like he was going to turn that kiss into my private hell. I could kick myself for being so stupid.

A few months ago, the antics of Riddick Avery, owner of A1 Recovery Agents and my peer, competition, and frenemy, sent me on a wild-goose chase that made me question my career choice, my faith, and the love I deserved with Justus. But if I had to come clean to Justus about the kiss, I would face the consequences. I really didn't have a problem putting my big-girl panties on.

"Maxim, I was told just the other day that you were still in the hospital," I said in a tone that appeared nonchalant, yet concerned.

"I got out early," he replied just as nonchalantly. I wanted to cut him.

"More like record time . . ." Justus said. "I'm sure Elaine is ecstatic to see you."

The Honorable Elaine Turner was the bride's mother, a Georgia state senator, and my mentor. I had captured and killed the man who murdered most of her staff, including her aide, Sean Graham. Maxim got shot saving my life.

"Yes, she was glad to see me." He looked at me and grinned.

I saw his eyes asking me, "Are you glad to see me, too?" I looked away.

"I don't want to take up much of your time, but can I speak with the bride to be?"

"Of course you can. While you catch up, I need to chat with the groom before the couple leaves," Justus said.

Justus wrapped his arm around my waist and kissed me on my cheek. It was not the kiss I had hoped for, but it was hot enough to hold me for now. He walked away and left me alone with Maxim.

I reached for my champagne flute and swallowed the last sip, then turned to Maxim. "Before you say anything, I need to get something straight with you."

Maxim furrowed his brow. "Did I do something wrong?"

"No, I did. Isn't it obvious?" I panted. I was beginning to feel anxious. I acted desperate when I felt anxious. I searched the room for Justus.

"No, not that I know of." He rubbed his chin. "The last time I saw you, I was crumpled on the ground and I saw you shoot The Knocker, a man I had been chasing the past two years. If there was anything wrong, it had to start with me. I owe you a debt of gratitude and an apology. I should have said something sooner, but I was embarrassed. A lady bounty hunter took my thunder."

I gasped, stepped back, and studied his eyes. Maxim didn't have a clue what I was talking about. He didn't remember our kiss. I didn't know whether to shout "Hallelujah" or lick my bruised ego for thinking that my itty-bitty smooch had it going on. But there was little time for any of that and

Maxim looked as if he had stood all he could take. Although he wouldn't admit it, he should have stayed in the hospital. He looked exhausted.

"You don't owe me anything, Maxim. If it weren't for me, you wouldn't have gotten shot and Marshal Sanchez wouldn't be dead." I referred to Maxim's right-hand woman, who died during a moonshine explosion. "Apparently, Bill lured me to the swamps to frame me. There's nothing special about that. If anything, I owe you for showing up when you did."

He chuckled. "Let's just call it even."

"I'll accept that." I smiled.

"Now I know that I'm asking under short notice and under awkward circumstances, but I need to ask a favor of you."

I was so relieved that he had forgotten the kiss that I would have signed up for almost anything he asked. "What do you need?"

"I need you to convince Reverend Romance to put off the wedding for a while."

I stared at Maxim so hard my eyes began to ache, but I was fully aware of what was happening around us. The servers were clearing the dinner tables, while the musicians and wedding singers talked of heading to Savannah for a midnight skinny dip. One of the bridesmaids whined and sniffled when she learned her groomsman escort didn't want her phone number. Justus was still away. Thank goodness.

"Are you going to say anything or just look at me?" Maxim asked.

I threw up my hand, to alert him to stop talking. "Before you say another word, let me suggest you choose your words wisely, because I almost forget that you can arrest me for slapping the taste out of your mouth."

He stepped back. "Hold on. Don't jump to conclusions.

I didn't say don't marry the man. I'm just saying don't set an early wedding date."

"Who do you think you are to ask that of me?" I hissed.

"I'm nobody and I'm desperate. What am I saying?" He closed his eyes and paused.

He wasn't acting like the suave and cool Marshal Maxim West that I knew. Something was very wrong.

I touched his shoulder. "Maxim, come over here. Let's sit down and talk."

"I'm sorry, Angel. I'm messing up my words. I don't want you to call off your engagement. No, nothing like that. I need you to do a favor for me and I need it now, so if you were planning to elope within the next month or sooner, then I couldn't use you. And I need you. . . . I need you badly."

His voice held so much desperation I shivered.

"There's something you're not telling me about this favor. Before I would even consider what you ask, I need you to tell me everything."

I felt Justus enter the room, so I turned to confirm for myself. He was walking toward us. Maxim and I were out of time.

"Meet me at DeKalb Police Headquarters in Tucker on Tuesday. I'll tell you what you need to know."

"I can't remember if I have plans for Tuesday."

Maxim glanced at Justus approaching. "Find out and text me. Don't call the office. You know why."

I nodded. "I remember."

During our manhunt, Maxim had revealed to me that he believed there was a mole in his office. After the time I spent with the team, I couldn't believe that any one of them would jeopardize each other. The only person I'd been suspicious of was Deputy Marshal Sanchez, but that was because she disappeared on us when we needed her. It turned out that she was following my hunch. Although I was right, my hunch had gotten her killed and Maxim shot, and revealed another person was involved. I couldn't see or hear the person, but I knew someone else had been out there with us in those swamps. So I understood where his distrust came from, because I had felt the mole breathe down the back of my neck.

Now I could feel Justus behind me. He placed his hand on my shoulder. I looked over it and up at him and smiled.

"The chapel director is almost ready to close this place down. Do you two need more time?"

"No." Maxim grinned. "I don't want to hold up you guys any longer. Again, congratulations."

As Maxim walked off, Justus turned around toward me. "Whatever he just asked you to do, you're going to have to do it with me."

"As nice as that sounds, honey, I doubt he can justify adding another civilian to SERFTF, but don't worry: Maxim is still on sick leave. You have nothing to worry about."
Not until Tuesday, anyway. . . .

3

Usually my day began before dawn, but something about last night made me rest longer. The cares of my world didn't burden me. Even Maxim's cryptic request didn't haunt my dreams. I stretched my arms wide across the bed and smiled. My mind hadn't felt this easy since before my dad died. I was engaged to my never-in-a-million-years crush.

The only reminder that my life wasn't perfect was when the face of my Uncle Pete, my father's brother, flickered through my mind, as I felt the sun's beam across my closed eyelids. Our relationship was strained. However, he had reluctantly helped me and Maxim find our wanted man during last month's manhunt. Yet his wife, my favorite aunt, Aunt Mary hadn't made contact with the family in a while. She hadn't been at home when Sanchez and I paid Uncle Pete a visit. That concerned me and that is what woke me up.

Perhaps if I did that favor for Maxim, he could do a favor for me. I needed him to find my aunt. Peace rushed over me again and I dozed off.

The hotel front office rang me for my nine-o'clock wake-up call. After I thanked them and hung up the phone, I noticed the large blue sapphire and diamond engagement ring resting on my finger. It looked like it had been there all along. I reclined in the bed with excitement and great fear.

"I've done it," I whispered to myself. "I'm marrying him."

Someone tapped on my door, then opened it. I wasn't startled, because it was either Whitney; my daughter, Bella; or Mom. Whitney was a late sleeper, and if Bella was going to wake me up it would have been around seven o'clock, because she wanted breakfast. Before Mom's classic Chanel No. 5 cologne perfumed my bedroom, I knew it was her.

Mom yanked the bed sheets off my body. "How could you still be in bed after all that has happened?"

"After what has happened?" I said, deciding to let Mom bring up the engagement first.

Mom's eyebrow rose high into that place that warned me to remember my place in her world. Yet, Mother's brow wasn't the only thing that caught my attention. I sat up.

My mom, Virginia, was a member of the almost-extinct Georgia Black aristocracy, a lineage of educated and wealthy blacks who changed the political landscape and culture of America for the good during the time of Jim Crow and the Civil Rights Movement. She came from privilege, brought up as a debutante, destined to be the wife of someone prominent. She had exhaled and married three important people. Her newest husband was a retired police chief and she took exceptional care of his money. But she wasn't wearing their wedding band this morning. In fact, she wore no jewelry at all.

"Mom, what's going on?" I asked.

"You tell me." She sat on my bed.

Her usually perfectly coifed golden curls, which framed her heart-shaped face, were pulled back into a banana clip.

She wore no makeup or shades to cover her aged, almond-shaped eyes. Her skin seemed pale, almost white. Although she was wrapped in her fur-trimmed, cream silk bathrobe, Mom barely resembled her doppelgänger, legendary actress Diahann Carroll. This morning she looked like me.

"You don't look like yourself." I placed my palm on her forehead.

She snatched my hand away from her face and then rolled her neck in that way that used to scare me, but now had me in awe. "This is me, Evangeline. I just have never let you see me as I am. There's nothing wrong with me."

I folded my arms over my chest and observed her body language. "Is everything okay between you and El Capitán?" El Capitán was my nickname for my new stepfather. He and Mom had married last year.

"Don't change the subject." She pursed her lips. "You act like getting betrothed to the most gorgeous and godly man of your generation happens every day. I would have shouted through the streets and woke up the island, if I were you."

"Did you do that when you got engaged three times?"

She slapped my thigh. "Now is not the time for sarcasm, dear. We need to get ourselves gorgeous before they return."

I crinkled my nose. "They return? Where are they?"

"Justus, Whitney, and Bella went for a stroll on the beach. You and I are going downstairs to finish off those pancakes and wait for the makeup artist who did Lana and Elaine's faces for the wedding. I've called one of the boutiques in town to bring over a few spring dresses to try."

"Maaaaa, that's too much," I whined. "Justus doesn't care about all that."

"But I do, and I want my baby to look like a princess on the first day of her engagement, and I want to put an engagement announcement in the papers as soon as possible, so we need visuals. I have also arranged for a local photographer to take some shots for the paper."

I tilted my head. "You want me and Justus to take engagement announcement photos today? We're supposed to be leaving here in a few hours."

"I don't mind paying for an extra day for the cottage. There's a spare room Justus could spend tonight in and we'll return back to Atlanta together tomorrow."

"Mom, he took a flight here."

"I'll reimburse him for the ticket." She slapped my leg again. "Goodness, Angel. Don't think you're the only one who knows how to cross your t's and dot your i's. I taught you. Remember."

"Yes, ma'am." I threw my head against the bed headboard. "But I don't want you jumping the gun."

She tightened her robe. "Why?"

"I'm not sure if Justus has shared the news with his family," I said. "Most important, I need to tell Bella."

"Too late for that." Mom leaned back and crossed her legs. "She already knows."

"What?" I stood up and began to pace the floor. "How does she know? Did you tell her?"

"Relax." Mom flipped my questions off with a wave of her hand. "No, I haven't told your daughter that you're getting married; she already knew. And before you go jumping to conclusions, let me warn you not to argue with Justus. He didn't tell her either."

"Then who did?"

Mom pursed her lips again. "I wondered when missing some of those PI certification classes would catch up to you. The only person left is Whitney, honey child. Whitney, your big-mouthed little sister . . ."

She referred to the state's forty-hour private investigation certification class I'd taken a few weeks ago. Ava had offered to pay for the class, as a gift to me. Maxim's uncle, Deacon West, was my instructor. However, I received the bulk of my training in the field with Maxim and his alphabet gang SERFTF during last month's manhunt.

"Whitney . . ." I shook my head. "She can't hold water. Mama, please keep her from telling Ava if it's not too late."

"Of course she can't. I think that's why she hasn't taken the bar exam yet. She knows that she must grow up quickly and keep her mouth closed."

"No, that's not it." I shook my head. "She's afraid to fail."

Mom's eyes widened. "That's ridiculous."

"No, it's not. Can you imagine the pressure she has put on herself, trying to please us? She definitely doesn't want to disappoint you, not because she knows you'll never let her hear the end of it, but because she thinks she failed you years ago when you sent her to me."

"I didn't send her to you; she was grown and still in college when she left. But she wanted to do things that I didn't approve of in my house, I don't care how old she was. If that's what you're referring to."

"I'm not referring to anything. I'm telling you what I know." I paused. "Since Whitney came into the world, she's been playing backup singer to me and Ava's performances. Passing the bar and becoming a lawyer takes Whitney out of the shadows. She'll finally get her own stage, but she hasn't had the practice. If it's anyone's fault, it's Ava's and mine, especially mine."

"So what do you suggest you do?"

I chuckled at how quickly she gave this task to me. "Give her wings before my wedding. I have important friends who owe me favors. Perhaps one of them can give her a legal eagle job she would be proud of."

I thought of Elaine. Since my fugitive murdered most of

her staff, she should have an opening. If she couldn't place Whitney, she could give her a great recommendation. And there was Maxim. I was sure he could pull some strings, or else I wouldn't consider his new offer.

Mom reached over and kissed my cheek and gave me a great hug. "You have really grown into a wonderful woman. I'm so proud of you."

"Let's just skip the pancakes, because I think you just gave me a toothache," I said.

Mom stood up. "I'll tell you what. I'll bring the pancakes upstairs so we both can wash up before everyone returns."

"Mom, please be sure to ask Justus about his plans for today. He does have a church to minister over. He may not have the time to afford an extra day here."

"Look at you sounding like a pastor's wife." Mom smiled and then began to tear up. "I knew it was in you. Your father would be so proud."

I smiled dryly as she scurried out of the room. Then I plopped back onto the bed. I wanted to marry Justus, but I still wasn't sure about marrying the church.

I shrugged the thought off and reached for my phone. I needed to call Maxim before Mom returned to my room.

He answered on the first ring.

"Got second thoughts already?" he asked.

I imagined his signature smirk on the other end of this conversation.

"Second thoughts about your favor or second thoughts about calling you?"

"You know what I'm talking about: meeting me on Tuesday."

I chided myself for thinking the worst of Maxim again.

"But if you have second thoughts about marrying Reverend Romance, I can understand."

"What do you think you understand?"

"I'm a single parent, too, remember. You're afraid about whether you're making the right decision for your entire family. It's not just your wants and needs in play here."

My neck felt warm. I tried to cool it off with a wave of my hand. "Something like that."

"See. I told you I understood. We're more alike than I would like to admit. Don't you think?"

"I don't know what you're talking about and that's not why I called."

"Very well." He chuckled. "Has anyone ever told you that your accent changes, depending upon whom you're talking to? I know it's human nature to do so, but wow . . . last month when we stopped over in your hometown to chat with your uncle, your accent dropped low and your diction sped up. The way you threatened your Uncle Pete was impressive; that drawl was sexy. And now you have a whiff of old Georgia money in your voice. I assume your mom is somewhere around. It would explain why you sound so controlling."

My cheeks burned with embarrassment as he nailed me to a T. I didn't like feeling this exposed, so I decided to end the conversation.

"On second thought, let's talk on Tuesday as planned."

"What? Come on, Angel. It was just a little ribbing. You know me. No harm done. I'm glad you called. I'm actually about to get on Bull River Bridge heading to Savannah and this water is getting to me. I don't want to get seasick."

"I would like to help, but I do need to go. I have to get ready to take our engagement photos."

Silence. More silence.

"Maxim . . ." I whispered.

"I'm here. I thought you had to go."

"I do, but then I didn't hear you. I need to ask you for a

favor. I need you to check in on my Aunt Mary before you head back to Atlanta. I need to know if she's all right."

"But she's in Valdosta. That's about four hours southwest of this bridge, to be exact."

"I didn't mean drive there, but ask your LE buddies if they've heard anything. Uncle Pete doesn't allow her to answer the phone, so I don't know . . ."

"Fine. See you on Tuesday." Then he hung up.

I looked at the phone, as if I was surprised by Maxim's abrupt end to the conversation, then I put it back in my purse.

After I showered and put on fresh clothes, someone knocked on the door. I assumed it was Mom with my breakfast. I patted my cheeks with my hands to pull myself together, but there was a rumble in the pit of my stomach that didn't sit well with me. It wasn't hunger either.

"Come in," I said.

The person cracked the door open. "It's Maxim. Your mom sent me up."

I clutched my tummy and turned around. "I thought you were driving up a bridge."

"Me, too." He glanced at me but wouldn't look me in the eye without bouncing his eyes back to the ground within seconds.

Something big was going on. I thought about what it could be, then gasped.

"It's about Aunt Mary, isn't it? Is she dead?" I asked, wondering if that's why she hadn't been heard from.

He shook his head. "Worse."

My leg twitched. My heart raced. I tried to stand up, but plopped back on my seat. "Worse, how?!"

4

Aunt Mary sat handcuffed to a small, bluish gray prefabricated wall, seated in a silver conference chair. Her free hand lay shaking on a plain wooden table, but her head was held high. Her mouth pinched tight as a drum. She wore a lavender seersucker house robe, black Hunter galoshes, and pink foam rollers in her hair. Why? I had no clue. And the whites of her eyes were the color of blood orange and her legs trembled.

According to the Valdosta Police detective, Lowndes County sheriff deputies had found Uncle Pete dead in his den sometime early this morning in Lake Park. The ME suggested that he drank a contaminated stash of fig chacha. It shut down every organ in his body and apparently, Aunt Mary's mouth. He had been dead in the house for days; Aunt Mary claimed to have been staying down the street at one of her bunko buddies' homes. The buddy confirmed her alibi, but the cops weren't letting her off the hook that easy.

Valdosta Police was investigating a suspicious death of a woman who died of a similar brew earlier in the week. Now they thought the two cases were linked and didn't believe that Aunt Mary knew nothing of Uncle Pete's moonshine and Mary Jane distribution enterprises. They wanted to know where he purchased the chacha and who he was working with, else she might be charged with drug possession and intent to sell.

Illegal alcohol and other depressants carry a one- to five-year prison sentence. However, there was so much crap on that property, who knew how many counts of that charge they would pin on her? Each count would carry a sentence. The sheriff's deputies transported her to Valdosta Police Headquarters for further questioning.

By the way Aunt Mary dressed, it didn't take a rocket scientist to realize that she couldn't spend a day in a women's correctional facility. I had to get those charges dropped, which meant I had to ditch Mom's engagement photos plan and come here with Maxim. But we weren't alone.

"How did you get the information on your aunt's arrest so fast?" Justus asked.

Justus had tagged along with us. Like he'd said before, I wasn't going anywhere with Maxim without him and he meant it. A slim, tall, and brown-haired detective chatted with Maxim just inside the threshold of the room Aunt Mary sat in. Justus and I stood a few cubicles back, definitely not within earshot, because we weren't allowed to come any closer to the interrogation room. It didn't matter to me because I could read lips.

Bail recovery agents never got this kind of access, because we had no reason to be in there. However, Maxim's marshal's clout coupled with Justus's minister badge opened doors I wished I could have had opened during my days as a journalist at the *Atlanta Sentinel*.

"I woke up this morning with Uncle Pete and Aunt Mary on my mind, so when Maxim called, I asked him to check on Aunt Mary for me. He called the sheriff's office and they told him what happened."

Justus frowned. "Maxim called you this morning?"

"Yeah. He was on his way to Savannah and became sleepy, so he needed someone to talk to, to stay awake."

"Wow. He was that far away and came back to pick us up? I didn't know that. I need to thank him. That was very nice."

"No need. Maxim drives about 100 miles an hour, as you noticed when he drove us to Valdosta. It wasn't that far, and he owed me for saving his life."

Justus chuckled. "Way to call in a favor."

"I needed him to come with us to straighten this out, because we made a slight deal with Uncle Pete during the manhunt. He wouldn't be arrested for helping us. But now that he's dead . . ."

"Aunt Mary is fair game," Justus whispered.

"Exactly." I scanned the department. It was mostly prefabricated walls, more corporate than small-town jail. Dad's hometown had grown and so had the drug trade.

"It's a good thing you trust your gut," he said. His words shook me out of my daydream.

"I'm not too sure about that," I mumbled. "I wish I could have thought about them before Uncle Pete took that fatal swig."

"From what you've told us, his unfortunate end seemed imminent."

I nodded. "Maybe . . . but as much as I despised Uncle Pete, I loved him. I didn't want him dead. Not like that. Contaminated moonshine? After all these years, he couldn't sniff out the rot?"

"Angel, his bad choices caught up with him. His experience didn't matter. At a certain point the universe pays us back on our investments. He invested in creating and drinking illegal alcohol and the payoff is eventual organ damage and death." He sighed. "I'm sorry, Angel."

"No need to apologize. But is there anything wrong with me mourning his death?"

"No, of course not. I hope you don't think that I was judging you, because I wasn't. I've been ministering to people so long, sometimes I forget that a life event isn't always a teaching moment." He lowered his head. "My sister has gotten onto me about that, and I stuck my foot in my mouth last year with you. I just . . ."

"You're fine, Justus. I understand what you meant. It made sense, which is good for me, because after Maxim shared the bad news with me this morning, I could barely get it together. I think I kissed Bella, Mom, and Whitney good-bye and packed my things, but I'm not sure if I did. I feel like I'm in a dream."

He took my hand in his. "Well, at least we're in the dream together."

I squeezed his hand and felt grateful, not terrified like I'd been on the drive here. Although the drive was short (thanks to Maxim's need for speed), I'd napped. The memory of Ava holding my brother-in-law's bloody body in her arms last year and the shooting death of Bella's father seven years ago had flooded my mind. I couldn't understand why this was happening again. Had we Crawford women been cursed?

"Actually, Maxim is in this dream with us, and I'm glad he's here. He can straighten this whole mess out for Aunt Mary far better than I can, especially since it was his task force and Uncle Pete was his informant, although I sort of forced him to help us." I turned to Justus. "That doesn't bother you, does it?"

"I don't talk to you about church business, so why should I be included in those matters?"

I cried a little. "Thanks."

While I waited, Whitney had texted me that she, Bella, and Mom had returned home. Bella had school tomorrow, so there was no reason to stay any longer. I had Whitney back to her role as Bella's live-in nanny. Although I promised her I would be home before Bella got out of school tomorrow, it didn't seem fair for my little sister to still pick up my pieces.

"First thing I'm going to do when we get back to Atlanta is find myself a mother's helper. It's time to get Whitney off my roller-coaster ride."

Justus glanced down at me with a wrinkled brow. He was quite a bit taller than me. "Where's this coming from?"

"While we've been waiting, I've been thinking. Lately she's been putting her life on hold for me and I don't want to stand in her way. She should be working at a law office by now."

"She will when the time is right," Justus said.

"I agree, but I think my life has been screwing with her life's clock. She's missing opportunities every time she has to take care of Bella for me, which seems to be a lot lately." I was referring to last month when I was on that manhunt with Maxim. "She needs her own space."

He lifted my chin with his finger. "When I asked you to marry me, I knew what I was getting into. Don't make this decision because you think I won't be comfortable with Whitney living with us. Our home together is Whitney's home, too? She'll have all the space and support she needs."

Justus was too perfect to be real sometimes. I smiled at him. "Our new home?"

"Yes, eventually." He grinned. "You just said yes, so I haven't thought everything out, remember. . . . I want us to start a life together that includes a home we build and furnish together, but let's discuss that later. Right now we need to help your aunt."

"I think it's too late for that. I honestly didn't see this happening. I thought it was going to be the other way around." I lowered my head on Justus's chest. "I thought I was going to be the one butchering Uncle Pete, not Aunt Mary. She wouldn't hurt a mosquito sucking blood from her hand."

"Babe, are you sure you can handle this? I know Uncle Pete was your dad's brother, and I know how much your dad meant to you."

"I'm fine. I mourned for him a long time ago." I straightened my blouse because someone was approaching us.

"Would you like to have a seat in an empty cubicle?" the female officer asked.

"No, I've been in a car for hours. My legs need the stretch," I said.

Justus raised his hand. "Actually, I would like a place to make a few calls. I need to check on the church."

"Yes, go with her," I told him. "I'm sure everyone is wondering where you are." I let go of his hand.

"The empty cubicle is just a few rows over. He won't be far in case you need him," the officer said.

I smiled. "Thank you, but I'm sure our church needs him more. If I get tired of standing here, I'll join him."

Justus kissed me on my cheek and I returned to reading lips.

"Miss Crawford?" The detective inside called my name.

I blinked. "I'm her."

He motioned for me to come toward him. I gulped and walked away from Justus. Once I stood in front of the detective, he shook my hand. He was bald by choice, a white man with green eyes, average height and build, and long brown eyelashes that looked like they were taken from a baby doll and glued onto his face.

Before he could open his mouth, I thought I would beat him to the punch. "Aunt Mary doesn't know I'm here, so I know she didn't ask for me, so . . . are you here to make me leave?"

He blinked. "No. Ma'am, I think you need to have a chat with your aunt."

I stepped back in surprise. "You're allowing me to talk to her?"

"I'm allowing you to keep your aunt from going to jail."

5

"What?" I glanced at Justus and waved him to join us. "You're not arresting her?"

"Ma'am, it doesn't take a can of common sense to know that she was forced into this situation. Excuse my French, but Peter Crawford has been whooping on your aunt for as long as I could walk. She has faded lacerations around her neck that lead me to believe that he tried to strangle her a few weeks ago."

"That explains why I couldn't find her last month when I stopped by." I looked at Maxim. "She was hurt and hiding from him somewhere."

The officer frowned. "She left him?"

I gasped; Maxim stepped forward. "No, she was hiding from her niece, most likely."

The detective nodded. "It's probably a good thing that she did, because from what I've read in the papers about Ms. Crawford here, Pete Crawford's death would have been a different story I'm sure. Well . . . if it was my aunt."

He babbled on. I didn't stop him. Police detectives being

chatty with bail recovery agents were the equivalent of a leprechaun taking you with him to the end of a rainbow. That junk just didn't happen.

"By the way, you might not remember me, but we were in fourth grade together." The officer smiled. "We were both in Mrs. Wetherington's homeroom class."

The detective's abrupt conversation change took me off guard. I studied his face.

"I'm sorry. My memory hasn't quite been the same since I became a mom," I said.

"My wife says the same thing." He chuckled. "Of course, you wouldn't with such a busy life as yourself. I'm honored to have played with you on the playground. You're a hero down here."

I exhaled. This was the first time since I'd worked for the *Atlanta Sentinel* that I'd been complimented by law enforcement. It felt good and not cursed after all.

After I introduced the sheriff to Justus (he had returned), I asked, "So, what do you want me to chat with Aunt Mary about, if she's not being arrested?"

"There's a lot of drug paraphernalia all over that house. Shoot. There is a marijuana farm in the kitchen pantry. Now we have our guys confiscating that stuff, but that house is so full of it we can't let her return to it. Plus she said something that means we'll have to seize it for a while."

I frowned. "Why?"

"She says that your uncle didn't drink the bad shine on purpose, but he was forced. She keeps telling us that some men broke into the house and tried to kill them both, but your uncle saved her life." He put his hands in his khaki pants pockets. "She said he never made or drank bad shine.

She got so cantankerous, I had to cuff her to the wall for her safety."

I'm glad he mentioned the cuffs before I did. If he thought Aunt Mary was combative, he hadn't read all the articles in the press about me. I threw my hands on my waist and sighed.

"Can she be uncuffed now?" Maxim asked.

"Sure thing," the detective said.

"Any evidence to support her claim?" I asked.

"Nope." He squeezed his lips flat and dropped his shoulders. "We combed that property top to bottom. Of course, we uncovered a bounty of weed and moonshine. But there was no sign of forced entry. We found no suspicious tire marks in the yard to suggest that there were visitors. The neighbors said they heard nothing out of the ordinary. All our evidence shows that no one was in that house but Pete and Mary."

"So why would she say that?"

"Angel, I think she's in shock. I have no problem admitting her to South Georgia tonight for observation. She needs to have her neck looked at anyway, but what I'm afraid of is that if she keeps talking like this, we may have to put her in Green Creek or charge her, because of her statement that she knows what her dead husband drinks and how it is made."

I sighed heavily. "Come on now. That sounds crazy."

"Now you get my point," he said.

Green Creek was the mental hospital. After all she had been through, I wouldn't be surprised if she needed some behavioral services. But she didn't need to be a ward of the state in order to receive it. And then to take her words and turn them around just to have a thumb on the situation wasn't fair. They wanted something and whatever it was had to do with me.

"Officer, can I speak to you in private?"

He looked at Maxim and Justus, then nodded. "Yes, it has gotten crowded in this area."

I motioned for him to follow me away from the investigation station to somewhere a few paces down the hall. Justus and Maxim looked at me with confused expressions on their faces. I put my hands in front of my chest, a symbol for them to stand down and mouthed "Be right back."

I followed the detective around the cubicle maze to an empty area of chairs and old computer equipment.

He stepped in front of me. "Now, let's talk."

"Although I didn't remember you, I haven't forgotten my roots and I haven't forgotten some understood rules down here. Cops don't throw folks that look like me and my auntie in Green Creek. They put us in jail. So . . . what do I have to do to change your mind about putting my aunt in jail?"

His cheeks reddened. "That's not what I meant."

"But it is what it is. Right?"

His mouth turned down at the corners. "Sorry, Angel."

"It's okay. I know you're a nice guy stuck in a jacked-up situation."

"You understand my predicament?"

"I'm human, ain't I?" I folded my arms over my chest. "So what do you want?"

"I need two things. One: I'm gonna need you to find my deadbeat brother-in-law before the bounty hunters get him. Two: I need your aunt to tell us where Pete's client list is."

"Before I can even consider your proposal, I have to correct you, sir. We're called 'bail recovery agents' and we don't like the term you used for the reason I may have to decline your offer."

He placed his hands on his waist. "And what is that?"

"I can't hunt for your brother-in-law without an agree-

ment from a bail bondsman in this county and I need a cer-
tificate of surrender from him as well. You see, the reason
why the word 'bounty hunter' doesn't stick is because there
isn't a bounty on his head. There is a warrant for failure to
appear, but I don't get paid for that either. I get paid when I
bring him to said bail bondsman for breach of contract
with said bail bondsman. Now, when will his bail be re-
voked? And why do you think Aunt Mary'll tell me anything?"

"Let's deal with your aunt first, since that seems sim-
pler," he said.

"If it's that simple, then what do you need me for?" I
asked.

"I'm hoping that if she sees you and you talk with her,
give your aunt some comfort . . . I'm sure she's full of guilt,
wives of addicts typically are. Seeing you might be the trick
that will make her come around," he said, then pointed his
chin in the direction of the interrogation room. "Let's get
back to the group before people start asking questions."

"Honey, whenever I'm involved, folks have plenty questions."

He snickered and I stopped myself from laughing with
him. Maxim was right. My accent does change when I need
it to.

"After you." I nodded at him, but I wasn't in total agreement. Why couldn't a Lowndes County sheriff find his
brother-in-law in this sprawled-out land of cotton groves
and hydrangeas?

The detective began walking back to the others. I tugged
his arm before we were too close to them, leaned closer to
him, and whispered, "Not for nothing, but what charge is
your brother-in-law running from?"

"Family violence battery. Aggravated battery. He stabbed

my sister three times before the neighbors pulled him off her. I'm gon' kill him before the recovery agents take him back in."

He continued walking; I stopped and looked at him like he was crazy.

6

"**D**etective, is Green Creek a strong possibility or were you just pulling my leg?" I asked.

From where I stood in the hallway, I could see through the window of the interrogation room and study Aunt Mary's body language. Although we hadn't been close since I had Bella, I remembered enough about her to know her moods and nervous twitches. Her feet were crossed and the front foot tapped the back foot rapidly. Moreover, my knowledge about the psychology of body language further confirmed that she was overwhelmed.

"It is. Like I said before, if I think that she's involved in her husband's death or if she appears to be a danger to herself. Usually we send drug addicts and those who have attempted suicide, but we also take persons of interest who may be traumatized."

"And if that person doesn't give you what you ask?" I scoffed. "Who would take her there, if you recommended it?"

"I can't take her there, but the sheriff's deputy who handles fugitive transport or your marshal buddy here can transport her at our request," he said. "Let me just say that your aunt's a good woman. She was my boy's Sunday School teacher a few years back. We kept her on our prayer list. I think she just needs a little rest and support from her family."

Maxim stepped forward. "So you knew what was happening to her all this time?"

"Everyone knew, but the law doesn't necessarily protect her, now does it?" The officer looked at me and sighed. "I'm dealing with the same thing with my sister."

I empathized with him a little. He didn't have to blackmail me into helping him pull his brother-in-law, but since he had, he didn't sit that well with me anymore. It's a good thing that I didn't bother remembering his name.

"The best consolation from this entire ordeal is that, now that Pete's gone, she can enjoy the rest of her life. If she gets admitted into GC it would be too sad."

"I don't know what to say to her." I turned to Justus. He had joined my side again. "What do you think I should say?"

"Since she's a praying woman, why don't you start there and then let her speak to you."

"Detective, how much time do I have?" I asked.

He checked his watch. "They'll be transporting her to the ER in about fifteen minutes."

"Well, that's good, because I don't think I could pray longer than two minutes."

"Are you charging her?" Maxim asked.

"Not yet, but we do need some medical reports to tell us whether or not she needs behavioral services."

I gasped. "Really?!" He was going to hold my aunt until I found that brother-in-law. I cringed.

"You can do this, Ang. You're going to have to dig deep and be objective. If you let your emotions cloud your perspective, you'll miss the clues to guide her into saying what needs to be said." Maxim rubbed my shoulders. "Relax . . ."

Justus cleared his throat.

I didn't bother to see how Justus responded to that, because it wasn't that kind of rub. He wasn't feeling me up, just relaxing my nerves. Unlike Justus, he had a sixth sense about my ticks.

"I'm good. Thanks."

I left Maxim, Justus, and the vigilante officer out in the hall and walked into the room where my aunt sat.

The cuffs dangled from her wrist like jewelry, but she wasn't the flashy jewelry type. All she wore was a plain gold wedding band on her ring finger and some CZ studs in her ears. As much money as Uncle Pete carried in his pockets, he never respected his wife enough to buy her diamond replacements. He and my father were like yin and yang.

There was definitely a look on Aunt Mary's face that concerned me. Her eyes weren't dilated, but her focus was off. She seemed to have been staring off into the blank, bluish gray wall. I uncuffed her and gave her a plastic cup filled with water from the water cooler near the investigations entrance door.

"Aunt Mary . . ." I said as I sat down beside her.

Her eyes were still bloodshot. Now that I saw her more closely I noticed the tiny line across her neck where Uncle Pete had tried to strangle her. It made me so mad that if he wasn't already dead, I would have saved the undertaker the service and stomped him six feet underground myself. Her hands still shook. Her left knee twitched like mine. Although we weren't blood relatives, I found that similarity comforting.

She looked up at me. For a few seconds she looked as if she didn't know me, then a glint, and a few seconds later her eyes twinkled like I remembered them doing. "Evangeline, is that you?"

Eve-Angel-Eye-N was how she pronounced it. She was the only one I would allow to mispronounce my name. I liked the honey-flavored slow drizzle of it coming off her tongue.

"Yes, ma'am. It's me."

"It's good to see you, baby." She patted my cheek with one of her hands. "But why are you here?"

"I was down the road when I heard what happened. How are you feeling?"

"Did they tell you 'bout your uncle?" Her lower lip quivered. "That fool . . ."

"Yes, ma'am." I sat back in my chair. This conversation didn't seem like a good segue into a prayer. "Did he tell you that I came to see you last month?"

"Yes, he told me. He told me what you said, too. But he didn't listen and now he's dead." She sniffled and then wiped her nose with a hankie that was in her robe pocket. "I left him a few weeks ago because of this foolishness. Did he tell you that, when he let you borrow his truck?"

"He said you weren't home, but he didn't share the details."

"He begged me to come back. Told me that you told him if I wasn't home the next time you came you were going to hurt him, but I didn't go back. I wanted to see what he'd do. . . ." She chuckled and then began wringing her hands. "I used to think Pete wasn't afraid of anyone except your father, and then you grew up and became his spitting image. He might not have showed it, but you kept him peeking out the curtains."

I leaned forward and placed my hands over her shaking hands. "What happened to him, Aunt Mary?"

Her hands stopped shaking and she looked into my eyes. "He didn't mean what he did to my neck. That's what he said. But God got tired of him not meaning to do bad. You know?"

"Yes, ma'am." Tears fell down my face. "Aunt Mary, what happened this morning? There must be more than what you said. Why did you tell the sheriff something different? Why did you say some people were in the house?"

" 'Cause it's true and I was scared. Every time I went to the police about Pete and his predicaments they sent me back. They sent me back for years. What would they do for me now? Blame me? Send me to a women's prison? That's what they do down here? Blame the women and let the crazy men go free?"

I turned around and looked toward the window where I knew they were watching. She had a point. "Aunt Mary, they won't be sending you anywhere but out of here."

Her bloodshot eyes widened. "I'm not in trouble?"

"No, but you won't be able to return home for a while."

She crooked her neck. "And why not?"

"Right now it's an active crime scene. Until they get down to the bottom of what happened, they will turn every corner in there. Who knows how long that will take?"

"They don't have to do all that. I'll tell them what they want to know."

"It's not that cut and dried. Your testimony isn't enough."

"What if I tell that I was in that house at the time Pete died?"

"Are you sure about that?"

"If that's what it takes, then yeah."

"Then that places you at the crime scene when Uncle Pete died and you'll possibly go to jail."

She clapped her hands around her cheeks. "I just want to go home."

"Honey, you haven't been home in weeks."

"Well, now that he's gone, I want to come back. Clean it up and make it look like I always wanted."

"Aunt Mary, you can't go back tonight, if that's what you're thinking. It needs to be cleaned up."

"You don't think I know how to keep a clean house?" She folded her arms over her chest. "Pete told you when you came over that I had gone, so the house didn't look too good when you were there. That's why it looked the way it did."

"No, Auntie. That's not what I'm talking about. I mean after the police complete their work in the house then a special cleaning service has to come and wash the dead out of your house. It's unfit to live in right now."

She frowned. "Who's paying for that?"

"Your insurance, and if they split hairs, I'll pay for the service myself."

"Oh my Lord." She gasped. "What am I gon' do now?"

"Why don't you stay with me for a while?"

She looked up at me with surprise. "Stay where—in the Big City?"

"Just for a little while until you're sick of me or until my wedding." I chuckled.

Her eyes perked up and she smiled. "You getting married, baby?"

"Yes, ma'am, and I want you to be there, but there's a problem."

She blinked. "What problem?"

I touched the paper that sat in front of her on the table. "I need you to tell these people who Uncle Pete was dealing with. I can start you off. The Calhouns up in Amicalola

Falls for one. Just put the names you remember him talking about from time to time."

"And then what will happen when those crazies find out that I was the one who put them in jail?"

"Aunt Mary, another woman died in the city from bad shine. The police could spin it that the information came from her, since she's dead. There are ways to hide who tipped the police off. Trust me. I know."

"Okay, but . . ." She shook her head. "I can't leave. I have to give Pete a proper homegoing service. This will be the first time he's been in a church in twenty years. I can't send him off looking disrespectful."

"Aunt Mary, Ava can help you with that. You'll need her help and she's up in Atlanta, too."

She nodded. "I forgot she's a lady preacher now. Maybe she can deliver the eulogy. Not sure how Reverend Campbell feels about women in his pulpit, though."

"That's not important to Ava. She'll do whatever you want her to do, whatever you need."

"I don't need her money for Pete's burial. I can tell you that. I had enough sense to put plenty of insurance on him when he was younger. Think I need to hire some maids to come over after them crime-scene folks or just bulldoze the place?"

"Good, maybe you can take what's left of the money and get you a new house with a gazebo like you always talked about."

"Don't they have houses like that up there with all of you?"

"What? Now you thinking of selling the place and moving?"

"I could see myself moving up to the Big City. I always wanted to live there before Virginia run off with you girls. Maybe me and your mama could be old friends again and travel the world. She always had good taste. She could help me with my wallpaper, but I won't let her go overboard. She spends way too much." She reached for the papers and signed them. "It might be best you help me for a while."

I turned toward the glass window again and gave the guys two thumbs up. The sheriff smiled, Maxim gave me a wink, but I didn't see Justus. He must have stepped out to check in on his congregation again.

7

Sunday, 6:00 PM
Aunt Mary's, Lake Park, Georgia

Aunt Mary was spending the night at South Georgia Medical Center for treatment of her lacerations and to monitor her anxiety. The psychologist on call was concerned that Uncle Pete's death hadn't quite sunk in yet. He wanted to observe her until the morning. To make matters worse, Aunt Mary had a slight breakdown just after the psych left. She still wanted to go home.

I went through the entire chat again as if she had hit a reset button, then she said, "I need to get something important out of there. A red pill box. What those fools came looking for."

Since the house was an active crime scene, neither Aunt Mary nor I could go back to the house without permission. Yet, to prepare for Uncle Pete's funeral, we needed her safe-deposit box that housed her insurance policy and we needed a powder blue photo album that Aunt Mary said she had good photos of Uncle Pete in. However, I wanted the mysterious red box.

Maxim stood in Aunt Mary's front yard trying to convince a Valdosta CDI to let him retrieve some items for her. Justus and I waited in Maxim's truck.

"So what's the plan exactly?" Justus asked. "You're staying behind to help your fourth-grade police buddy kill his brother-in-law?"

The tone in Justus's voice made me giggle, although what he meant wasn't funny. "He's not going to kill him. I'm sure that's just an exaggeration. That man doesn't want to jeopardize his career. He just wants to be the one to drag his brother-in-law's butt back to jail. And to tell the truth, I don't blame him."

"And when do you plan to do this?"

"Later, once you guys are settled in for the night. He's picking me up and we're going to distract the sister and round him up. Apparently, he is most inebriated on Sundays."

"No way." He jumped in his seat. "There is no way I'm letting you go out in some strange place with a strange man with a badge to pick up a knife-wielding fugitive who doesn't like women."

"I can handle myself, Justus."

"Is that why big, burly, capable men constantly ask you to put yourself in harm's way? To see you handle yourself?"

"No, baby. It's the same reason your phone buzzes all night and day from members of the church. Everybody needs a hero. I'm good in these situations 'cause I look like just a pretty face. I can get my catch to let his guard down."

"They need Jesus. That's what they need," he grumbled.

His voice still held skepticism and doubt in it. It had been like that since we'd left Aunt Mary at the sheriff's department, but now I could hear it loud and clear. He was afraid that I was going to get hurt.

"Justus, a few days ago you said that you had no problem with my life and now we haven't been engaged for a solid twenty-four hours and you're tripping."

"I'm not tripping, woman. This is different."

"The only thing that's different is that you put a ring on my finger, not a ball and chain."

"I put a ring on your finger because I want you and me to have a life together."

"Then share my life with me."

"You're usually running with Tiger or those Bad Boys in Atlanta, not with people you don't know, and definitely not with men more dangerous than the next."

"The guy stabbed his wife. That's not dangerous. That's being a wimp." I scoffed. "I should have brought my knives from home. I could show you some things with a dagger."

"I can't . . ." Justus scooted farther away and mumbled something under his breath.

We sat in silence inside the extra cab of Maxim's truck.

His words knocked the wind out of me. "You can't marry me now?" I asked.

"I didn't say that." He glanced at me. "Where did you get that idea from?"

"Because you just said that you couldn't."

"I meant . . . the conversation was going nowhere, so what was the point of continuing the talking about it when it's obvious that *I can't* win any argument with you."

"This wasn't an argument. It's a kink we need to iron out before we marry. That's why we need premarital counseling."

"Premarital counseling? You're overreacting." He reached over and took my hand in his. "You can't blame me for being overwhelmed by this impromptu recovery assignment. We're supposed to be celebrating our engagement, not this."

"Do you think I planned this? The guy was going to make Aunt Mary pay for Uncle Pete's sins. That wasn't fair."

"And so you'll be the sacrifice instead."

My nose wrinkled. "I don't understand."

"Now *you're* paying the price for your uncle's sins." He looked up. "Baby, you're constantly paying for someone else's troubles. Last year you almost died trying to clean up Ava and Devon's situation. Last month Sean and Rosary's secret love almost got you and Maxim killed. My skin crawls thinking of what could happen to you tonight because of your aunt and uncle."

"You're right. I have a bad habit of solving the wrong people's problems, but it's fulfilling—like when you help a congregation member through a tough time." I sighed. "This is what I mean. We need premarital counseling. I'm already learning something important about myself that needs to be corrected before we marry."

"Angel, what are you talking about? Anyone who thinks that you're supposed to be perfect before you marry is setting themselves up for failure."

"I want to be the best wife I can be for you before I marry you."

He turned toward me, lifted my hand, and kissed it. "Woman, I take you for better or worse."

I smiled. He had me speechless.

"I know I can't convince you to not do this, but I hope you begin to think about how your decisions affect your family, Bella and me."

"I understand. In fact, I thought about my invitation for Aunt Mary to come stay out my home. I texted Ava on the way here and asked her if she could stay with her instead."

Justus sat up straighter. "I thought Aunt Mary was staying with you."

"I did, too, until I realized how tragic this situation is for her and the lack of resources I have to help her. Ava deals with this kind of thing all the time and I have a lot to do to prepare for this wedding."

"Okay. As long as you didn't make this decision because of me," he said.

"You're cute, but not that cute." I tried to twist my engagement ring around my finger.

He caught my hand and lifted it. "Did I get your ring size wrong?"

"No, it's a nervous twitch thing. I'm not used to wearing it."

"Aunt Mary is okay. Why are *you* nervous?" he asked.

"I feel partly to blame." I sighed. "I could have had Uncle Pete arrested last month for all that crap he had in the house. Instead I helped him become an informant and gave him a free pass to hurt her again."

"Don't beat yourself up about this. From what you just said, you couldn't help your uncle if you tried. But you are here for your aunt now and that is enough."

I liked when Justus made my life seem so simple and easy. Maybe if I spent more time with him I could believe it.

"The plan for now," I said, "is Maxim is going to try to pull some items for Aunt Mary and then we're going to check into a hotel. While you guys become best friends, I will be out on a short jump."

"Maybe I should spend the night with your aunt at the hospital. She shouldn't be there alone."

"Aunt Mary has been a ward clerk at the hospital since Ava and I were kids. She has many peers who volunteered to check on her for me. I think everyone is breathing a sigh of relief." I shook my head. "We thought she wouldn't be the one to make it out of that marriage."

"Angel, I want you to know that I'll never lay a hand to you."

I chuckled.

He frowned. "What's so funny?"

"I'm the one in this relationship to be feared, Justus." I turned toward him and caressed his cheek. "I'm the one capable of hurting you."

"I don't believe you, because when you had your chance to break my heart, you said, 'yes.' " He moved closer and kissed me in a way that made me forget that we were making out in front of a crime scene.

Someone tapped the truck's hood. I jerked out of Justus's embrace and blushed.

"I think Maxim saw us," I whispered.

"Good." Justus kissed my neck.

I giggled and took his hand in mine as we watched Maxim slip on overshoes and blue gloves and follow the CDI inside.

8

"**A**s tempting as this situation is, I can't kiss you good night," Justus said as he held me close in his arms.

We stood in the hallway between our adjoining hotel rooms. Maxim and Justus would be roommates for the night, while I would be off in the back woods with a Valdosta police officer.

"I know." I pouted.

He whispered, "Because I'm still a little angry with you about sneaking off with another dude and, the real reason: I'm not going to have the strength to stop kissing you. I want more and it will be harder to resist what I want. I couldn't put you in that position, because I know I can get it if I wanted it."

"Sh . . ." I squeezed him tight. "I'll be so glad when you stop worrying about my virtue. I'm a single mom or have you forgotten?"

"That doesn't mean that I get a pass to not treat you like a woman . . . and you're not a single mom. You're a mom, raising your daughter on your own, but not for long, because you're my fiancée and Bella will be my daughter, too."

"Fine," I grumbled. "I give up."

He kissed my forehead. "Good. Now go get the dead-beat and get back here safe."

"And fall face foreward in my pretty hotel bed," I said.

"That reminds me . . . I know you'll be tired when you return, so I'll check on your aunt in the morning. The doctors can tell me if she can travel with us to Atlanta or if she'll have to stay here. Are there any relatives here that you want me to call, to let them know what has happened?"

"Oh, thank you so much. There are." I wanted to hug him again, but he stepped back. "I will jot the list down and slide it under your door. I hope she can come with us."

"I know, and I want whatever will make you happy."

"Justus Morgan, you're spoiling me. Do you know that?"

"That's what I'm supposed to do." He grinned. "Now go before Maxim disturbs this groove."

A thud hit my gut. It was my guilt again over that kiss that even Maxim couldn't remember. "Justus, I think we need to do some premarital counseling."

He stepped back some more and furrowed his brow. "Wow. We're back to this again?"

"Isn't that what you require everyone at church to do?" I asked.

"Yeah. Yes. Sure." He nodded. "I just thought that I would be the one to bring it up."

"Well, I beat you to the punch."

"Yeah, you did three times today." He tilted his head and lifted his brow. "Is there something you need to tell me?"

"No, yes. I don't know. I don't know what I'm supposed to tell you now that we're engaged. The last time someone asked me, he died, so . . . I have a lot of skeletons in my closet. I don't know if you can deal with the body count."

He rubbed his chin. "Woman, I told you I can take whatever you got."

"There are bad things about me that I wish I could keep from you, but you need to know whom you're marrying."

"I'm marrying my Havah, my Eve. I know who you are. Trust."

I wanted to believe him so badly. I also wanted to tell him about the kiss when he said that, but then I remembered that he was bunking with Maxim for the night. Not an opportune thing to do on my part. Besides, like I said before, Maxim didn't even remember. Perhaps God was giving me a pass in the Sea of Forgetfulness. If only I could let it go.

Justus touched my cheek and knocked me out of my daydreaming, a bad habit of mine. "Are you all right?"

I jumped. "My mind is on strategy mode. I need to figure out the fastest and safest way to pull this guy out."

"So what's the plan exactly?"

I shook my head. "Not sure . . . He texted me before we said good-bye to Aunt Mary at South Georgia. He said that since it's a full moon, his brother-in-law, Jagger, will be hanging with the Sunday Night Fishing crew in some fishing hole near Jennings, Florida."

"He would have a name like Jagger," Justus huffed.

"Yeah, and it explains why my buddy is concerned that his brother-in-law won't get the justice he deserves. Jagger only shows his face on the Florida line, which Valdosta almost sits on. Unfortunately, Jennings is out of this jurisdiction, so he can't pick him up and the recovery agents in this county can't get him, because Florida law doesn't allow a Georgia fugitive recovery agent to chase a guy in their state, who has a case in this one."

"So this guy could continue to roam free because of red tape and state's law."

"Pretty much."

"Are there any bail recovery agents with state licenses in both Florida and Georgia?"

I raised my hand. "Let's just say that I wasn't the apple of Uncle Pete's eye."

"Now I get it." Justus chuckled and shook his head. "Now I get why Tiger, Maxim, and now this VPD officer want you in their back pockets."

"And I want you." I blushed.

He lifted my chin, leaned toward my face, and whispered, "I love you and can't wait to show you how much."

Then he kissed me. He kissed me so soft and tender that when he released me I stumbled into my room and fell face forward on the bed. I was in the middle of a honeymoon dream with Justus when my cell phone rang.

I assumed it was the VPD guy, so I answered. "I'll be downstairs in five."

"Angel, let me be understood. If you ruin this wedding for me, I will kill you."

It was Mom. I scrambled myself up on the bed.

"What did I do?" I asked.

"What you always do: put everyone else first and spite your happiness."

"But Aunt Mary needs my help."

"No, she doesn't. She did a good job helping herself out of that marriage this morning—no offense to your dead uncle. But you have a marriage to prepare for, so I'll spare you the unnecessary drama. Mary's church and I will take care of Peter's funeral arrangements. She'll spend the rest of the week with me. I'll fly you all back to say your good-byes to your uncle on Friday, unless the funeral home can't seem to put him back together by then. If her home isn't ready after the funeral, then she'll stay in my guest house for as long as she needs."

"Mom, Ava had agreed to take care of Aunt Mary."

"Not you?" There was a glint of surprise in her voice.

"No, I was just going to help her through tonight and bring her back to Atlanta with us tomorrow, if the doctor releases her. Ava was going to take her from there."

"Oh well. It's good to see you and your sister working together again."

"So it's all good. Ava and I have it under control."

"It's good, but my plans trumped both of you. Like I said, I'll take care of this. A driver will be pulling up to the hotel in the morning at nine AM for you and Justus. And please wear one of those spring dresses I had packed for you. Let Justus envision you as his bride, not his homeboy."

"Yes, ma'am." I rolled my eyes at the fact that this woman was still telling me what to do as if I were a child, but never said two words to Whitney, who was still young enough to be advised. "What about Maxim?"

"Let that man return to his world, Angel."

"What does that mean?"

"No man would be hanging around and doing favors like this for just a peer. He has feelings for you and you need to cool him off. The drive back to Atlanta or where he was heading to in the first place will give him the time and distance to do that."

"Mom, you have it wrong. Maxim . . . it's strictly professional. He's being helpful because I saved his life."

"If that's the case, then give him his life back." She hung up.

My jaw dropped; I looked at my phone. Was she serious?

The phone buzzed again. Crap! It was time to go. I grabbed my hotel key card, my purse, and my cell phone, and left for downstairs.

The Hilton serves fresh cookies in the lobby just before midnight. Mom's meddling had me famished. The detective could meet me in the lobby. That would be better anyway and I would stash a few cookies for him, too. By the time I made it to the front desk, there were two chocolate chip cookies left. I reached for the one on the left and Maxim reached for the one on the right.

"Since we both don't believe in coincidences, this must mean good-bye." He grinned.

"You make it sound like we did something wrong," I said, as I sat in a floral lounge chair near the fireplace.

"No, nothing like that. Just tying up loose ends. You asked me to check on your aunt. I did that and now it's time we part ways. Doing it over a fresh batch of warm cookies is a nice way to do it. Don't you think?" He placed his cookie on a napkin and looked at me.

"What? Are you leaving tonight?"

"I thought about it, but Reverend Romance begged me to tag along with you and the boy in blue." He grinned and took a bite of his cookie.

My cookie fell out of my hands and landed in my lap. "What? He asked you to do what?"

"He loves you and he did a good thing." Maxim snuggled into the chair. "Besides, I learned long ago not to offend a man of the cloth. So I'm going to don my badge and do you this favor."

"The favor you want to talk to me about on Tuesday . . ."

"Mhmm." He bit another piece of his cookie.

"I hope you brought some galoshes with you. We're going fishing tonight." I pointed at the ones on my feet. "Aunt Mary let me borrow hers."

"I'm glad you gave me an explanation for why you were dressed like one of the swamp people." He grinned. "My boots will do."

"I bet."

"Yeah, I have a few rods in the back of my cab, if you need them."

I frowned. "And why would you have those?"

"After Lana's wedding, I was going to head up to Tybee Island to do some fishing. As a matter of fact, I'm ducking out before dawn, once I know you're back in your room safe. I need to pick up my son before I report back to work. He's in Savannah with his mom for the break."

"You don't talk much about your son. . . ." I bit my cookie. It fell apart in my hands.

"I do, just not with you." He chuckled.

"Well, maybe you will when we see each other Tuesday. If you want, I'll bring Bella. They could play together."

He cleared his throat. "You're trying too hard, Angel."

"Trying?" I shook my head in confusion. "Trying too hard for what?"

"Trying too hard to move forward. I'm not going to be your detour this time. When I asked you to help me, maybe I was being selfish. I don't know. I'm reconsidering whether I should involve you. You're involved in enough."

"What does that mean?"

"It means let's get this guy so that your aunt can spend the rest of her life in peace and you can make Reverend Romance the happiest man on this planet." He tipped his hat to something behind me.

I turned around. The VPD officer stood in the front of the lobby.

"Let me tell him about me joining your posse while you finish your cookie," Maxim said, then stood up and walked away.

The farther away he got; the colder the room felt. It was as if the fireplace didn't roar in front of me and I knew why.

My ego was bruised and I was shamefaced, because he hadn't remembered that kiss and I shouldn't be thinking about it at all. Perhaps I was the one who needed counseling, but I couldn't get it from Justus. I thought of Ava and suddenly my chocolate-chip cookie didn't taste so good.

My phone buzzed again. Maxim's face popped up. I looked up and waved at him and the VPD officer. It was time for me to hunt.

9

Monday, 12:17 AM
The lower 30 Sante Fe River before it bends into the
Suwannee, North Florida and South Georgia

When my dad was alive and before the visions of pretty bad boys flooded my mind, he had taught me the secrets of night fishing. The bigger fish, the trophies (bass, trout) didn't hang in shallow water and they hid from a bright, full moon. They didn't feed until they saw rock and tree shadows. We used earthworms and minnows, any natural thing the bass ate to bait them to the boat. We saw our lines clearly at night. We didn't tip the boat, because we wanted them to think it was a big rock, a home for the food trophy bass fed on. We waited in silence.

Uncle Pete sometimes tagged along and pissed the fish off with his fake wobblers and flashlight on the water, and he chunked shine jugs at whatever moved. He was a first-class butthole. It was hard to mourn a man like that, but I tried. I carried some of his fishing supplies along for the excursion, mainly the blue flake bass slug, some blue spinner lures, and a bucket of catfish. All attracted bass.

Maxim said I was a chameleon. I hoped I looked like the perfect lure to catch this guy.

Tonight we were deep into a river I vaguely remembered, under a warm breeze and a cloudy, quarter moon, searching for a boat and the owner, a person who I'd been told can skin a catfish in under a minute. I clutched one of Uncle Pete's bleach buckets for fishing and dug Aunt Mary's galoshes into the boat's floorboard, as we veered into deeper waters. I hadn't been swimming in a while, either.

"All right, guys. Obviously we won't be jumping him in the water and you won't need to fish. We're going down these waters so that you can pull him out of his watering hole around the bend. It's a nip joint," VPD guy said, as he drove the boat toward the Limestone Spring Belt, which wasn't far from Fargo and Okefenokee Swamp, where we had just busted a motley assortment of moonshine stills.

I couldn't help but look at Maxim when he mentioned "nip joint." My first assignment with Maxim had been to shut down a highline nip joint in Atlanta. To know we were heading to one in swamp country was ironic and scary. What if someone recognized him? What if someone here recognized me?

Maxim tapped VPD officer's shoulder. "It would be best for you if I don't follow you into the nip joints. To ensure my presence doesn't tip your guy off and I don't arrest you for not doing your job."

The VPD guy cleared his throat. "No, your being here is a part of the plan. Someone will spot you and clear that whole place out, but Jagger will be so caught up with Angel here, he won't notice. We have to get his guys from around his perimeter. You're the best bait for that. I have a guy with a truck on the other side of the watering hole so that Angel can drive him back into Lowndes County."

"A guy? No." I shook my head. "If I'm bringing him in, I'd rather Maxim ride along. No offense, but you have us in the middle of sinkhole Georgia in the darkest night of the quarter. I'm a tough girl, but you're asking too much. Besides, who's to say I won't be recognized?"

Maxim sat back and grinned at me. "You're not as dumb as I thought."

"Angel, his kind don't watch the news or read the paper. Looks too much like a family scrapbook. If anything, he'll see your uncle in your eyes, which would be good. Instant vetting for you."

I rolled my eyes. "I hope not."

"Why not?"

"I don't want to be associated with that man and I don't look like him." I looked down at my clothes. "Actually, I don't look good at all to crash a nip joint down by the river."

"What? Why not?"

"Well, look at me. I'm wearing old lady galoshes, my traveling jeans, no makeup, and a college sweat shirt. Nothing sexy about that."

"Honey, you look like the outdoor girl of the week. That's pretty big down with the Sunday night fishing crew."

I shrugged. "If you say so."

"Angel, you know you look good. Now relax," Maxim said.

I could see him staring at me in the dark. I gulped.

A nip joint at the edge of a lake in South Georgia looks like a broken-down shack in the middle of noswampwhere. The night's darkness made the place shimmer against some strewn Christmas lights attached to the outside pillars and the roofs made it appear better than I knew it would had I stumbled upon this hole-in-the-wall in the daytime. We Southern people are very creative. Yet I couldn't, for the life of me, understand the want to travel in twelve-foot fishing boats to the edge of a marsh to trade fish, drink, and tall tales.

We stopped at a bank near a clump of fallen trees to drop The VPD Guy off. A water spout had knocked them down years ago. His buddy with the transport vehicle could be seen above the bank. His dim lights flashed twice, and then darkness.

"We'll be waiting on the other side and will take my boat back, while you drive him to where I can arrest him." He looked over my shoulders to Maxim. "The nip joint is ten minutes around that bend. You gotta float in. They don't like to hear motors."

"Sheriff, you and I are going to have a talk when this is over," Maxim said.

"You got that right," I mumbled.

As we had floated up to the spot, I wondered if the fact that both Maxim and I were black people would offend the Sunday night fishing crew. However, as I studied the picture of Jagger that VPD slipped me before he ran off to the back and saw the people hanging around the hut, I soon realized that I was right at home. This nip joint was for black people. It was a juke joint.

Now his reason for me being here made even more sense. Maxim didn't have to worry about folks not knowing who he was. He had more than likely captured a quarter of the people in the room. It was a good thing I'd decided to bring my Kahr, my Glock, and my stun gun, and that I'd had Maxim lift Uncle Pete's pocketknife when he'd got that box for Aunt Mary. I hoped Maxim was well enough to take care of himself, because we might be entering a trap.

There was no phone service out here, so I couldn't make contact with anyone. I missed saying good night to Bella. Out of all that I had done today, I hadn't done my most important assignment, mother my child, and now I was out in the middle of nowhere living on a wing and a prayer to get back to her. This was definitely my last time doing a favor to save someone else's behind.

I pulled one of my sleeves off a shoulder, reapplied my lipgloss, then picked up Uncle Pete's bucket and made my way inside.

Inside, the place was the size of Bella's dollhouse times two. One wall had two-by-fours hammered into the walls, to serve as shelves to hold the fishermen's brew. Everything on the shelf was either in mason jars, porcelain mugs, plastic jugs, or glass flasks. There was a working light bulb in all four corners and a cement pole in the middle that kept everything from imploding. I was afraid to walk inside, but the mosquitos were so bad around the place I had very little choice.

There didn't seem to be a woman inside or maybe there were a few in one of those dark corners. I wasn't sure if that was good or bad.

However, Jagger Jones was easy to find. He wore corn-row braids that fell past his shoulders and almost into the small of his back; a white, sleeveless, ribbed T-shirt; dark fishing pants; boots; and a gold wedding band on his finger. He was a handsome devil. Even in the dark I could tell that he was a lady-killer, literally. He stood on the other side of the makeshift bar and pointed for me to come over to where he was. Men mumbled and a few women followed me with their eyes as I plodded toward the bar. The place smelled like fish, musk, and ish. Thank God for the holes in the walls.

"Baby doll, do you know where you are?" he asked.

I lifted my bucket and put it onto the bar. "No fins; no gins."

He peered into the bucket. The eight-pound bass that the VPD guy had caught earlier while I waited at the hotel flipped around inside and must have impressed Jagger. His eyes widened and then he laughed.

"We've never seen you before, so how do you know about Sunday night fishing?"

"I was down here for family reunion years ago and remember the place."

He stared at my face for a few seconds, but it felt like hours. "You're one of them Crawfords. Your uncle Pete was found dead this morning. Damn, y'all having the funeral already? That's cold."

My knee twitched. *VPD was right: this fool hasn't read about me in the papers. He's as clueless as he is dumb.*

"No, no, just here to comfort Aunt Mary. She's not taking it so well."

He nodded, then poured me a glass of something clear into a mason jar. "So what you been up to, girl?"

"You know her?" one of the hovering men asked him.

"She's good people. You know them Crawfords got a lot of folks. They don't come here no more, though. Pete done run 'em off, ornery fool. But he's dead now, so I ain't gon' lie. I'm gon' miss that fig chacha, but I ain't missing him, spesh if more relatives come back to town that look like you, baby doll, then I'll mourn with y'all ladies. Shoot. I know how to help you get over your loss." He chuckled with a husky voice.

"But you married, so you can't help me much." I took a sip.

Everyone laughed, while heat shot through my chest. It was apple-pie moonshine. I planted my foot on the barstool to keep from jumping out of my skin.

"Oh, she doesn't get jealous. We're separated. She's where she wants to be and I'm where I want to be tonight." He circled my bare shoulder with his finger. "I'll have her fry your catch for you, if you want."

I bit my lip. "You're bad."

"I'm very bad," he whispered. "But I'll be good to you."

"Stop talking to me like that, because you're drunk and that's not good. You don't want to be drunk running this place all night. You need to mind your p's and q's."

"Look at you. Sounding all concerned about my welfare and ish." He smiled, then poured his flask out on the floor. "I don't mind being sober if I'm coming home with you."

"It's not that . . . uh . . . you remind me a little of Uncle Pete when he was younger."

He stepped back. "I don't know if that's a compliment or a backhanded slap."

"He was handsome back in the day and wasn't much trouble. I like a little trouble." I squinted behind him. "Who's supplying your chacha now, by the way?"

"Not your uncle anymore, that's for sure."

"Well, I'm not into this stuff, but I do know the recipe. Grab my bucket and help me to my boat and I'll tell you how to get it."

"What's your name? I don't walk off with strange, hot women unless I know their names."

I gave him my most devilish grin. "Peaches. Peaches Crawford."

"I like Peaches." He almost stumbled from around the bar.

BINGO.

10

"Angel, you're a natural at this," Maxim said.

VPD Guy, whose name is Ray by the way, brought us back to the hotel as soon as the Clinch County sheriff's deputy who supplied us the transport vehicle took Jagger into custody. Poor guy didn't give me a struggle, more than likely because family battery charges never yielded long sentences. He'd be back out whooping Ray's sister's behind before Christmas. However, the look in Ray's eyes told me that Jagger might not make it to VPD lockup.

Maxim and I sat in the empty hotel lobby. There were no more cookies, but we didn't want to go to our rooms yet. Or at least I didn't.

"That's what Tiger said when I helped him capture my first fugitive." I sat back in the lounge chair. "I was pregnant with Bella then."

"Yeah, I know . . ." His voice trailed off. I could tell he knew a lot more about me than I had told him myself.

He looked up at me and smiled. "I can't let anyone be a part of my task force without a thorough background check."

I nodded. "I do that from time to time for Tiger."

"You should do that for a lot more companies. I told you that you're better than this. I hope Pastor Morgan will help you see that." He stood up. "Good night. See you on Tuesday."

I didn't watch him walk away this time, because I smelled Justus's cologne (bergamot, sandalwood, amber). He was in here somewhere. I didn't move.

"Is there something you need to tell me?" Justus's voice cracked the silence.

"Hey." I pretended to be surprised. "We just got in and I was too tired to go up to my room and my phone's dead. It's been dead since—"

He walked around to where I sat. His eyes were puffy and red from lack of sleep. His head tilted to the right. "What are you talking about? Maxim texted me when you two were on your way back."

I tightened my neck. "Then I don't know. What are you talking about?"

"Your mom called. She said that she was sending us a driver in the morning to bring us back to Valdosta. You didn't say anything to me about it. And why is Maxim staying behind?"

I sighed with relief. "Mom is being Mom. If you need to leave in the morning, by all means let her drive you back to Atlanta. But I'm not leaving until the doctor releases Aunt Mary. That's what I came for." I turned my head up to the ceiling and shook my head. "Maxim had other plans before I dragged him and you into this mess."

"That's what I thought and that's what I told her." He sat beside me. "If your aunt is okay to fly, I can pull some strings and get us home before Bella gets out of school. If not, we'll pile into Maxim's."

I jumped from my seat and into his arms. "You're the best boyfriend in the world."

"I'm your fiancé, not boyfriend." He kissed my forehead. "I know how to take care of the people I love. I can take care of you better than your mom can. I think her call was a test for me to prove it."

I kissed him and held him tighter and didn't respond. Deep in my heart I knew that wasn't a test. Mom was trying her best to remove Maxim and any other distractions from me marrying Justus from my life. But she didn't need to worry. First thing I was going to do once I got back and hugged my daughter was visit Ava for some Good Bride 101 training. The best decision I'd made since having Bella was saying yes to this man.

11

I put my thoughts of Maxim and Aunt Mary on hold to visit my twin, Ava, who was senior pastor of Greater Atlanta Faith Church, one of the largest megachurches in the city. She became the pastor a year and a half ago, after my brother-in-law, Devon, was murdered. It was still hard to believe that Devon was dead.

As I stepped onto the campus, it was even harder to believe he was no longer here. Ava had done a great job of continuing Devon's legacy. The last time I spoke with Devon—some seven years ago—he mentioned that he had a vision to have a religion library that theologians and the community could use. Bulldozers were breaking ground to my right. A sign stood in front of the construction site that stated "future home of The Devon McArthur Library for Christ."

When I walked toward Ava's office a shiver ran down my spine. I had almost been murdered near this spot.

Ava's receptionist smiled when I entered the office lobby. "Morning, Miss Crawford."

"Angel." I stopped her with a wave of my hand and continued walking toward Ava's actual office. "You don't have to be formal with me."

"Yes, ma'am," she said.

I stopped and paused.

"Leave her alone." Ava chuckled. "She's doing her job and doing it well."

I harrumphed. "Tell her to relax on the ma'ams and misses. She's making me feel old."

"You ought to be thankful that you're getting old." Ava threw her hand on her hip and shook her grinning face at me. "Lately all you do is throw yourself into dangerous situations. You should be thankful to be alive."

I raised my ring hand up to my face so she could see. "So then this must be very dangerous."

"Hallelujah!" She squealed, then began to jump and step around like she was the Holy Ghost dancing.

"I'm surprised Whitney or Mom haven't spilled the beans." I giggled. "You better stop playing with God."

"Playing?! Honey, I'm rejoicing. I never thought I would see this day."

"You never thought I would marry? I was engaged to Gabe."

"Not for nothing, and please understand that I am not disrespecting the dead, but any man who would impregnate a woman before he married her, it doesn't seem like his intentions were pure in the first place."

"Have you ever considered that maybe I delayed things?"

"Angel, you're tough, but when it comes to men . . ."

I frowned. "Are you kidding me?"

"No, I'm not. Gabe had you playing hooky from work. Tiger convinced you to leave a promising journalism career to run after convicts. Then the marshal, who was supposed to be helping you get your PI license, took you by the hand and you skipped off into the woods to chase a crazy man."

"Hold on, now. You're mixing things up and taking them out of context."

"Maybe, but there is a thread of truth in there. However . . ." She pointed at me with her index finger and then waved it in the air like she was drawing a huge zero. "Justus has never steered you wrong. He's supportive. He's a praying man. I feel safe when you're with him, because I know that his feet are heading down the safe and right way."

I rolled my eyes. "Come on now, Ava. Don't put Justus on this huge pedestal. It's not fair to him. He doesn't want that."

"Obviously not," she scoffed.

"Seriously, I want you to feel comfortable with him. Don't do that bishop stuff you did with Devon. Please."

I was referring to Ava calling her husband Bishop instead of his first name. She felt she was duty bound to call him by his status; I felt she was peacocking.

"Don't be ridiculous, Angel," she said.

"Don't dismiss me, Ava. I don't like it and I don't like when you do it. It makes me feel like I'm not good enough and I already feel like that, especially now with this ring on my finger." I felt a tear rush down my face. I shook my head. "Why am I being so emotional?"

"Because you're in love and you're afraid. You've always had to be the tough one. I guess that's my fault. . . ." Ava touched my shoulder. "I'm sorry."

She wrapped her arms around me and we hugged. I don't think we hugged when I saved her from that murder wrap or at Devon's homegoing service. As I squeezed her tighter, I felt like a puzzle piece had finally been found.

"Okay . . ." She pulled away slightly. "What's this about you not believing that you're perfect for Justus?"

I nodded. "You're right. I'm not."

"I never said that."

"You might as well have." I stepped back.

"What?" She folded her arms across her chest and stared at me.

I knew that stare. It was our twin-tuition activating.

She sucked her teeth, pursed her lips, and tilted her head. "What have you done?"

I looked around her office for the nearest chair and plopped on it. "I kissed Maxim."

"Help me, Holy Ghost." She gasped.

The tears returned. I grabbed a paper tissue from her disposable hankies box on her tea table. "What's even sadder is that Maxim doesn't remember the kiss. It's like I'm a masochist, a glutton for punishment."

Ava sat beside me. "There is no judgment here, Angel, but I'm curious. Why did you kiss him?"

I shrugged. "Biloxi shot him; I shot Biloxi. I thought Maxim was dying, so I held him. It was dark and smoky. All I could see was him on that ground and I didn't want him to be alone. So I gave him what I thought was a harmless peck on the lips. He kissed me back and I let him."

"I thought you said he didn't remember?"

"He doesn't." I shook my head. "He came to Lana's wedding, then took Justus and me to Valdosta to see about Aunt Mary and treated me like nothing ever happened. I felt embarrassed."

"You sure he wasn't just keeping it to himself because you had just gotten engaged to Justus?"

"I thought about that, but every time we had some alone time together . . . nothing."

"Or the kiss could have been horrible and he doesn't want to hurt your feelings."

I pursed my lips and tilted my head. "Don't go there, okay?"

"I'm just putting all options on the table."

"Take that one off."

Ava sat farther back and placed her hands in her lap. She did that when she was thinking hard and forming a judgment. She could call me what she wanted, because I deserved it.

"If you thought Maxim was dying, he had to be wounded pretty badly. More than likely he was incoherent. He could be telling the truth, which is good for you."

I turned my head toward her. "Why is that good for me?"

"If he doesn't remember it, then you won't have to deal with him bringing it up."

I nodded. "Okay . . . That's it?"

"No. We don't know if that's the case and we may never know. Meanwhile, we need to get to the bottom of what's going on with you."

"That's why I'm here."

"Good." She smiled. "Well, you got me on a good day. Before you showed, I had an appointment cancellation."

"I only have about two hours before I need to get back to Bella. School ends a little after two."

"Oh, don't I know it." She stood up and walked toward her desk to pick up a picture of her two children. "Since Devon's death, I've become more active with Taylor and Lil' D than before. I make it a point to be home when they get home, so don't worry. My days of living in the church are over."

I smiled. "Good for you."

"Tiberius and I have been teaching them how to run kites," she said.

When she mentioned Tiger's true first name, I did everything I could to keep from flipping my wig. I needed help and I had promised myself to stop meddling in everyone's life, but this Tiger thing had weirded me out.

"Tiger has been doing that?" I asked. "Cool."

"Now, enough of that. . . . Before we begin I'm bringing in my ladies to help us."

"Your ladies? The armor-bearers!" I stood up. "Ava, no. I need strict confidence on this matter of Maxim."

"Maxim isn't the issue. You would have kissed Tiger by now, if he wasn't preoccupied with other things. No, honey"—she pulled some papers from her desk and reached for a book off her shelves that stood behind her desk—"this is a soul issue and you've come to the right place. Give me six weeks and by the time I'm done with you, you're going to be the best wife you can be."

"Um . . . Whitney and I'm sure some of my friends in the Ladies Communion and Brunch will want to help me with wedding plans."

"That's bridal stuff." A familiar voice jolted me. I turned around.

It was Mrs. Loretta. She looked just as stoic and busybody in the name of the Lord as she did a year ago when I'd considered her an accomplice in Devon's murder.

"How are you?" I walked toward her and shook her hand.

She pulled me close to her and gave me a hearty hug. I definitely wasn't expecting that.

"Your friends will help you with your bridal stuff. They will make you a beautiful bride, but your sister and we ladies will make you a good wife; more important, the person you want to be."

"And who is that?"

"Someone who can go to sleep at night with peace in her heart."

I hugged her again. "Where have you been all my life?"

She chuckled. "After what you did for Lady Ava, you know I will protect you, too."

My phone began to buzz. I looked down and frowned. "Ladies, I really wish I could stay longer, but I have an emergency."

Ava huffed. "If you're leaving to chase some poor man who's afraid to go to jail, then reconsider and stay."

"No, if it were that simple . . ." I looked up. "It's Detective Salvador Tinsley. He never calls me. "

Mrs. Loretta harrumphed. "Is that the detective who put Ava in jail twice?"

"Now, Mrs. Loretta, if you hadn't been holding out on me, that last arrest wouldn't have happened."

"Amen to that." She nodded reluctantly.

"It must be important, if he's calling you," Ava said.

I shrugged. "I hope not, because I've been thinking about actually taking a vacation. Bella's spring break is coming up."

"Sounds good, but don't forget Wife Boot Camp with us," Ava said.

"Don't worry. I'll make sure she doesn't miss a session." Mrs. Loretta winked.

I rolled my eyes and chuckled. "Lord, have mercy on Justus."

"Amen to that." They laughed as I race-walked out, wondering what Salvador could possibly want from me.

12

Atlanta-area bail recovery agents and local law enforcement weren't strange bedfellows, but they did have a peculiar relationship. Fourteen counties comprise the Atlanta area with six of the larger ones spilling over each other and dipping into the smaller ones. Sometimes an agent would pick up his principal, who had a bond in Gwinnett County, to later learn she had a warrant in DeKalb. So who gets first dibs? Therefore, to work as a bail recovery agent here, you had to also be registered with the Georgia Association of Professional Bondsmen. This ensured that all bail recovery agents would work alongside LEs (law enforcement) and be on the up-and-up.

Back in the day, bail recovery agents got bad reps for excessive force. They blamed LEs for releasing hardened criminals from jail without a bail arrangement. It was a hot-mess situation that both sides still hadn't completely gotten over.

However, my strained relationship with Detective Salvador Tinsley had nothing to do with the old bad blood between recovery agents and sheriffs. Our rift stemmed from my days writing at the *Atlanta Sentinel*. However, we mended fences last year when I investigated my brother-in-law's murder against his wishes. Like I said before, we had a peculiar relationship.

I parked my car and headed toward the front entrance of police headquarters.

Justus called just as I stepped into the lobby. I answered with my hands-free device.

"I was calling to see if you were available to have a late lunch with me," he said.

Since we'd returned to Atlanta on Monday, Justus had been swamped every hour with one church member dilemma after the next. Last night he'd fallen asleep while calling me to say good night. I felt sorry for him, and guilty. A good fiancée would have tried to make today easier for him. I should have brought him lunch instead of him asking me to eat with him. I would do better the next time.

"Babe, I don't know if you can wait for me, because I'm at DeKalb County Police headquarters in Tucker. Why don't you order some takeout for yourself so you can rest a little at the office and tonight I'll hook you up with a home-cooked meal?" I asked.

"I'm not at the office. Actually, I'm near you. I'm at DeKalb Medical Center. Mrs. Marbury is getting ready to go home soon. They are setting up papers for her to have a hospice nurse at her daughter, Carmel's, house. Carmel lives in Tucker."

"My prayers to Mrs. Marbury and her family."

Mrs. Marbury was one of the founders of our Ladies of Sugar Hill Communion and Brunch. She had been sick for a few weeks, but I didn't know her illness was that bad. It didn't feel right for me to ask Justus why she was dying. It didn't feel right for me to ask about anyone's personal life.

"She seems in good spirits about the news. In fact, she

said she was supposed to die years ago when she was pregnant with Carmel. Mrs. Marbury is an exceptional woman."

"Justus, I'm sort of new at this pastor's wife duty thing, but I really like Mrs. Marbury, so tell me what you need me to do."

"Pastor's wife duty thing . . ." He chuckled. "Can we get down the aisle first before we even consider having this kind of discussion?"

"No, seriously. I want to do this right. In fact, before I arrived at police headquarters, I was getting advice from Ava and her armor-bearers. I'm going to make you proud once she's done with me."

"Angel, you don't need to do that. . . ." He sighed. "Let's talk about this later. Call me when you're done. Is someone picking up Bella from school?"

"Yes, my new assistant."

"You hired a real assistant?" He referred to my office assistant, Cathy Blair. She worked mostly at her home, but she did her job well. I worked at my house. Why couldn't she?

"Cathy is real," I said. "No, I hired a mother's helper. Someone to help me around the house and give Whitney a break."

He snickered. "It's not your Aunt Mary, is it?"

"No, it's Whitney."

He laughed.

"Don't laugh. I'm paying her now. That way she doesn't feel like I'm using her."

"Fair enough. Actually, that's good. We can meet at Matthews Cafeteria around two and bring some pizza home from Enzo's."

Matthews Cafeteria and Enzo's Pizza were the choicest and cheapest eats in Tucker. Matthews didn't serve cafeteria food, but good, Southern cooking and Enzo's was an Italian jewel of a pub. Coming out here to see Salvador had perks after all.

I smiled. "I like that."

Before Salvador called me I had heard there were rumors around town of his retirement. But from the urgency in his text message to me it didn't seem like he was slowing down.

Taking a cue from Maxim, I wore my bail recovery agent badge as a belt buckle, but no one paid attention to it or even knew what it was, which was a good thing, since in Georgia we're not supposed to look like law enforcement or risk being jailed. However, the snarls I received from the people waiting in the lobby made me snatch that thing off and put it back in my wallet.

This was probably the best way to go, just in case there was someone in here hiding from me. You would be surprised at how many skips hung around the jail without the police knowing about it. Mostly they had failure-to-appears in other counties, outside this jurisdiction. I hadn't had plans to tag a jumper, but I would if I could.

Salvador's office was in the SVU department. Unlike the popular television show, these sex crimes weren't so intricately planned. Mistress fed up with boyfriend, who won't divorce his wife; pimps kidnapping teen orphans; domestic violence; crimes against children. The list was long and all ended up on Salvador's desk. I hoped this request to see him didn't have anything to do with the last one.

When I walked inside and shut the door, I almost backed into it. Salvador stood in front of his desk, along with Maxim and the late U.S. Deputy Marshal Kalinda Sanchez. For a second I thought I had seen a ghost, but I had never seen a ghost before, so how would I know what I was seeing?

"Cat got your tongue?" Salvador asked.

He still looked very much the silver fox with a South

American groove. He wore his customary Brooks Brothers pinstripe suit. This one was gray, which made him appear even more debonair. His matching gray fedora hat rested on the top of his coat rack.

Maxim stood up. "I hope not."

He wore his blue marshal's bomber jacket, blue jeans, and his badge as a belt buckle. He didn't wear the hat, but a blue skull cap. It was a new look for him and it fitted him very well.

However, despite the handsome men fashion in this room, I couldn't stop staring at the woman. Lieutenant Marshal Sanchez had died last month; I still felt at fault. I hugged the wall. "Maxim, what's going on here? Who is that?"

The woman looked at Maxim and smiled. "I knew she would react this way."

"You knew what?" I looked at Maxim and Salvador, a little too weirded out to look at the ghost of my old swamp running buddy again.

"Angel, she made it after all. Sanchez didn't die."

"Stop." My head began to swim. "April Fool's Day was a few weeks back, so stop with this foolishness."

"Angel, I wouldn't have called you here if this was a joke," Salvador said. "Come over here and sit down, because we don't have much time."

"Sanchez, you're really alive?" I walked slowly toward her.

"In the flesh." She smiled, then shook my hand. "Congratulations on the engagement."

I yanked her hand and pulled her into a hug.

"Oh my word!" I squealed and squeezed her tighter after every squeeze.

She wiggled from under my embrace. "Are you trying to squeeze me to death?"

"No, just excited." My heart raced and I felt light headed, so I sat down in a burgundy wing chair near Salvador's desk. "But you died in the swamps. I was there."

My mind quickly recalled the events and conversations that happened the day of Sanchez's supposed death. Every memory had the same result. Sanchez had died in a moonshine still explosion near the Okefenokee Swamp. Her charred clothes were used as evidence to buttress that conclusion.

"I made myself look dead when I heard The Knocker coming," she said. "Although I carefully parked your Uncle Pete's truck on the other side of the highway about a half mile away from the stills, my gut told me that someone saw me. They must have called The Knocker to get rid of me. . . . I threw my blouse down near one of the stills and worked my best to clog the worm, so that it would blow up. I left the truck and hiked to a safer place. You must have showed up about an hour after the explosion."

"The timing seems right," I said. "But why didn't you come forward after The Knocker was killed?"

"Angel killed Biloxi 'The Knocker' James, by the way," Maxim mumbled.

Sanchez's smile widened. "I knew you were deadlier than you looked."

"Never mind that." I waved the compliment off. "Why didn't you come forward until now?"

"Because I haven't come forward. . . ." She stopped smiling and looked at Maxim. "Not yet anyway."

Salvador stepped forward, addressing me. "And you have to promise us that the truth that Sanchez is alive cannot leave this room. Don't even share that Maxim is no longer on medical leave. This is very important. No one must know she's alive."

"What?" I frowned. "Is that why Dixon isn't here? You don't trust her?"

Salvador's partner, Francine Dixon, was that itch in the middle of my back that was hard to scratch. She had a thing for Justus, and if she wasn't here, she was somewhere plotting a way to steal him from under me the first chance she could get. But other than that, she was a solid police officer. Yet I was curious why she wasn't in on this. Why keep her on the hush?

"I know what you're thinking and why." Salvador winked. His Peruvian accent made his words sound like small rolling thunder during an afternoon spring rain shower, easy on the ears. "But you're wrong about Francine. I couldn't work with a partner I didn't trust. She's good."

"She wants my fiancé."

"There's no secret about that." He lowered his head and chuckled. "However . . . Marshals West and Sanchez and I agreed to include only you in this matter."

"What matter? You still haven't told me why we're hiding Sanchez."

Maxim sat down in the opposite chair to my right. "The reason why Sanchez didn't come to the task force after you killed Biloxi was because she ID'd my mole."

During the manhunt we had discovered there was a leak in Maxim's special task force. I had assumed it was Sanchez until she was killed—I had assumed—by Biloxi at the moonshine stills we had also been searching for.

"She did? Who was it?" I asked.

"It was Ty," Sanchez said. Her jaw was tight. She bit her lip. "I still can't believe it."

I gasped. He was such a steady guy. Ty was my buddy. I thought we had a connection.

"Are you sure?"

"Just as sure as I'm alive. He was the one I told where I was heading when I left. Shortly after I got there, Biloxi showed up. By the look of the still, the shine wasn't ready, so there was no reason for him to come out there. In fact, when he came he appeared to be looking for someone, because he had his gun out in plain view. That wasn't a coincidence." She nodded, then shook her head. "What's the world coming to when the good guys are worse than the bad ones?"

"So where have you been all this time?" I asked. "Why did you have us think you were dead?"

"I was long gone when you came to the woods, but I was afraid to go back to our mobile station and the B and B. I texted Marshal West to let him know where I was, but he didn't respond."

"Because I was shot," Maxim said. He looked like a man filled with guilt.

"Right. I didn't know that West was shot, so I waited for contact. I waited in a hotel in Folkston until I saw on the local news what had happened. Ty was standing behind the Charlton County Sheriff during the press conference. Although we've worked together on some projects, he's ATF. I wasn't sure if Ty was acting alone. I didn't trust anyone at that point. I decided to lie low until God gave me a sign."

"But you could have trusted me. Why did you go out alone instead of waiting for me or Maxim?"

"Wait for you? Ha. None of you did that." Maxim harrumphed. "Both of you are the most hardheaded women I've ever met. I told you to stay put."

"But we solved the case, Boss, and Angel popped The Knocker. We did good." Sanchez popped her collar.

I wanted to giggle, but Maxim's eyes were bulging a little. He didn't find this funny one bit. I decided to change the subject.

"So how did you capture Ty?"

"ATF agent Tyrone Davis slipped up trafficking ciga-rettes into my jail," Salvador said. "And that's where Braden Logan comes in."

Salvador took a TV remote from his desk and pointed it at the television in the corner.

13

Tuesday, 1:00 PM
DeKalb County Police Department, Tucker, Georgia

On the tape, Ty sat in a small, white-walled investigation interview room, much like what I had seen at the Lowndes County Sheriff's office when I went to help Aunt Mary. This one was at the U.S. Marshal's office downtown. I had seen it a few months ago before I went on the manhunt with Ty, Sanchez, and Maxim.

Typically bail recovery agents weren't privy to these interviews, so I was very curious why they were sharing this with me. I assumed Ty would not be released on bond, because he was definitely a flight risk and had the means and the skill set to disappear into the world if released. So I wasn't here to bring him in; why was I here?

"Should I be watching this?" I asked.

"Angel, if we didn't want you to know, would you be here?" Maxim asked.

I relaxed my stance and watched. "All right."

Maxim and Ty had sat at opposite ends of the table. Ty's arms were folded across his chest; Maxim had his hands clasped together on top of the table. There was a notepad and two pens on the table beside his black Stetson hat. Ty kept his attention on a spot on the table.

The time stamp on the video read a few days before Lana's reception. I glanced back at Maxim with surprise. This whole thing went down while I was playing bridesmaid and didn't have a clue. Maxim shrugged.

"Pay attention, Angel," Salvador said.

I shut my mouth and watched the video.

Maxim: Brother, let's not do this thing we do with convicts, who dodge and play games with us across this table. You've already told us about your involvement with the fireman and obstructing Sean Graham's case. Let's just lay all the cards on the table, so we can start the rest of our lives.

Ty (head hung low, he begins to shake his head): I was losing my house, man. After all these years putting my life on the line for ATF, I couldn't keep my own house. My bank didn't care about the circumstance and there was a freeze on overtime. Becca threatened to leave and take the kids if I didn't fix things. My back was against the wall.

Maxim: You could have come to me. I could have helped.

Ty (scoffing): Bro, you didn't have 75K hanging around. You had just paid Vanessa to get out of your life and leave Noah with you. I couldn't ask you for anything.

Maxim: You didn't have to ask. I had the money. Whatever you needed.

Ty (sits back): Please don't tell me you're rich and chose to be a marshal for fun.

Maxim (nods): Okay.

Ty (leaning forward): I was joking, but you're not. You're rich? Seriously, dude?

Maxim: This isn't about me. Who were you working for and are you alone in this?

Ty (snickering): I thought we were putting it all on the table.

Maxim (clearing his throat): I belong to a wealthy family. I have not acquired my own wealth yet. Now can you answer my question?

Ty: Sh . . . Now I feel even more stupid.

Maxim: Don't be. No one knows but you. How did you get involved with the Crawfords, Biloxi James, and the illegal moonshine syndicate?

I turned away from the video and glanced at Maxim again and wondered how many secrets this man could keep.

Salvador tapped my shoulder and pointed at the television screen with this finger. "Here's the good part."

Ty: It's not hard to find ways to get your hands dirty in this business. Pawn shops, gun dealers we're investigating, even LEs have approached me about side hustles. I didn't have to look far is all I can say about it.

Maxim: LEs? Are there more on the inside? Tell me.

Ty: Tell you? If I don't mind having my wife and daughters murdered by hit men, then sure, I'll tell you everything you need to know. Look. I knew when I signed on to this that if I got caught I would fall on my sword.

Maxim: We can put your family in custody right now. They'll be safe. You'll be protected.

Ty: WITSEC? And Becca would leave me, as soon as we got new identities. Once she knew what I did, they . . . (He sighs.) She would request that you guys not tell me where she and my babies were. I would lose them.

Maxim: But you're gonna lose them anyway in jail.

Ty: Right now I still have her heart.

Maxim: Until she reads about you in the paper, until she hears the testimony we have on your involvement . . . Your best chance is to work with us and tell your wife, man. She loves you. That I know for sure.

Ty: Is there a way she can't know? (His eyes look so desperate. I felt sorry for him.)

Maxim (shakes his head): Buddy, that's one thing I can't do. Skeletons have no place in a marriage, no matter how hard you try to bury them.

Ty (begins crying): But right now I still have her heart. (He says that again, then bends over in his chair, looking like he's tying his boot, but slumps over, then falls on the floor. Looks like he's having a seizure.)

Maxim: Ty?! (He jumps up and runs toward him.)

The television screen turned to black and white fuzz. Salvador turned the television off.

"Is he dead?" I asked.

"He died before he hit the floor," Maxim said. "Someone on the inside had sent him some poison to take. He must have taken it when he pretended to tie his shoes."

"Someone sent him poison in the federal building?" I asked.

"I didn't give you the location of where we were. More than likely he already had it, in case something like this happened," Maxim answered.

"Are you kidding me?" I asked. "Who does that?"

"Don't act so surprised," Sanchez said. "I'm sure you've witnessed worse in county lockup."

"Sure I have, but this is Ty. It's very sad. He was so nice and in love. . . ." I wiped a tear from my eye and hoped no one saw me when I did it. "He did that for love."

"He made a bad choice and he made an even worse one taking his own life into his hands," Maxim said. I could tell by the gruff edge in his voice that he was still angry.

I turned to Salvador with folded arms over my chest. "So how was Ty's suicide the good part that you wanted me to not miss?"

Salvador frowned. "You didn't catch the clues?"

"Clues?" I rolled my eyes over everyone in the room and winced at them all. "Is this what you brought me here for, to decipher a code from his body language, because you may have to rewind. I stopped paying attention when Maxim revealed he was a secret millionaire."

"So why were you just crying?" Maxim asked.

I wiped my eyes again. "I'm still crying."

Sanchez sucked her teeth. "She's getting married. Maybe she doesn't have the heart for this right now."

"She's fine." Maxim stood up, then looked down at me. He placed his hand on my shoulder. "You're fine. Right?"

I nodded. I wasn't fine. "I just don't know why I need to be here for this. Ty was the mole. Okay. Let's move on. Honestly, I wish I didn't know that, because he was a nice guy. I liked the memory of him that way, not as a dirty, heartbroken agent."

"Your friendship with Ty clouded your perception. Since you missed the clues, let me break it down for you. Ty told Marshal West—in his own way—that he wasn't alone. There is another mole out there," Salvador said.

Sanchez began to pace the short distance between my chair and the door. "And we don't have a clue who it is, which means I have to hide my shadow for another night."

"Don't worry, we'll have you back into the world in time for some serious shoe shopping. But seriously, I don't know if it's ATF, someone from my crew, GBI, sheriffs from any of the counties . . ." Maxim looked at me.

"This task force has members from every branch of law enforcement in the state," he continued. "There could be more. That's why we're meeting at Detective Tinsley's instead of my place. That's why to everyone else Sanchez is dead and I'm still on medical leave. I don't know who to trust outside this room."

"After today, I don't think we should meet here either," Sanchez said. "We don't know if the leak is here at DeKalb and we can't do anything until we have some real hard evidence. Bringing Internal Affairs into this will cause a media firestorm and more unnecessary layoffs. We don't need that."

"Okay . . ." I was still confused. I turned to Maxim. "But I still don't understand. Why are we meeting here? And why are me and Salvador involved?"

"There is a person of interest in this new investigation who has ties with DeKalb County Detention Center and Ty," Maxim said. "I asked Detective Tinsley to pull you in, because both of you have a past working relationship with our person of interest and among yourselves *and* we need a bail recovery agent who works this jurisdiction."

"Okay . . . so I'm not needed as a PI this time?"

"When we picked Ty up he was here at DeKalb County adding commissary on a Braden Logan's account. We later learned that Logan was his brother-in-law."

"Becca's brother?"

"Yep." Maxim nodded. "Upon further investigation we also discovered that Ty transferred a nice lump of change to Braden just before we headed for the swamps. Three days after Ty's suicide, Braden bailed himself out of jail and disappeared. His court date was today; he skipped. No-brainer. But get this: the bond was with Riddick Avery."

I rolled my eyes as soon as I heard the words "Riddick Avery." "Why didn't he bail himself out earlier? Why sit in jail for three more days?"

"We'll ask him once you bring him back." Sanchez smirked.

I shook my head. "I can't do that."

"Angel, don't you remember who Braden Logan is?" Salvador asked.

"Please don't take me around a bush and up the corner to tell me. Just give it to me straight. I have to meet Justus soon. Who is Braden Logan and why should I care?"

"I agree with Angel. Seriously, I don't think she can do this." Sanchez stopped pacing and sat down in the chair that Maxim was sitting in. "No offense, Angel."

"Your slight disdain for me is the reason why I sing, Sanchez." I rolled my eyes. "Do you know I cried for you when Biloxi told me you died in that still explosion?"

She smiled nervously. "Like I said, no offense."

I pursed my lips and looked away from her. "Salvador, you have about two minutes and then I'm out."

"Seven years ago when you reported for the *Atlanta Sentinel,* you uncovered some questionable activities inside some megachurches that operated nonprofit foundations. Your source led you to Braden Logan, a CPA who specialized in setting up nonprofits for churches."

My source? They referred to the last investigative journalism piece I worked on before I chose early retirement from the *Sentinel.* They were also referring to Gabriel Hwang, my source in that case, who was also my first fiancé and Bella's dad. I was getting tired of Salvador's name-dropping when I was trying so hard to move past the memory of Gabe.

"No!" I stumbled up out of the chair. "Don't you dare bring Gabe into this."

"Angel, we're not." Maxim walked toward me. "We just need you to use your new PI skills and that special thing that you do to bring Braden back. He's on bail for an obstruction of justice charge. One of his clients, a minister, was accused of molesting teen boys in his charge. That should be bad enough to bring him back, but Ty told him something about our leak and we need to know what that is. We need to know who the leak is."

"Even if I would agree to this, I can't." I checked my watch. It was definitely time for me to go. "I'm not contracted to work with Riddick, so I couldn't help you if I wanted to."

"Surely you didn't think we'd ask you to do this if we hadn't cleared up that minor technicality," Salvador said. "Riddick has subcontracted this recovery to one Tiberius 'Big Tiger' Jones of—"

"BT Trusted Bail Bonds," I completed his sentence for him. "Hold on, why don't you send your Boys in Blue to get this guy?"

"No one behind this room must know."

"Yet Avery knows."

"He's not law enforcement. He's not our leak. Besides, we have so much crap on that guy he's lucky he hasn't lost his bail bond license," Maxim said.

"But if this leak is caught, we agreed to credit Riddick for the capture." Sanchez rolled her neck and gave me that sisterhood solidarity look.

"Then the deal is off." I continued my walk toward the door. "I have no incentive to do this."

"It's a $125, 000 bail bond. That would be $30K give or take for you," Sanchez said.

"I'm getting married, so I won't be hard up for that kind of money any time soon."

"Riddick said that you would say that, so he had a message for me to give to you," Salvador said. "If you agree to this, then he'll introduce you to the person who sent you those flowers."

I closed my eyes and said a quick prayer before I slammed the door and walked out of there.

"Angel . . ." Sanchez called after me.

I hadn't made it to the double doors leading to the lobby before I heard her shoes clicking behind me. She must have been lightly jogging. She ran in front of me and stopped me when she placed both hands on my shoulders.

I grabbed her hands, pushed her into the corner near the water fountains, and whispered, "Sanchez, if you're supposed to be in hiding, don't you think running behind me defeats the purpose?"

"I might as well come out for everyone to see, if you can't help. I'm dead anyway."

"Unbelievable." I took her hand and marched her back to Salvador's office before someone in the lobby could spot us.

"Did you change your mind?" Maxim asked.

"Nope, but if she pulls another stunt like that I'll kill her myself."

14

Justus promised he was okay with me being late when I texted him before I left the parking lot of DeKalb County Police Department. The nerve of Salvador, Maxim, and Sanchez ganging up on me to hunt someone who should have been put under the jail years ago had frustrated me. Even worse was that Riddick Avery was using that mysterious note card over my head like it was a dog chew toy and I was the dog. After Sean's funeral he had revealed to me that the floral card I received last year wasn't a ploy to scare me out of doing bail recovery upstate, but that it was a message he chose not to tell me for my benefit. However, now he was more than willing to share where the card came from. It was too much. I couldn't wait to share this news with Justus. He would agree with me and be happy that I'd turned them down. He had been right for a long time: my career was taking over my life and it shouldn't be that way.

I hurried into the restaurant to find Justus sitting at a table with someone I couldn't stand, Detective Francine Dixon. No wonder she wasn't slinking around Salvador's office like I had suspected she would be. She was, yet again, trying to steal my man. Today she wore an even tighter skirt suit than the last time I saw her, but I was dressed cute, too, so she had better back off. I walked toward them and practically sat on Justus's lap when I greeted him with a kiss.

Justus fumbled with his hands on my body as he scrambled out of his chair. "Wow . . . you can be late more often, if this is your version of saying you're sorry."

"No, I just missed you, that's all." I glanced down at Francine and turned up my nose at her.

He glanced down at Francine. "Detective Dixon bumped into me while I was waiting for you. She's a fan of Matthews, too."

"I'm a fan of many things." She stood up to shake my hand. "Congratulations on your upcoming nuptials."

I looked down and noticed her skirt was shorter than before. I felt a little sorry for her because she was a beautiful, competent, and strong woman who tried very hard to get a good man's attention. You would think that working around many men would yield many dating opportunities. However, even I knew that all bets were off living here in Atlanta. She would steal the thunder of a regular Joe Blow, even if she didn't try. Most men couldn't deal with a woman that powerful. I was still surprised that Justus had attached himself to me like a moth to a flame.

Usually I would shake her hand and then wipe her slime onto my dark-washed jeans, but this time I shook it firmly and then touched her shoulder, to let her know I was glad to see her.

I could tell she was shocked by my response to her. Her eyes widened. She gasped and then chuckled.

"My, Pastor Morgan, your influence on my old friend is impressive."

"I'm his Havah. He knows that I bend toward his will," I said in that tone that Ava has used sometimes when she's trying to sound all holier than thou.

"I don't want to hold up your time." Francine smiled and removed her hand from mine. "Again, congratulations to the two of you. Hope we'll run into each other again in the near future."

I don't plan on it. "Of course we will."

Matthews had a simple design that bolstered its down-home community feel. It wasn't trendy like some of the new Atlanta hot spots. Nope, this was respectably Southern: wide-open spaces, no booths, well lit, white walls, wood tables, wooden red bottom dining room chairs, and red gingham table covering. That was just the dining room. You had to go through a cafeteria line to order your food. No fancy design in there; everything is situated to get you in and get you out. The staff knew everyone and everyone knew the staff, even if you'd never met them before. It was a great place, if you were in a great mood or needed to get into a great mood.

After we'd walked through and ordered our meals—I won't reveal mine, but let's just say my plate had a yellow theme with a little bit of mac-n-cheese, squash casserole, banana pudding. Justus ordered fried chicken and mashed potatoes—Justus blessed the food, but we barely touched it for guzzling down their sweet tea. That thing should be a food group.

"I have to ask . . ." Justus prefaced his questions to me in this way when he knew he was about to ask me a question that might strike a nerve. "What happened at Salvador's?"

"Don't be mad, because I can't share much. This is super confidential."

"Okay." He nodded and then continued eating.

I frowned. "That's it?"

He placed his fork down. "What, Pretty?" His new term of endearment for me.

"You don't even want a clue about what we discussed?"

"Woman, I told you that all I want is you. As long as you come back to me and Bella at the end of the day, then I'm good. I know, in your line of work, you have to keep some things secret, because lives are on the line. And I don't tell you everything I'm privy to, either."

I pouted and sipped some more tea. "I want to tell you a little bit, at least the part that I'm concerned about."

"You think I can help you with that?"

I shrugged. "Let me share something with you about most women. Ninety percent of the time when we say we need help or advice, we really mean we want you to just listen. I need to get the issue out of my brain so I can hear it, to help me solve my own problem. I actually just need an extra ear."

"Fine. Can I eat my chicken while you solve your own problem, then?" he asked.

"Of course." I nodded and smiled. "I'm liking this lunch thing with you."

"Me, too." He paused and drank from his cup. "Before you begin, let me share with you something about men."

"Oh boy, I can't wait," I quipped.

"We like for you to get to the point, at least before the mashed potatoes get cold."

"You got jokes." I nudged his foot with mine under the table.

He chuckled and kept eating.

"Salvador wants me to pick up an important guy to a federal case, who just skipped on his bail for a county charge. I'm concerned about doing this for a lot of reasons, but the biggie for me is that your pal Detective Dixon can't know about it."

Justus stopped eating. "Why would her not being on this case bother you? It should make you happy instead of suspicious."

"I'm happy, but also wondering why."

"Did Salvador give you a reason?" he asked.

"Yes." I waved my response off with a flip of my hand. "It makes sense, but then again I can't believe she's out of the loop?"

"Why should it matter?"

"It didn't until she showed up here. Now I'm suspicious."

"You think she came here to spy on you?"

"That's crazy. I just don't believe in coincidences, but she definitely didn't come here for me. There's no way she knew we would be coming here for lunch. That's crazy. I was thinking that God was trying to tell me something . . . give me His decision about whether I should take this case or not."

Justus's face got so bright. He was a beautiful man, but when his face lit up like that it made me think that an angel lived inside him.

"Are you listening for God's voice or are you trying to be what you think I need in a wife?"

I shook my head. "No, I'm telling you the truth. When I left Salvador, I had not given him my decision. Then I walked into Matthews and there is Francine. God knows I don't like that woman, but she's here and she has no clue where I have been. She has no clue that her partner wants to work with me without her. That delights me."

"So your answer is 'yes.' "

I shrugged. "I don't know yet. I need a less petty alternative to do this."

"Well, I'd rather you do it because of something silly like this and not because you need to avenge a harmed family member. Lately you've been on personal vendetta missions, which must be stressful. I need you stress free for this wedding."

"I was thinking of not doing it because it's personal."

He wiped his mouth. "Now I'm definitely surprised by you."

I clapped my hands. "Good, I'm glad I keep you on your toes."

"Please don't keep me in suspense about a wedding date for us."

My gut twinged. "I won't. I just don't know how to do this wedding thing."

"You don't know how to pick a wedding date with me?"

"No . . . I was never the girl who pretended to be a bride as a child. I never had visions of walking down the aisle. I didn't go to college to find a husband who could afford the lifestyle I wanted for myself. I don't know how to be that woman."

He lifted my ring hand and kissed it. "Is that why you wanted the premarital counseling? Is this that hard for you, because if it is, then let's do that."

"I just don't want to mess up. I don't plan on getting married again."

"I don't either." He kissed my hand again.

"Let me reassure you that I won't let you wait long, because I don't know how long I can keep myself from throwing you over this table and having my way with you."

He growled softly. "So what's next? Are you hunting this guy down or what?"

"I take it that this is your version of a cold shower for me."

He laughed. "No, it's a cold shower for me."

I laughed back. "So waiting a year is definitely out of the question. We have to get married sooner rather than later."

15

In Georgia, especially in the Atlanta area, a bail recovery agent must contract with an approved bail bondsman. For the past six years, I have kept a contract with Big Tiger. He didn't teach me everything I know, but he gave me a start when I didn't know what I was going to do with my pitiful self. A few months ago we had a bump in the road over my contract and his involvement with Riddick, but we mended fences. Real talk: I didn't want to work with anyone else, but it was time he paid me what he paid The Big Bad Boys.

Tiger's office sat a few miles away from DeKalb County Jail in the Avondale Estates area off Memorial Drive. It looked like a bricked white box with smoke puffing out the back. His mom and part owner, Mama D., also ran a soul food kitchen on the back side of the bail bondsman office. On Tuesday mornings, she served free pancakes to the needy. I wondered if she would give me a stack, because the scrumptious smell of cane syrup, butter, and warm sweet bread coming from that side of the office had me needy and greedy.

"It must gon' rain today, if you're showing up this early," Tiger said.

Tiger was not wearing a stuffy suit like the last time I'd seen him, but he wasn't wearing his signature velour track-suit either. Today he wore black designer jeans and a snug black T-shirt that spotlighted his massive arms and accentuated the huge dagger tattoo that was etched into his dark chocolate skin. He wore a black skullcap and now sported a goatee. My old friend looked better than wow, and to my happiness, was no longer under my sister Ava's holy water.

"You know why I'm here. You have a jacket for a Braden Logan that has my name on it."

He folded his arms over his chest, then looked down at me. "When did you and Avery kiss and make up?"

I raised my hands over my shoulders and hoped I looked surprised. "I told you that Avery and I came to an under-standing at Sean Graham's funeral."

He leaned forward and then squinted. "What is that on your hand?"

I looked at my hand and flipped my wrist. "Oh that . . . Justus put a ring on it."

"Angel Soft, how could you?" He stood up from his chair.

He called me Angel Soft when he was being sensitive.

"So that means you won't be giving me away?"

"H to the No." He grabbed me and lifted me off my feet. "You're too badass to be a bride."

I patted his hands. "Don't curse around me like that."

"There you go." He scoffed.

"Seriously, this isn't new. You know I don't like that stuff, especially when we're around Bella. You know how she mimics you."

"How is my baby?"

"Excited about finally having a father."

"Is that why you said 'yes'? Soccer mom peer pressure?"

"If that was the case, would I be a recovery agent?"

He shrugged. "Lately, I don't know why you do what you do."

"Are you going to continue being a pouty second-grade boy about this or are you going to give me my case?"

He looked back at his desk, then reached for his cell phone. "Give me your phone."

"Why?" I pulled mine out of my jeans pocket and handed it to him.

He lightly touched them together, then gave me my phone back. "All the information you have about Braden is in your phone: last known address, map of the residence, his mug shot, that small cut just under his left eyebrow, even his babies' mamas' names."

I chuckled at "babies' mamas." From what I remembered about Braden, he wasn't the pulling-chicks type. "Does he have a lot of kids?"

He shook his head. "No, he has just one with his wife."

"So what's he gotten himself into?"

"Angel, what was the point of me zapping all that information to you, if I have to stand here and tell you?" He grinned.

"That never stopped you before." I pulled up a chair and sat down in his office.

He threw his hands behind his head and cleared his throat. "You already know a few things about Braden. He was a decent guy until the bottom fell out, actually a little time before."

"Gabe had said that he was some kind of audit consultant for churches. I interviewed him briefly and thought he was clean. I dropped my story after talking with him."

"I never understood why you did that."

"He had explanations for everything and Gabe couldn't find one questionable tax code being used."

"If it were me, I would have stayed on him."

"Why?" I asked.

"When tax records are that clean, something is up." He dropped his arms. "You have to be a robot to be that good."

"That's what I said to Gabe, but he was adamant that Braden was a dead end."

"Hmm . . ." He sucked his teeth. "Don't seem dead to me."

"Well, I hope not. I need to find him."

"I hope you remember that I warned you about Hwang, but you didn't listen. I'm warning you now about jumping the broom with Pastor Pretty, so will you listen to me this time?"

"Yeah, about that: I'll listen to you about Braden Logan all day long—in fact, I'm hoping you'll help me track him down—but I'm not talking to you about my love life."

"I'm not seeing Ava," he said very matter of factly.

"I can tell, but I can also tell by your body language that you want to."

He sighed. "I don't like it when you do that. It's creepy."

"Then don't blame me for whatever is not going on be-tween you and my sister."

"I'm not good for her. I don't have a problem admitting that."

I frowned. "Did you hear what I said? I'm not talking about Justus with you."

"You have me all wrong; hear me out. I want you to be happy. If I thought this guy deserved you, I would run you down the aisle to meet him. You're playing it safe because you think you're going to make the same mistake you made with Hwang. But Justus Morgan is no Prince Charming. Prince Charming don't exist this side of Heaven, Angel."

I stood up and almost stumbled over the chair. "All you

had to say was 'no,' you couldn't partner with me on find-ing Braden."

"I'm in love with your sister and you know I'm your huckleberry," he yelled as I walked out of his office.

Frisco, a new member of The Big Bad Boys, stood near the water cooler when I stomped away from Tiger. He didn't have a cup in his hand. He leaned against the wall with his arms folded over his chest. I suspected he wasn't there to get a drink.

I slowed down, stopped in front of him, and threw my hands on my hips. "Now what do you want with me, baby?"

He blushed, then rubbed his neck with his hand. I hoped this wasn't his tell but a nervous tic associated with the blush in his cheeks. "You need a partner on the Logan jacket?"

I turned to get a good look at him. Whoever said there weren't nice-looking straight men in Atlanta didn't spend much time around bail bondsmen offices. These guys were tough, hard to pin down for two good minutes, but were al-ways ruggedly handsome and had no problems talking to strong women. Such was the case with Frisco Cabral.

He had the same coloring as Sanchez but with a little more cinnamon color to his skin. He wasn't as tall as Tiger or Justus but taller than Salvador. He wore a Caesar buzz cut that showed off his thick arched eyebrows and honey brown eyes. He had a smaller build than most of The Big Bad Boys. Nonetheless the ribbed T-shirt he wore revealed a very toned and muscular man underneath. If he wasn't dressed down in jeans and work boots, I could see him in a black suit looking like a Hispanic 007. He had that look about him that fit the bill.

I smiled. "I do, if you say 'no.' "

16

Wednesday, Noon
Alon's Bakery & Market, Ashford Dunwoody Road, At-
lanta, Georgia

After Frisco and I discussed the particulars on Braden Logan, I had to meet Mom. She wanted to discuss wedding plans and I wanted to discuss Uncle Pete's funeral. We agreed on Alon's at Perimeter.

Alon's at Perimeter was a second location for the popular Atlanta bakery. I chose this one instead of the Virginia Highland location because you could watch the chocolatiers make chocolate while you have lunch. Although I hadn't made many plans for this wedding, I knew I wanted chocolate wedding favors and Justus agreed.

"When you agreed to meet me here, I was overjoyed because I was concerned that you had gotten preoccupied with other, less important things," Mom said.

"Mom, I don't know what I'm doing, so Ava's helping me with the 'becoming a wife' stuff and I plan to ask the ladies at Sugar Hill to help me with the bridal stuff."

"Fine, just as long as everyone's clear that I will spearhead the wedding stuff. Outside of your prayer buddies at church, who'll be in your bridal party?"

"Mom, there are about six ladies in the church group. I won't be inviting all of them to be bridesmaids, but I was hoping they would hostess. Whitney, Ava, and Charlie will be my bridesmaids."

Mom almost spat out her tea when I said Charlie's name. Charlie Fairchild had been my best friend since college, so I don't know why she was surprised.

"Where is Charlene now, by the way?" Mom asked.

"She's in Cologne, but she'll be returning to Atlanta at the end of the month. Her job is transferring her back to the states. Isn't that great news?"

Charlie was an executive administrator for a German and Japanese engineering company. She split her time between Cologne, Germany, and Kyoto, Japan, where her boss, the chairman of the board, lived.

"Is she still having an affair with her boss?" Mom asked.

"I wouldn't know. She doesn't discuss those things with me anymore, at my request."

"Well, you better hope she still does, because I don't think it's prudent to be best friends with a kept woman. She may try to put her claws in Justus."

"Come on, Mom. Everyone makes mistakes. I'm sure that's long been over."

Mom raised her eyebrow and sipped more tea. "If she's returning to Atlanta, I'm sure it's over between them."

"Mom, I trust both of them. Trust me for a change. Now, how are things with Aunt Mary and Uncle Pete's funeral?"

"It is what it is. I told your aunt to have that funeral tomorrow, but she wants to wait until the weekend. By the time this funeral happens, Pete will be unrecognizable. The man will be darker than a silk chocolate pie." She shook her head. "Why can't we do like everybody else and say our good-byes the next day?"

My phone vibrated. I picked up the phone and looked at it. It was a text from Frisco.

"I don't know, Mom. I thought it was a tradition that started back during slavery," I said. Then I read the note.

braden has a girlfriend on the side

I frowned.

"What's in that text to make you look like that?" Mama asked.

"I just learned that my convict has been skipping out on his wife." I shook my head. "He didn't seem the type."

"They never do. That's why you need to keep an extra eye on your jet-setting friend," Mama said as she stirred her tea.

"Very funny," I grumbled.

Since Whitney couldn't do au pair duty for me today, I texted back to Frisco to meet me at the house in four hours.

"So what are we going to do now?" she asked.

"Get you to stop stirring trouble and help me pick out a chocolate keepsake before I have to do Bella's carpool."

17

My office was in my backyard. Whoever had the house before I bought it had built a guest bungalow for their in-
laws. I turned the place into my version of super PI central.
I nicknamed it "The Office." It held my collectible daggers
and swords display case, a sauna to relax my muscles, a fit-
ness room, a war room with a SMART Board and artillery
closet, a front office, a separate bedroom, and my computer lab.

The only problem with it was that I didn't have a separate car entry. Frisco would have to pull into my drive, open
the gate near the garage after I unlocked it via remote, and
walk through my backyard garden. Bella's tree house hov-
ered over the garden, which meant she would see him. I
didn't like that. Now that she was older and more obser-
vant, I didn't want her noticing the strangers coming in and
out of my gate. I had enough trouble with my neighbors.

Since Justus and I were getting married and we were
likely moving from this house, I needed to get a new office.
Bella didn't need to know too much about what I do. As I

watched Frisco trample my pink dahlias with his boots, I knew I needed a new office like yesterday.

"Does Frisco have a woman?" Whitney asked.

I was standing on the back porch with her when Frisco came inside the gate.

"Let's revisit this subject after I get Ava's scent off of Tiger."

Whitney flipped her brown hair across her shoulder, then pursed her lips. "If I keep hanging back for you and Ava, I'm gonna be an old maid. Nope. Not happening. He looks single to me."

"Stop flipping your hair. You look ridiculous."

"Not until you introduce us."

I motioned for Frisco to meet me at The Office, then I turned to her. "So what do you think you're going to do? You think I'm going to let you interrupt my meeting with Frisco to play matchmaker between you two?"

"No, nothing like that, Big Sis," she whispered. She waved at him as he continued past my back porch, wiggling all the fingers on her hand. "Give me something to do with the case. That way I can meet him on my terms."

I looked at her and wanted to slap her. Whitney had been trying to find a way to get into bail recovery ever since The Knocker had almost killed Elaine. She might have had an interest in it earlier, but I wasn't paying attention then. Today, however, I saw the game she was playing and I didn't have a problem giving her what she asked for. She had it coming.

"First off: Mom would have my head if she knew that I let this foolery happen between you and Frisco. Number Two: Someone has to watch Bella while Frisco and I work. And Number Three, my most important point: You don't know if Frisco wants you."

"I have number two covered. Remember our neighbor across the street invited Bella to Monkey Joe's for Jacob's birthday. They'll be picking her up any minute now. I was nice enough to pick up a present for him. You owe me ten dollars. Number One: Who cares what Mama thinks? And Number Three . . ." She smiled. "Frisco has walked over every pink flower in your garden because he can't take his eyes off me. I think I got me a date for Friday night."

"I think you're about to get popped in the eye. Leave him alone."

"Can I work this case with you?"

"Only if you agree to keep it on the hush and do what I ask."

"My lips are sealed unless he plants a hot kiss on my lips; then all bets are off." Whitney hopped off the porch and skipped toward The Office.

I couldn't snatch her because my front doorbell was ringing. Jacob's parents were here.

After I signed a parental waiver for Bella to play at the indoor jumping bounce house arena and kissed her goodbye, I met Frisco and Whitney in The Office. When I walked inside she was showing him one of my Scottish Dirk daggers.

I snapped the case of daggers shut. "Let's meet in the War Room."

The War Room wasn't like the ones seen on television. It wasn't tough or high tech, but pretty girly actually. In the middle of the room was a long white IKEA conference table, powder blue Eames molded plastic armchairs, and my giant whiteboard on the north wall. The walls were blue damask wallpaper. The War Room was once a living room. I didn't have the heart to cut damask. Just too pretty. However, the wall behind the north wall was a lime green for balance.

"Whitney, hit the lights," I said before I turned on my whiteboard.

Bella's first-grade teacher used a SMART Board to teach her class. A SMART Board was an interactive whiteboard that did cool things like store lessons, sync with other computers, and monitor computers in the classroom. I needed something like that for my office. Sometimes I hired a skip tracer and needed her finds synced with my project software. Sometimes I needed to pull files I'd left at Tiger's to my office. However, I couldn't afford a SMART Board, so I hooked up a Wii player to a projector, set the projector to light up on the big whiteboard, downloaded the whiteboard software, and used the Wii uDraw pen. Whoever said kids' tech toys were a waste of time weren't creative.

Whitney and Frisco sat in chairs next to each other. I didn't like that arrangement, but I felt secure that Frisco wasn't as interested in my little sister as she believed. Men like Frisco were used to women's advances, especially the nontransparent ones Whitney was giving off.

"What I will share on this wall will sync to your phones if you turn on your Bluetooth or a similar wireless open technology device." I pointed the remote at a manila envelope projected on the whiteboard until it clicked open. "We are searching for Braden Logan, for a failure to appear for a racketeering charge in DeKalb County. Both of you are new to working with me, so let me just say from the jump this case can't be shared. Frisco, that means no one at the office except me or Big Tiger. Whitney, keep your mouth closed. Period."

"Why is this guy so important?" Frisco asked.

"I don't care. His bail recovery comes with a bonus. That's all I care about," I said.

Of course that wasn't the entire truth. White lies kept me in business.

Whitney raised her hand, thereby proving my point that she wasn't cut out for this business.

"So this guy is like a white-collar criminal? He's not dangerous."

Frisco smirked. "Who said white collar wasn't dangerous? These are the masterminds, the weapons designers . . . the dinero. Don't be fooled. They are the most dangerous, because they are always one step ahead and you never know what they're packing."

Whitney scooted her chair closer to Frisco. "If that's the case, I need some personal protection."

He grinned; I mean mugged Whitney.

"What you need to do is pay attention. Frisco has learned that Braden has a wifey."

She leaned over to Frisco. "How did you find out?"

"Logan had a cell phone confiscated when he was in county lockup. Because he was charged for racketeering, the jail checked out the phone to see if it was evidence for the case, but they found nada. I asked for the cell-phone number from one of my staff buddies. Get this . . ." He sat up straighter. "The phone number didn't match with the carrier he uses for his wife and daughter, Cheyenne."

Whitney glanced at me and then back to Frisco. "So they're on a different family plan than Braden?"

"No, he has a phone with them, but . . ." Frisco jumped and begin drawing on the whiteboard. "The phone that was confiscated wasn't his family phone. It was the phone he used to call his wifey with."

"Wha?!" Whitney leaned forward. "How would you know that?"

Frisco raised his hands up to his shoulders, popped his collar, and grinned. "It's a man code thing. I can't share because I'm sworn to secrecy."

"Man code my butt." I patted his back as he sat back

down in his chair. "It's simple. Braden's a smart guy, but he isn't smarter than me. He bought his chick a separate phone so that the wife wouldn't be on to him. Which begs the question: what happened to the family phone?"

"He either left it at his office or left it in his car when he was taken in," Frisco said.

"In either case, wouldn't that be confiscated, too, either by the county dicks or county impound?" Whitney asked.

I was hoping that our shop talk would scare her off her new distraction to become a recovery agent instead of a lawyer.

Frisco threw his hands up. "Could be, not sure, but I didn't need to know what was on that phone. That wasn't what I was after."

Whitney looked at me with a confused expression on her face. "Then what was the point?"

"Be patient, hermanita." Frisco touched her knee with his hand, looked at me, and chuckled. "The first rule of thumb in this game is to know your convict's family dynamic. Who's he dealing with? Who's he living with? Who's his confidant? My instincts told me that this guy's family was too lily white for him to sleep peacefully at night. All the charges stacked on this cat. He had to be spilling his beans to somebody. I just needed to know if there was a plausible reason he had a woman on the side. The extra phone gives me motive."

"And everybody knows that the mistress knows everything the husband is too afraid to share with the wife." I grinned. "If we could get to the wifey, we would find our man."

"Bingo, which means she's probably hiding him or had helped him dip and dodge out of town." Frisco licked his lips and rubbed his hands together.

Tiger did the same thing when he thought he was on to

something. Frisco was definitely a Big Bad Boy, but Whitney and Ava wouldn't have any part of it on my watch.

"I checked with my sources at Hartsfield Airport. They found no one fitting Braden's description had come through their terminals. However, there are about ten other airports in the area."

"We have to get the flight schedules from them and you know that's hard to do," Whitney said.

"Exactly, Whitney, and this is where you come in. I need you to use your legalese to get those guys to tell us whether or not Braden's flown out from their spot, and if he hasn't flown the coop, then I need you to use your hairography and hot sauce to charm them into keeping us on their speed dial in case he comes through," I said, hoping Whitney would find my plan too hard to execute.

"I doubt they would share that info with an (excuse my French)"—she raised her hands and made quote marks with her fingers—" 'bounty hunter.' "

"Don't worry. You're not a bail recovery agent and you won't be traveling alone. We have some friends in high places who will escort you there." I reached into my pocket and handed her Maxim's business card.

"Dang, okay." Whitney stood up. "I need to find the right outfit for this."

"You look real good like that," Frisco said.

The boardroom got quiet real fast. Frisco looked at me until he read the "I will kill you if you flirt with my little sister again" stare.

He cleared his throat. "I mean, you shouldn't go in there looking like a lawyer. That coed prep school girl with a dash of hot sauce look you have going for ya will do just fine."

"So what are you guys doing, while I'm tracking down flight passengers?"

"We need records of that secret phone just in case you find a dead end," I said. "We need to find the paper trail; we'll start with a Dumpster dive. Frisco, do you have rubber boots on you?"

"Is this payback for flirting with your sister?" he asked.

I tapped his knee. "No, sunshine. It's me working my case."

While they were out searching for Braden's paper trail, I went into my attic. The night he died, I had smuggled Gabe's disk drive out of his computer before the Feds ripped his apartment apart. I had buried it in the back of Aunt Mary's closet when I was distraught and pregnant. Maxim had made sure he retrieved it for me when he took Aunt Mary's personal items from her house. Now I had the box in my hands.

I prayed to God that Braden Logan had nothing to do with Gabe's death, else Maxim would have worse than a leak to plug. He was going to have to mop what was left of Braden Logan, Ty, or anyone—I mean anyone—who took him from Bella.

18

Justus knocked on my door one minute shy of midnight. I was a ball of nerves when he arrived. He stepped through my front-door threshold, lifted me toward his lips, and kissed me softly. As good as he felt around me, I couldn't stop shaking.

He released me back to the ground and shut the front door. "You're shivering."

"I know . . ." I walked toward the living room.

The box was in there.

"It is a little cooler than usual." He followed me toward my living room. "I'm sorry I couldn't come at a more respectable hour. There were so many things going on at the church. Everyone is excited about the wedding, by the way."

I stopped and turned around. "I thought we agreed to announce our engagement this Sunday."

"I didn't announce it to the congregation, but I thought it would be only fair that I told my staff. They're organizing an engagement brunch for Sunday also. Tell your mom. I know Ava won't be able to make it."

"Justus, stop." I sighed. "I didn't call you here to discuss our engagement. I called you to keep me from killing a former ATF agent with a bald head, who looked me in the eye for almost a week when the whole time he knew who killed Bella's father."

Justus's eyes widened. He walked toward me and helped me sit down on the couch beside him. "What are you talking about? What guy? I thought you killed Gabe's killer?"

"I thought there was more than one shooter, but I couldn't confirm it or I didn't want to admit it. But today . . ." My hands shook as I pointed at the white storage box on the table and then I dropped my head into my lap and began to cry.

"Baby . . ." Justus touched my shoulder. "I gotcha."

I turned toward him and let him grab me up in his arms. I fell asleep there until I felt the shivers again, but this time it came from somewhere deep in my mind, a memory that wouldn't let go.

Seven years ago . . .
The parking garage outside Buffalo Wild Wings Grill &
Bar, Buckhead Atlanta, Georgia

It had been storming and too cold for March mornings in Atlanta. Fortunately for me, it was also too wet to do the first part of my assignment covering Filene's Basement Department Store's annual Running of the Brides event for the *Atlanta Sentinel.* So to pass the time before the brides ran, I called Gabe. (The stupid things you do when you're in lust.) He had whisked me to a private parking garage within earshot of Filene's, then surprised me with a hot breakfast and a long good-morning kiss. Everything was perfect until the barrage of bullets from both sides of his truck made Gabe push me to the floorboard of his truck.

My heart pounded. After the last shots, I knew better than to scream. Everything was happening so fast. I had to take a slow breath to calm down and find a solution. Then dark red liquid oozed down my shirt sleeve. It wasn't my blood. It was Gabe's. I trembled. I heard him whimper. He was face down, but breathing. Afraid for him I began to cry.

"Don't worry. You're going to be okay." I sniffled as I slid my hands along the carpet for his gun.

He kept a Kahr under his driver's seat. I knew this because we had just had an argument about the gun two days before. It creeped me out that it was in his truck.

The Kahr felt cold against the leather holder it had been resting inside when I found it. I slid it out and eyed the rim to see if it was cracked. As many dirty-south deeds I had reported on for the *Atlanta Sentinel*, I had never needed a gun. I inserted the clip and released the slide with the slide stop. I couldn't remember everything Daddy had taught me, but I remembered that. I also remembered that I needed steady hands. I gulped. My hands began to tremble again.

By now I had managed to scoot myself toward the back of the truck. There was more room and the back windows were tinted. I could peep out without being noticed, but I didn't know where the shooter was or if the shooter was plural. I heard nothing, not even Gabriel's shallow breathing. I swallowed more tears down, took a deep breath, and peered through the back passenger door again. No one was there. Not one single person in the parking lot.

I stepped out of the truck, but didn't close the door in case I needed to jump back in for cover.

I ran my fingers over the phone's keyboard so fast. A 911

operator picked up. As I began telling her our whereabouts, I heard footsteps coming from somewhere on the dark side of the parking garage. A lump lodged in my throat. Yet I refused to drop the phone or the gun.

Adrenaline and anger rushed through me. Before I could remove the thick lump from my throat, I dropped to my knees, dropped the phone, and unloaded and reloaded the clip. I didn't stop shooting until I heard a groan, a thud, and then silence. I smelled lightning crackle around us but heard nothing. Not even the thunder rolled again.

I opened my eyes to see whether my nightmare was over. A man dressed in a black hoodie sweater, black leather gloves, and black jeans lay sprawled on the pavement. Dead.

In the close distance, somewhere in the parking lot, I had heard the click-clack of stilettos and then the burning rubber screech of a motorcycle peeling out.

The sound woke me. I sat up, pushed Justus's arms off of me, and ran to my living room window.

"What was that?" I peered through my drapes.

It was the neighborhood motorcycle club heading out for their Wednesday Morning Ride, a tributary drive through the city in honor of their founder who was battling cancer in Northside Hospital in Atlanta.

"What? What's wrong?" Justus panted. He was now standing behind me.

I closed the drapes and turned toward him. "I was right. There was another shooter in that parking garage with me and Gabe."

"Do you think the other shooter is Ty?" he asked.

"Huh-uh . . ." I shook my head. "The shooter was a woman."

"Okay. Then it's not the guy you're looking for."

"Right, but it could be our leak. It could be the person Braden Logan is hiding from."

"How can you know that, because of a dream?" Justus asked. "How are you putting all of this together?"

"I don't believe in coincidences . . . and the box on the table." I tilted my head in its direction. "I wanted to show you what was inside last night, but I was too overwhelmed."

Justus's warm brown eyes washed over me. "Are you sure you want to share that with me?"

"Of course I do."

My gut kicked me because it felt like another opportunity to tell him about me kissing Maxim. Yet again. I heard the pitter-patter of Bella's feet moving around upstairs. "Mommy."

I picked up the box and handed it to Justus. "Can you take it to your office? I'll be there after I drop her off at school."

"I can make breakfast," he said.

"Not wearing the same clothes you had on yesterday, you can't." I grinned.

"I guess not." He leaned down and kissed my cheek. "We're going to have to stop waiting to see each other at the edge of night."

"Sure, but no wedding talk. I want to spend time with you, not deal with that stuff."

"Angel, it's our wedding you're talking about. If we don't plan it, who will?"

"Mom, who else? I'll ask her to stop by the church and help the staff with the brunch."

"And what about your new case?"

"Frisco, Whitney, and I are sniffing out a decent lead on bringing in Logan. I feel pretty good that this thing will be over soon after I show you what's in that box."

"Fair enough." He leaned his forehead toward mine. "Get to the office as soon as you can. I'll have breakfast there for us."

"Good, and bring some more of those kisses you had with you last night, too."

19

Thursday, 8:00 AM
Sugar Hill Elementary School, Sugar Hill, Georgia

I called Salvador's office after Bella hopped out of my SUV and headed to the school's front door. He picked up on the first ring.

"Ms. Crawford, how may we help you?"

I gasped at the sound of Francine Dixon's voice on the other end of Salvador's phone.

"So you've been demoted to office assistant. That explains bunches." I smirked.

She chuckled, but I heard it drip with contempt for me. "Well, it's a good thing your sense of humor isn't what endeared Justus to you. As a matter of fact, I don't know what he sees in you."

"Don't be bitter, B—"

"Angel . . ." Salvador cleared his throat. "Angel, is that you?"

I exhaled. "Is today April Fool's, because you just made a fool out of your sidekick."

He laughed. "Sorry, dear. Dixon and I sometimes cross our phones when we're meeting in the mornings. What can I do for you?"

"You can do a better job about holding on to your phone."

"Anything else . . . ?"

"I need to talk to you about our case. There have been some developments and I want to run them by you, but in private, like we agreed on yesterday. If you know what I mean. . . ."

"Of course, that will not be a problem. I will rearrange my calendar to accommodate."

"Actually, I wonder if you can come to me instead of me coming to police headquarters. After what happened yesterday, I don't think any of us should be hanging around there."

"I understand and agree. When do you want to do it?"

"Either within the hour or after your workday. Since we live within minutes of each other, you could always stop by on your way home."

"No, the sooner the better. We've lost enough time on this."

"Great. That works for me."

"Thanks, Dixon," he said.

His voice sounded distant. I assumed he had removed the phone from near his head.

"Are you still there, Angel?" he whispered.

"I'm here and will be waiting on you when you come."

"Do you want to see just me or everyone?" he asked.

"Just you and Justus," I said to him, while I pulled into the parking lot of Sugar Hill Community Church. "Don't ask."

Thursday, 8:30 AM
Sugar Hill Community Church, Sugar Hill, Georgia

It was hard for me to admit that love at first sight was possible. When Mom met my dad, she thought he was a

Podunk preacher farmer straight from the South Georgia cotton fields. Dad thought Mom was a bourgeois old maid from Atlanta who needed the stick pulled out of her backside. They got over their prejudices, fell passionately in love, and lived a good life together. When Ava met Devon, he thought he was still talking to me, which worked in both their favors, because he was too boring for me.

But when I saw Justus, the first Sunday he was introduced to the church as our new pastor, he took my breath away. When he looked my way, I turned to stone. That man had me under his spell since the beginning and I was super scared when I learned he knew my name, when he told me he wanted to know me, and I think a part of me was still on the floor when he asked me to marry him. Dreams like that don't come true for girls like me. I knew I was stalling on the wedding date for fear that I would wake up.

Mrs. Lewis, the church office manager, hopped from her desk and greeted me with a smile as I walked down the narthex.

"Evangeline, dear, why are you hiding from us?" she asked before she hugged me.

A high pitch held her Southern drawl in the air longer than Mom's. I deduced that she must have some Savannah roots.

"I'm sorry. Since I returned from my friend's wedding, I've been swamped with my client work and my uncle died."

Her jaw dropped and she pulled me into an even tighter hug. Yep. I'm pretty sure she was from Savannah. "Oh dear . . ."

"It's okay, Mrs. Lewis."

"Oh dear, Brother Morgan told us about your uncle and

I totally forgot the moment he shared that you two were engaged. My apologies. No wonder you've been out of sorts. How are you feeling today?"

"I'm fine." I squeezed her hands to reassure her that I was well past grieving for Uncle Pete. "In fact, Justus and I are having breakfast together this morning."

Her face beamed. "To finalize the wedding plans."

"No, ma'am, but my mom, Mrs. Virginia Carter, will be by this afternoon to help you with Sunday's brunch."

She shook her head slowly and had a puzzled look on her face. "You're not cancelling?"

"No. Why would you think that?"

"Well, your uncle's funeral for one thing, and Brother Morgan mentioned this morning that the timing may not be the best for you two."

I looked over her head. Justus stood behind Mrs. Lewis. She noticed my eye movement, turned around, and jumped.

"Brother Morgan, you scared me." She gasped, then looked back at me. "He does that all the time. I can never hear him walking around."

I chuckled. "He does have quiet feet. Doesn't he?"

He smiled in such a way that I had to remind myself that we were in church and I had to table those thoughts for the honeymoon.

Justus touched Mrs. Lewis's shoulder. "I'll remember to stomp the next time."

She placed her hand over her chest and laughed. This whole thing had tickled her.

"Justus, Mrs. Lewis and I were talking about Sunday's engagement brunch. I told her that it was okay. Uncle Pete will be buried tomorrow. Mom and Ava are flying out to say their good-byes and to bring back Aunt Mary, but I won't be going."

"And why not, dear?" Mrs. Lewis asked.

"We had already said our good-byes a few weeks ago and I'm at peace about it," I said.

"Well, good, then. The brunch will be lovely. Mrs. Carter is very elegant and efficient. We'll get along real good."

"I know you will." I nodded.

Justus slid his arm under mine. "Mrs. Lewis, can you handle my calls this morning?"

"I think that's my job, Brother Morgan."

He sighed with a smile. "You know how to keep me on my toes."

"And I know how to pick out a good wife for you." She winked.

I giggled. "Are you talking about me?"

"They don't call me the Magnolia Matchmaker for nothing." She winked again. "Y'all better get to it before the world wakes."

Justus led me to his office, then stopped. "I had a feeling that you would be chasing your guy today, so I made sure that we had a fun but hearty breakfast."

I chuckled. "Oh boy. If it's Krispy Kreme, then let's elope right now."

He opened the door and I almost fell on my face. A large Mimi's Café bag sat on his settee table. The aroma of bacon, eggs, and something spicy filled the air. I skipped toward the table until Justus caught my arm.

"Hold on, Skip to My Lou, you mean to tell me if I had gotten Krispy Kreme Doughnuts, we would be married by tonight?" he asked.

I shrugged and smiled at the same time. "I was just being bad. No, this is much better. What is it, eggs and bacon? I love Mimi's Café."

"No, it's two Monterey Omelettes, watermelon, and strawberries. However, you haven't answered my question, woman. Do I need to make a quick run to Krispy Kreme?"

Justus's intercom buzzed. "Brother Morgan, a Detective Tinsley is here to see you."

Justus sighed and lowered his head. "Paradise lost."

I chuckled, then kissed him on his cheek. "I forgot to tell you that I asked Salvador to come over."

"To discuss the box. That makes sense."

"He was the first person on the scene when Gabe was killed, so . . ."

"No problem, but I'm not sharing my breakfast."

"Now you're being bad." I giggled.

"No, that's me being hungry and you learning the hard way that we're a team now."

I stuck my tongue out, then ran to the bag, lifted out an omelette tray, and began eating.

Justus bent down and laughed. "Bad bride to be. Bad bride to be."

Salvador knocked on the opened door. "Did I come too early?"

Justus turned toward him and shook his hand. "No, sir. You're just in time. Angel wasn't sure if you liked omelettes, so we also brought some pancakes."

I frowned, then looked around the room. What was he talking about and why was he lying in church?

"Babe, the other bag by my briefcase on the windowsill." Justus pointed behind me and smiled.

If my brown complexion could show how hot my cheeks felt, it would have looked fire-engine red. I didn't know how he knew that Salvador would be coming here, too, but he had me good. Maybe we should elope tonight.

We didn't discuss the box until after we had that yummy breakfast. There was no need to have indigestion. After I cleared the breakfast trash off the table, Justus placed the box back on the table. It was time. I opened the lid.

20

"The day Gabe was murdered, I went to his apartment and took all the things we worked on together."

Salvador cursed and threw one hand in the air. "Angel, don't say anything else before you get yourself in trouble."

"What did she do wrong?" Justus asked.

Salvador pointed at the box and then glared at me. "She hid evidence that could have led to Hwang's murderer. Evidence tampering is a felony."

"You can't be serious, sir." Justus scoffed.

"No, I'm very serious. Angel could get a year to ten if convicted for hiding this."

"What?" Justus hissed. "You would arrest her for this? She's bringing this to you in God's house? Shouldn't that count for something?"

"Don't do that to me, Justus. You know I'm Catholic and yet I respect your church. But this is different and she knows it." Salvador's Peruvian accent got heavier when he was upset.

He looked at me, then huffed. I stepped away from him

because he looked like he was about to explode. I began to tear up. I hadn't really thought this thing through.

Justus came over and took my hand. Both hands shook now.

"Maybe I shouldn't have included you in this," I said.

He squeezed my hand and grinned. "Detective Tinsley, why don't you hear her out? She didn't have to tell you any of this. She could have kept it to herself. There must be a reason for Angel to jeopardize all her hard work and a future with her family, if she is coming to you now about this."

"Justus, I know what you're trying to do, but the sooner you realize that Angel knows how to dig her own self out of a hole, the better." Salvador turned his attention toward me.

"Is that why you asked me to meet you here, Angel, to back me into a holy corner?"

"No, I asked you here because I didn't want to kill Braden Logan when I catch him."

"What did you say?" Justus asked.

"I didn't stutter. . . ."

"Murder, theft . . . do you realize what kind of trouble you're getting me into?" Salvador asked me.

"I wasn't thinking. I'm sorry." I wiped my eyes with my sleeve. "When I took the box, I thought what I had didn't lead anywhere—until yesterday after you mentioned Braden Logan."

"How in the world did you not think that stealing the last thing Hwang was working on wouldn't be considered evidentiary material?"

"I didn't take the last thing he was working on. I only took what he had been working on for me, and you had proven a long time ago that his work with me at the *Sentinel* had nothing to do with his murder."

"That's because I didn't have the box you've kept all this time."

"Come on, Sal." I rolled my eyes and sighed. "The story never made it to print and Ava and Devon's church was the focus of it. They didn't have Gabe killed. That's preposterous and you know it."

"I don't know it. I don't know anything right now."

"Know this, Sal. Gabe was a private investigator. His specialty was white-collar crime and he kept his work close to his vest. He never told me anything about work. Who knew who he was working with or what he was doing? His credentials were incredible and he was always in demand."

"No offense, but if that's the case, why did he choose to work with you on a church scandal news story?" Salvador asked.

I shrugged. "He thought I was cute. I don't know."

"And it's beside the point," Justus interrupted. His eyes showed a great deal of concern for me.

I blinked. *Please, God, I don't want to tell him everything, so he needs to stop looking at me like that.*

"Doll, I need you to give me something better than 'I don't know.' I need proof that Hwang had another client at the same time he was working for you."

"What?" I could feel my chest puff up in anger. The tears fell from my eyes faster now. "I never asked him about his other projects. He never asked me about mine. That's not right, Salvador. You're asking too much."

"Fine." He took a handkerchief out of his jacket pocket and handed it to me. "What else do you know?"

"All I knew at the time was that the box contained mainly the stuff I had hired Gabe to find on the church tax fraud story. It was my assignment at the *Sentinel*. Remember I canned it when it led nowhere?"

"It led to your sister Ava and brother-in-law Devon getting added to the Senatorial probe," Salvador said.

"Right, and my poking around cost my sister five years of strife for nothing. Thanks for reminding me." I plopped down on Justus's settee couch. My whole body trembled.

"Angel, you're safe here. Tell us what happened," Justus said.

"I was so sure that Devon was hiding money, but we didn't find it. You know why? Because I was too busy trying to get back at my brother-in-law instead of having his back. If I had done my job, I would have known about Elvis Bloom a long time ago. I would have stopped him long before he hurt Devon. My brother-in-law is dead because of me. That's what it led to."

I put my head in my lap and cried. I felt Justus's arms around me. I picked my head back up and looked at Salvador. It was hard to do because my eyes burned from crying.

He now sat on the other side of me. "Go on."

I cleared my throat. "I was just trying to protect Ava and Devon by pulling those files. Instead, my mistakes just kept piling up, Sal. I know that. But I promise if I knew that what I had taken would lead to who killed Gabe, I would have been the first person to give it to you. He's Bella's father. Back then he was the love of my life. You know I've been trying to find out who wanted him dead since he stopped breathing in my arms. Why would I intentionally keep that from you? That's why I pulled the box. Perhaps there was a clue in there."

"I get it now." Salvador sat down. "When you learned that Ava and Devon weren't involved, you backed off the story."

"Yeah. Like I said before, I told the *Sentinel* I had a personal conflict so I couldn't continue. By then I already knew that Devon and Ava were on the up-and-up. I didn't care what they uncovered thereafter. Ava was in the clear."

"Is that why you resigned?" Justus asked.

"No, I resigned after Gabe was killed." I sat down opposite Salvador. "I was traumatized; I was pregnant; and let's be honest, I had become a headache of an employee. I knew that my position was in jeopardy after I dropped the investigation of Ava and Devon. Yet I didn't care about playing hooky with Gabe."

"You had gotten cocky," Salvador scoffed.

"Don't believe what you see when it comes to me," I said. "I had become jaded with the concept of journalism. That's different from being cocky. Nonetheless, my attitude had become a problem."

"Still, you haven't proven that Braden is connected to Gabe's death. Could this be a coincidence?" Justus asked.

"There are no coincidences," Salvador and I said in unison.

"Jinx," I said.

Salvador chuckled.

Justus frowned. "What else could it be, if not a coincidence? If this guy was connected to setting up fraudulent tax shelters seven years ago but didn't get caught, why would he not be involved with another white-collar crime like hiding alcohol tax revenue from moonshine sales with the ATF guy y'all apprehended?"

Salvador tilted his head at me. "Didn't I tell you not to take this case outside the loop?"

I rolled my eyes. "Justus is not the mole and he doesn't have any ties to DeKalb County Police."

"Don't worry, Detective Tinsley. I learned the hard way,"

Justus said. He referred to that time he almost got Ava convicted for a triple murder when he shared some information I gave him with Detective Dixon.

I squeezed Justus's hand to remind him that all was forgiven.

Salvador looked down at our hands, then grinned. "It works every time, and here's something else you can learn from your fiancée: Angel is right about coincidences. When you've seen what I've seen, you're left with little truths." Salvador folded his arms over his chest and sighed. "How is Braden Logan connected to all of this?"

I lifted a manila folder out of the box and placed it in Salvador's lap.

"I don't know. He may have nothing to do with Gabe's death at all. However, he is connected to him somehow. I remembered hearing his name during a conversation between Gabe and someone he talked to on his cell phone. I thought if I retrieved the box from the attic, it would refresh my memory. But it didn't. Instead, I found this."

"Is this right?" He frowned as he flipped through the folder. "Why didn't we know about this?"

"Know about what?" Justus asked.

"This file is an info dump on Braden," I said. "He was a CPA with a JD from Louisiana, but when he relocated to Georgia he never applied for the state bar. He never worked as a CPA. He worked as an accountant specialist for the DeKalb County Department of Motor Vehicles. But he wasn't an employee; he was contracted through a temp agency."

Salvador nodded. "He definitely knows something."

"And what does that mean?" Justus looked confused. "How are you two making assumptions?"

"Baby, the only reason a JD/CPA is working at the DeKalb DMV is because he's hiding. If the DMV knew about his great pedigree, he would be working for the Tax Commissioner's Office. The reason they don't know is because he's not Braden Logan. He's either a former WITSEC client that has left the farm or he has an expunged record and the offense would be found out if he worked in a government-sector job."

"That would explain why he appears to be a ghost." Salvador rubbed his chin. "Since Tyrone was his brother-in-law and working with ATF, he more than likely helped him cover his tracks once he got here."

"Although Braden and Ty became family because of marriage, they're more than likely 'play cousins.' They grew up together or have some other strong tie that has lasted for years."

"That would also explain why Ty gave all that money to Braden instead of his wife, before he killed himself," Salvador said.

"Did the folder tell you Braden Logan's true identity?" Justus asked.

"No, but I was hoping that with this information, Salvador could look into this. It could lead to your leak or be used as leverage to get Braden to tell us who the leak is."

"I'm beginning to see the light at the end of this tunnel." Salvador sighed, then grinned. "However, the best people to look into this are the marshals."

"So you think I'm on to something?" I asked.

"I think so." Salvador nodded. "But I also think that somehow Logan has a connection to Hwang's death. I don't know how, but there is something there tugging at me. I'm sure you feel it, too, Angel."

My chest tightened. "That's why I'm giving you the box. No matter what happens. . . ."

"Wait a minute. You were cleared from that a long time

ago; why would you want to open that back up?" Justus looked at me, then Salvador. "She killed the person who shot Gabe. What's his name . . . Shouldn't that be the end of it?"

After killing Elvis Bloom and Biloxi James, I still found it hard to think about or mention the name of the person I killed that day Gabe was murdered.

"His name was Ephraim Collier, and no, that wasn't the end of it, even if I wanted it to be."

"But why?" Justus asked.

Justus's voice had risen to a pitch of aggravation. I didn't want him to think I was saying this to stall about setting a wedding date with him. In fact, I wanted very much for the Gabriel Hwang chapter to be closed.

"It can't be, because there was more than one shooter there that day," I mumbled, then slowly looked up at the two. As I suspected, their mouths were dropped. "I don't know if I was so flustered over what had just happened to Gabe that I didn't notice it when you interviewed me at the crime scene, Sal, but there was someone else there. I think this box triggered my memory last night. So take it, like I said, and see what it may lead to, because if I keep it here, I will."

"Have mercy . . ." Justus released my hand and backed himself into the wall. His eyes were wild and tired, more than likely tired of my constant ball-drops.

Salvador leaned back in his seat, opened his jacket, and reached for a red lollipop. His mannerism reminded me of the late actor Telly Savalas's portrayal of the hit television detective Kojak, back in the day. Seeing that red lollipop pop out of his coat pocket sealed the deal for me.

"How do you know that what you think you saw last night was what actually happened? It has been a long time.

I can barely remember what happened that night. You could be putting people there who weren't there."

"And why would I do that? Up until you asked me to find Braden Logan, his name had dropped off my radar. Shoot. He's an accountant, nothing dangerous about that. But he was a trigger somehow."

"Yet you think he's Gabe's killer," Justus said.

"Of course I don't. Braden didn't shoot at us. He wasn't in that parking deck."

Salvador scratched his cheek. "So you saw who did it, then?"

"No, it wasn't Braden. I know that for sure, because the other shooter was a woman."

"Angel, I'm glad you did wait to tell me all of this until after breakfast. I think this news will definitely cut into my dinner," Salvador said.

"I aim to please." I smiled short, then looked over at Justus.

He was looking at me, but I couldn't read his face.

"Justus, please don't be mad. I just want this part of my life over and—"

My phone buzzed. I reached into my pocket to see if it was Bella's school calling me. One thing Ava and my mom didn't tell me about becoming a mother was how tied to the phone you become when your child begins school. Although I didn't expect the worst, I tried to be prepared for anything and everything.

I looked down at the phone and gulped. "I'm trying not to kill Braden Logan when I find him."

Salvador coughed. "And why do you think you'll find him."

I put my phone on top of the box. "Frisco has found where his girlfriend is hiding him. They're in Alpharetta in some affluent subdivision that I'm sure will try to give me a hard time when we show up. I'm about to go out and drag him back to your house, Salvador."

"You'll have your work cut out for you. Some of these security staffers are laid-off Atlanta city police officers. They know search-and-seizure law like you know your ABCs." Salvador stood up and adjusted his belt. "Although it's out of my jurisdiction, I'll call Fulton County for you, so they get a heads-up that you're coming."

"Please do." I shook his hand. "Sorry about all of this."

Here in Georgia, bail recovery agents can't pick up skips without notifying the county what their plans are. It's a safety measure for both the recovery agent and the skip.

Salvador dropped his empty lollipop stick in a wastebasket, nodded, and showed himself out of the office. I reached for my bag and car keys. They sat on Justus's desk.

Justus lunged forward and touched my elbow. "Don't go yet."

"I've been here long enough. Don't you think?" I slid my keys in my jean pocket. "I know you had other plans for today."

"I do, but you're more important. Tell me. What do you need from me? How can I make this new drama easier for you?"

"You're too sweet." I checked my watch. "Can you check on Bella and Whitney for me later? If Braden is where Frisco states he is, then I know I won't be home when Bella arrives."

"No problem. I'll relieve Whitney and make them both a nice dinner." He pulled me closer and kissed my forehead. "I know things have been hectic. If you like, I can pick Isabella up from school for you. Just add me to her school contact card."

I cupped both sides of his face with my hands and planted a big kiss on his plump lips.

He chuckled, then looked at me with those brown eyes that melted me all over. "You better go before I marry us right now."

"It's good to know that I'm not the only one thinking about the honeymoon." I giggled.

21

Thursday, Noon
Crabapple Orchard Country Club Community
Subdivision, Alpharetta, Georgia

Alpharetta was one of the most affluent cities in the Atlanta area. Before it merged into the north side of Fulton
County, Alpharetta was the seat of old Milton County until
the Great Depression. Back then the county had almost gone
bankrupt. As I drove past one multimillion-dollar, azalea
garden–themed estate after the next, it was hard for me to
believe this town had ever had a financial problem.

It was even harder to believe that a woman who lived
this well would be in a relationship with a tax geek on the
lam. I wondered what the woman looked like.

When I arrived at the subdivision, Frisco flagged me down
at the security gatehouse. It was very sunny outside, so I
saw it all and maybe too much. He stood next to two security officers who looked like they were expecting me, in a
bad way. Their necks were twisted, their eyebrows furrowed so low that they almost met the tips of their scrunched
noses.

"I haven't gotten out the car yet and they've already

given me shade," I grumbled to myself and hopped out of my SUV.

The reason I offered to split the commission on this with Frisco was twofold. I needed a heavy for protection purposes and I needed to reduce my time on this contract. Minor activities like meeting with the country club subdivision public safety and calling the local sheriff's department to let them know we were apprehending a fugitive took time away from me, Bella, and Justus. After the kiss Justus had given me a half hour ago, I needed to make sure I had time for one of those every day. Frisco needed to do better, and Salvador—I hoped—had made that call.

"Do we have a problem?" I asked the officer whose tan pants were pleated and crisp.

I wouldn't say that I'm a good judge of character, but I doubted that the shot-caller of this duo was the one who looked like he'd just rolled out of bed. His pants were a wrinkled hot mess.

"No problem at all. We just need to see your bounty hunter's badge," he said through gritted teeth.

Usually I would say something smart alecky about his "bounty hunter" remark, but I didn't want Braden to jump the back gate or hang glide out of here. These men were just doing their jobs. Unfortunately, they had prejudices and misinformation about who we were. If I lived up to their expectations, how would that benefit me?

I wouldn't, so I had to play by their rules. However, once I understood the rules, I would use them against the officers later. Just watch me.

The officer with the crisp pants had dry, calloused hands. I handed him my state bail recovery identification card, a certified copy of the bail bond, and the wanted poster Salvador had provided me from DeKalb County. When his hands touched the paper, it made a soft scraping sound that made me close my eyes for a second. This man needed a manicure and a nice bottle of cocoa butter hand lotion, stat.

He looked at me with surprise and bitterness. "What can I do for you, Agent Crawford?"

"We're here to bring in Braden Logan. He's wanted in DeKalb County and we have confirmation that he has been living in this subdivision for at least two months."

He lifted the paper and squinted, then lowered it and showed it to his partner. The wrinkled-uniform officer mumbled something incoherent and tilted his head toward the gatehouse. The pleated, crisp, and bitter officer excused himself to go to the gatehouse.

"He had to go get something," Wrinkled Officer Dude said to me as if I were blind or couldn't figure that out on my own.

I looked at Frisco and rolled my eyes at him. What in the world had he been doing before I got there? Trading baseball cards? I shook my head. Why was I splitting my money with this cat? I seriously couldn't remember.

Crisp Pleats returned with a clipboard. He had a lean in his walk that reminded me of Denzel Washington playing Easy Rawlins in *Devil in a Blue Dress*. I stood straighter. He cleared his throat and looked down at the clipboard. "We have no record of this man here."

I leaned over and glanced at the clipboard, then scoffed. "Sure. You have no record of someone by that name driving in here, but you don't know who's in the cars that have come through."

Frisco folded his arms over his chest. "That's what I told them before you arrived."

Yeah, right, I thought to myself. I studied the expression on Frisco's face. He looked more annoyed than before and I didn't know why. It wasn't like I was coming for him.

"It's okay, Frisco. He's just being thorough." I smiled and batted my eyes.

I hoped that if I seemed more girly he would relax a bit. It wasn't working. I sort of wished I still had my long hair. Halle knew how to rock this pixie cut, but I didn't.

"Did Fulton inform you that we were coming to capture this fugitive?" I asked.

"The only people we've talked to about this today are you and your homeboy."

I didn't like the way he said "homeboy."

"Frisco, will you do me a favor and call a sheriff out here."

"Ma'am, that would be a waste of time," the security officer said. "They pretty much don't care what happens out here, because we're on the edge of Fulton. That's why the subdivision hired private security officers. We don't need the sheriff to tell us you're not allowed inside the gate. This is our domain and our call."

"Like hell it is," I shouted.

"Angel, you're losing time," someone said from behind me.

Frisco, the security officers, and I spun around in the direction of the voice. Maxim stood there dressed in rare form: navy blue tee, dark blue jeans, black Teflon vest that had the word "U.S. Marshal" etched in big, bold white letters, and those black cowboy boots. I chuckled at the sight of him.

He walked toward us slowly, holding up his marshal badge wallet, revealing his bright, gold, five-point marshal star. He flashed it around in case we didn't see it. That made me laugh a little. Maxim was the master of the LE Peacock, my term for when law enforcement types like district and state attorneys, fixers, handlers, and your occasional

Maxim strutted their legal authority around us mere mortals.

"Marshal West, what can we do for you?" Crisp Pleats asked.

"You can let my partners help you remove a wanted man out of your nice neighborhood. We're sure you wouldn't want the nice folks of Alpharetta to know that you have willingly let this fugitive spend another minute in their safe country club community. It would tarnish your criminal record and I reckon it'd mess up the property value of your employers."

Crisp Pleats looked around. I couldn't read his mind, but by the way his eyes wandered off into the oak trees around us, he seemed to be thinking about what Maxim had just said.

"By the way, it's not your call, buddy." Maxim tapped his badge. "It's ours."

Crisp Pleats glanced at me and Frisco, then turned toward Maxim and handed my papers to him. "We were just doing our jobs."

"Of course you were and I appreciate you guys for what you do. Just remember this isn't a competition. We all have our roles." He took the papers out of the officer's hand and gave them to me. "We all are the good guys."

Then he turned to me and leaned toward my ear. "Why were you cursing? You know that's my job."

"Because Frisco wouldn't do it." I ribbed Frisco and chuckled.

Frisco didn't smile or laugh back, but he didn't frown or argue either. He had the good sense not to disagree.

22

"Open the gate, gentlemen, and we'll take it from here," I said to the security officers.

"Yeah, you guys man the gates for us. Make sure Logan doesn't sneak out while we're heading that way," Frisco said.

"Sure thing," Crisp Pleats said. "We'll help in any way we can."

"We would expect nothing less." Maxim tipped his hat at the men.

We turned around and walked back toward our trucks.

I said to Frisco, "Now you decide to speak up."

"You know good and well it wouldn't have mattered what I said to them top cops. They weren't hearing me—or you, for that matter." He looked over at Maxim and stopped walking. "Thanks for helping us out, bro."

"No thanks needed."

I touched Maxim's shoulder. "Well, I want to thank you anyway. I asked Sal to call Fulton for me, but I guess he hadn't gotten around to it yet. You sped things up for us, which rarely happens between bail recovery agents and law enforcement officers. You made us look legit."

"Bump all that. Like I said before, everyone has a job to do. Those guys had no reason to be that way with you," Maxim said. "But you have to admit there is stigma attached to you guys, and the reality television shows don't help."

"Like that's my fault." I huffed.

"Perhaps you should have worn one of your low-cut, high-thigh dresses. You know . . . to change the image."

"You won't let it go about that dress. Will you?" I scoffed and rolled my eyes.

Last month, Maxim had asked me to pretend to be a moonshine runner for his task force. I'd worn a blue halter sequined mini dress that he hadn't liked or maybe liked too much. It was short and got our job done in a short amount of time. Yet he was still licking his wounds over being wrong about the dress.

"Should we leave your SUV here since my truck is equipped to transport a fugitive?" Frisco asked.

"Yours is equipped?" I frowned and turned around. "What gave you the impression that mine isn't?"

"Because Tiger usually brings in the guys you tag for us. And come on . . . You're like a soccer mom girl scout. Your daughter and her brownie scout friends sit back there." He scrunched his nose. "I wouldn't have white-collar trash sitting where my kids play."

"Soccer mom girl scout. Are you kidding me?" I stepped back in surprise.

"Why don't you use my vehicle?" Maxim asked. "I can go in there with you."

"No, I can take it from here. Thank you."

"Are you sure? I mean, right now you seem to be off

your game." His mischievous grin had returned like it had before I got engaged.

I chuckled. "Don't mistake the pressure you put on those two wannabe LEs with me being off my game."

"If I hadn't shown up, then what would you have done?"

"I would have called the Fulton County Sheriff's Department to come down. If push came to shove, the sheriffs would have put them in check."

Maxim shook his head. "Not good enough. I'm tagging along with you guys."

"You can't do that." I threw my hands on my hips. "Frisco, tell him. The last thing we need is you scaring the rich white lady. She may go ballistic."

"And Frisco isn't scary looking?" He rolled his eyes toward Frisco.

Today Frisco wore his Big Bad Boys black T-shirt, a pair of dark wash jeans, and workman boots, and he carried his cuffs in the small of his back. He didn't look that bad. You could hardly notice the large dagger tattoo on the side of his neck.

I shrugged and dropped the corners of my mouth. "Nah."

Frisco tapped my shoulder. "If he comes along, then we'll still get credit for the capture?"

"I didn't say he was coming with us," I said loudly enough for Maxim to hear. "But if he does, don't worry. He can't go with us to DeKalb to take Logan in because Maxim is supposedly still on medical leave."

"And I can't come off leave until Logan is captured and he gives me what I need." Maxim chuckled. "So can we do this now?"

I nodded. "Let's."

23

Thursday, 1:00 PM
Crabapple Orchard Country Club Community
Subdivision, Alpharetta, Georgia

According to one of Frisco's tipsters, Braden Logan was hiding in plain sight with Allison Kim. She was a new divorcée, thirty-something, petite, blond, gymnastics mom, who once made the LPGA tour in her heyday. Her ex-husband was the king of orthopedic surgery in Atlanta.

They were almost perfect for each other except for the tiny issue of him leaving her for a younger, plump, almond-eyed brunette medical assistant, who was expecting his first son. Allison's consolation prize for playing a round of marriage with Dr. Kim was a three-million-dollar English manor–style mansion built on the ninth hole of the golf course, and a cure from golfer's elbow.

If circumstances had been different, I would have tried to be her one black friend. You know, the sistah sidekick in movies who helped the pretty, white lead actor find self-worth after heartbreak, job loss, or a tragedy that only white women related to. As we pulled into her cobbled drive, I felt more confident that I could definitely be that friend for her.

Whitney had called me on the drive to Alpharetta to let me know that Allison had chartered a private Cessna jet to depart tomorrow from DeKalb Peachtree Airport with a destination to Saint Petersburg, Russia. With that information, Frisco and I had until today to get Braden Logan back to County. Yet I couldn't stop thinking that I needed to find a way to get in with Allison.

Usually when I visited a home that might be suspected of harboring a skip, we planned a method of capture. One of us would make sure that someone was in the vicinity of any exit door, window, or roof. But this place was too huge for all of that and I was sure that Allison had a surveillance room inside. At least that's what the surveillance center company said to me when I called to inquire about a new service for my estate, while Maxim and Frisco were taking their dear time meeting me at my truck.

"This place is pretty, isn't it?" I smiled.

"What's your plan, Angel?" Maxim asked.

Frisco turned toward Maxim. "How do you know she has a plan?"

"She's smiling."

"Don't think you know me, Marshal." I blushed. "We're going to ring her doorbell. If Braden doesn't answer the door, then we'll introduce ourselves to her and tell her why we're here. Maxim, I want you to take off that marshal belt buckle, and Frisco, turn your shirt inside out. Once we're inside, Maxim, I want you to monitor the surveillance center and use your walkie-talkie feature on your phone to tell us where he is. Frisco, you and I will retrieve him."

"Sounds simple enough," Maxim said.

"What? No rebuttal? No better game plan?" I asked.

He shook his head and grinned. "You're the coach this time and I'm following your plays. Just remember that the next time I call you in for task-force duty."

"I'm pretty sure you'll remind me." I patted my Teflon vest.

I discreetly wore the vest underneath my button-down white sweater. I definitely didn't want Allison on the defensive. We walked toward the front door together; I rang the doorbell.

Thankfully, a woman fitting Allison's description answered the door.

"Mrs. Kim, I presume?" I asked.

"The former Mrs. Kim . . ." She sighed. "Your boss said you would be here within the hour to pick up the boxes, but I wasn't expecting you to be here this fast."

"We pride ourselves on the element of surprise," I lied.

I had learned from both Tiger and Sergeant Deacon West (Maxim's uncle) to listen and pay attention to the people you need to solve your case. If Allison assumed we were some private courier service, then that's what we needed to be. The fact that the real couriers wouldn't show up for another sixty minutes was like icing on the cake.

"Then you must have met my husband. He should win an award for being full of surprises." Allison nursed a margarita glass in one hand, and opened her door wider and waved us in with the other.

She led us to a staircase in the corner of her grand dining room. I pretended like I walked around million-dollar estates every day, when I wanted to drop my jaw after I passed every fine piece of art. My sister Ava's McMansion was what I said it was. The Kim estate was the real deal, a quarter-pound Angus beefburger of a place.

Allison stopped at the staircase and pointed downward. "The boxes are in the cellar down these stairs. They are already ready to go, but you seem to be short one guy. We need these boxes to the airport by two. Are you sure you have enough people for this?"

"Just in case we need an extra hand, would you be up for it?" I asked.

"That's what I hired *you* for." She smiled coldly.

"Right." I chuckled. "No offense, but you placed a service order with our boss at the last minute. This change required our other guy to get things squared away with TSA. He's at the hangar right now clearing this shipment with your pilot for no extra charge. You can't just decide to ship cases of wine at the last minute. We are the best in the city, but ma'am, give us a break."

I lied again, but this time I hoped I was right. The flight schedule Whitney had e-mailed me did not have a large shipment of wine flying with them. TSA rules were stricter since 9/11. There had to be some grumbling on the carrier service and the Cessna captain on the back end about this.

"My apologies. I do have a guest here who will oblige me. Braden!" she yelled.

I turned toward the men and smiled big with my eyes. Frisco licked his lips again, just like Big Tiger did before a chase. Maxim nodded at me and looked just as cool, calm, and collected as ever. I then realized the reason he'd wanted to tag along was because he missed the chase. He had been out of commission and probably wanted to see if he still had it. By a quick glance at his toned, muscular physique, I determined he looked like it. My heart began to race. It was about to get fun.

It took Braden thirty seconds to meet us near the cellar staircase and about five to realize that we weren't from a licensed wine shipper. He took off running down the stairs. Frisco bounded behind him and Maxim ran toward the front entrance to catch him on the other side.

I called Fulton County myself, to verify that they had received a call from Sal.

Allison snatched the phone out of my hand.

"What do you think you're doing?" she yelled.

"Ma'am, Braden Logan is a wanted felon. If you cooper-ate with us, then you won't be charged with harboring a fugitive."

"A fugitive? What? I . . ." She looked downstairs. Her margarita glass trembled in her hand. "Does every man lie about who they say they are?"

"No, just the bad guys do." I thought of Justus and im-mediately thanked God for him.

She looked at me with tears in her eyes. "But why would they lie to me?"

"Bad boys lie to rich women because they want a nicer place to hide. Don't take it personally. It happens to the best of us. Stay upstairs and we will get him out nice and quiet." I patted Allison Kim's shoulder before I slid down her cast iron, cellar railing, to run after Braden Logan myself.

24

Thursday, 1:30 PM
Crabapple Orchard Country Club Community
Subdivision, Alpharetta, Georgia

If circumstances were different, I would have told Allison the truth. Bad boys lie to privileged women because they know that they're no different from the rest of us. They just have more money to blow. I felt sorry for her, because I knew about her background. She had been betrayed before and was left with a lavish lifestyle. This time she was left with a fueled Jet with nowhere to go.

This was where the Sistah Sidekick came in. She would hold Allison's hair while she cried her sorrows away and convince her to take that trip to paradise despite her misfortune and bad luck with men. She'd even take an early vacation to join her on the excursion. They would spend bucketsful of money on clothes the size of one of my handkerchiefs. They would drink mimosas like water, have affairs with men twice their age, and then find a small, seaside, white church on a hill to repent their debaucheries in. It would be good movie fun. But that wasn't the way the real world worked, was it?

In the real world, most stupid and smart, rich and poor,

old and young, pretty and homely women have been conditioned to hunger to belong to a man and for that man to belong to them. It was bored into our psyche from listening to fairy tales when we were too young to read, reading them once we could, and then watching them play out in cartoons, movies, and the news. I've tried not to teach it to Bella, but I'm only one woman against a sea of many.

If they saw what I saw, women who did stupid things like risking their jobs to sneak off to be with him or lying to the police about how many people were actually in the parking lot when he was murdered, they would understand that they never win in the end. There's no happily ever after when the relationship is founded on lies and fairy tales.

See, I knew the bewilderment in Allison's eyes very well, and I also knew that it didn't matter what I said to her, she would do just about anything for another night of pleasure with Braden Logan, including fight me. But I didn't want to clock this chick. Besides, she looked like she might be packing a Glock under her cashmere sweater. So I lied and kept it moving.

I had a precocious first grader waiting at home for me and a good man waiting to build a life with us the minute I gave him the word.

Surprisingly, Braden was nothing like his jacket said. He must have been working out while hiding out. He wasn't as white bread as I thought. He definitely wasn't 150 pounds. He was quite built and jumped those stairs like an Olympic hurdler. The geeks of today were athletic and hot, a bad combination. No wonder rich Allison was so mind blown.

Once I reached the bottom of the stairwell, all I saw was Frisco. Braden was nowhere to be seen. That was because the wine cellar was dark.

I flipped on the lights. Things didn't get much brighter. Allison had dim lights installed. The light bulbs gave a bluish tint to the room. As I looked around, I noticed three walls were painted in navy blue and one wall was decorated in a plum and cobalt blue velvet draping. All the walls except for the draped one were covered in custom-built wine racks. A rustic wooden table with matching velvet chairs sat in front of the draped walls next to a wooden, bowl-shaped sink. This was the wine-testing area.

I looked closer, then frowned. "Where is Braden?"

"Your guess is as good as mine. I haven't been able to find him. It's like he vaporized. I think this dude was on meth or worse." Frisco panted.

I think Braden's bolt had knocked the wind out of him. Not a good look, if he wanted to join me on another hunt.

"Nah. He just bit off more than he could chew and you need to lay off the space movie marathons," I said.

"Dude jiggled and flip-flopped down those stairs like a Jamaican bobsledder in the Winter Olympics," he said. "He's probably hurt and wants to surrender by now."

I chuckled, but my gut told me that Braden Logan had no intention of going quietly with us back to DeKalb County Jail. However, tiptoeing in a wine cellar in pursuit of a wildflower skip wasn't my idea of a good time, so I needed to stir the pot.

"Frisco, I don't spend much time on skips. Let's set a world record tonight."

When a skip missed his court date, he breached his bail contract with a bail bondsman. Braden Logan had been released on bail to appear in court three days before Ty had committed suicide. If we caught him before DeKalb County did, then Salvador could release him into Maxim's custody for safekeeping until they found the leak in the department. Salvador used us to keep things under the radar. I hoped it worked.

"Braden, this is Angel. I'm not destroying Allison's nice

wine cellar to find you. That would be stupid and neither one of us is stupid." I sat down at the winery tasting table and motioned for Frisco to sit down with me. "Let's create a treaty. You turn yourself in with us and we'll keep you from returning to County lockup."

Frisco shook his head. He didn't want to sit down. I was eyeballing him to follow my lead when the lights went out. I hopped up. I guessed Braden wasn't up for any peace talks.

The cellar was pitch black. I didn't like pitch black. In fact, I had bad memories of pitch black, so bad it made me angry just to think about it.

I searched my body for a flashlight, but I couldn't find one. I'd left it in my truck. As a matter of fact, I'd left many of my usual capture trinkets in the truck. My pocketknife, pepper spray, and nunchucks were missing. I think I subconsciously left them, because I felt safer than I did on most hunts. This was the first time I had a team to back me. However, I'd just put us all in danger because I dropped the ball.

Instead of letting my guilt get the best of me, I tiptoed away from the table and searched for Frisco with my nose. It was too dark to do anything else and my partner smelled good: a mix of bergamot, cinnamon, and something muy caliente. I found him on the other side of the table.

"Are you carrying a flashlight?" I whispered.

"No, mami," Frisco said. "I only carry it at night or when we're going into basements."

I had to keep myself from heavy sighing after that remark.

Maxim was still outside waiting to catch Braden if he ran out through an exit door. Because Braden had hit the lights, I assumed that there was no exit. He would also have probably been at least two miles from Allison's house by now if the cellar had an exit. The only way in was upstairs, which made great sense since Allison had us go through the front entrance to retrieve the wine, instead of on the side or in the back. I hoped Maxim would join us any second. If he came through the stairwell, he would light up the place.

So now Frisco and I stood back to back, eyeing that dark shadow near the wine racks, hoping Braden didn't do anything stupid that might get him killed.

Frisco didn't have the patience I did. He didn't have any kids or meddling sisters, but he was a sweetheart and a godsend. I had been searching for a heavy, a brawny tough guy to tag along with me on manhunts. I needed him to watch my back, because I was tired of worrying about someone taking me out before Bella grew up. Now that I was engaged to Justus, I was afraid I wouldn't meet him down the aisle if I kept going it alone.

I loved my work and I had finally gotten my bounty-hunting groove back. Now, if we could get Braden to DeKalb County Jail in time . . .

"Braden, darlin', we don't have all day, so let's drop the games," I said to the shadows on the wall to my right, underneath the stairwell, and the large one waiting for us at the end of a long creepy hallway.

I didn't have a clue where he was. As large as this cellar was, there had to be more than one light switch in it.

"Logan, no me hagas venir en pos de ti en ésta oscuridad," Frisco said.

"Can we kill the Spanglish, Frisco?" I felt my eye roll. "Allison obviously speaks English and Braden isn't Latino."

"We don't know that," he hissed. "This man is an alias on top of an alias. His skin looks like family to me."

"The man's been living on a golf course with a ginormous pool out back. He's probably tan from luxuriating up in here," I whispered. "My phone has a flashlight feature. I'm going to switch it on and talk him down from Crazy."

"These rich people don't like us muddying up their tile." Frisco sucked his teeth. "Stop placating this fool. Let's get paid."

"I'm not placating him, but he needs to come on. . . ." I mumbled.

Before I'd left for work, I'd promised Bella that Justus and I would take her for ice cream this afternoon. Although I hadn't given Justus the time he deserved this morning, Bella wouldn't suffer because of my penchant for chasing Bad Boys. But if I was going to make good on my promise to her, I needed to get Braden out of this mansion like right now. If I was getting out of here in time, I had to take charge.

I felt something cold and hard on my back. It was in Frisco's pocket, but it wasn't a gun.

"Do not make us drag you out of the dark, Braden. I'm counting to three. If you don't turn that light back on, it's your ass. One, two, three."

I pulled the flashlight out of Frisco's back pocket, turned it on, stuck it in my mouth, and raised my stun gun from my holder. I heard feet scuffling and bottles crashing in the back.

"What the—" Frisco huffed. "I thought I left this in the truck."

As the flashlight pierced the darkness, I sprinted toward the wine racks with my stun gun ready to fire upon anything uncorked. Then I saw Braden's red eyes. Frisco was right. He was definitely on something.

He stumbled against the rack. A bottle crashed to the hardwood floor, but I kept my eyes on Braden. "Allison is going to hurt you for busting up her Bordeaux."

The lights came on. I jumped in my shoes, hopefully not high enough to give Braden the impression that I wouldn't shoot his hide-and-go-seek behind. It was more than likely Maxim.

I spat the flashlight out of my mouth. It popped when it hit the ground. "Braden, do you know that I'm close enough to tase you? I could have you gyrating all over Allison's gorgeous floors and foaming at the mouth like a junkyard dog. Is that what you want?"

He shook his head, then lowered it. His shoulders had slumped into a defeated stance. I would have felt bad for him, but he had just played with my time and I have a problem with folks who mess with my time.

He stepped forward, his head still low but his arms outstretched for me to cuff him. "No, Angel. I want to be with Allison. Can you get me back tonight?"

"For you to catch your flight to Russia? Uh . . . nah." I cuffed him. "I have a better offer for you, one that won't have you hiding out."

"Ty said you guys would say that."

"Ty lies a lot." I huffed. "Does it run in the family or are you not related to him?"

"What do you think?"

"I think you're not who you say you are." I pushed him forward and began walking him toward the exit. "You're not Ty's brother-in-law, you're not Braden Logan, and you're not in WITSEC anymore. You're unprotected and there's a bounty on your head."

His walk began to slow. We were now near Frisco. I mouthed to Frisco to go get his truck and find Maxim. Frisco nodded and headed up the staircase first.

After Frisco opened the exit door and went inside, Braden stopped and clutched the rail.

I sighed. "Braden, besides carrying this stun gun, I have a

gun. If you try anything funny up these stairs, you will either be crippled or dead," I said.

"Angel, can we talk now?" His voice was low, but loud enough for me to hear. "Just me and you."

"You missed your chance to talk when you shut the lights off on me. Darkness makes me angry. Ty should have told you."

"Ty's dead." His voice cracked.

"My condolences . . . Now, let's move," I said.

"I shouldn't be in this situation again." He whimpered. We were now three steps away from the top. "Angel, I want to make a deal. I'll tell you what you need to know, but you can't let me go back to County. I need to work a deal with Tiger."

"Braden, I'm just a recovery agent. I don't make deals." We stepped back into the dining room. I was so glad to get out of the cellar.

"You do if you're looking for a bigger fish to catch."

"I'm looking to get you out of here. Move." I nudged him toward the foyer.

"You really don't want to know who's playing the fence on both sides?"

I walked around from behind him to look him in his eyes. "I don't care, but someone else does. If you pick your feet up, I can take you to them and then you can make your deal."

"Are they waiting for me at DeKalb County? I don't want to be hemmed up in holding."

"To have all these demands . . . I don't understand why you don't have a lawyer."

"Ty was working on it for me."

"Is that why he wired you the last of his savings account?" I asked. "To retain a lawyer?"

"Something like that." He nodded. "Look, Angel. I'm not a criminal. I'm just a guy who's good with numbers in a bad way."

"Cute." I chuckled. "I'm curious. What's your relationship to Ty?"

"Leave my man alone!" Allison yelled from behind me.

She was so close to me I could feel her desperate breath on the back of my neck. *Where in hell were Frisco and Maxim?* I didn't turn around.

"Allison, I hope—for your sake—that you're talking to my buddy Frisco, because if you're talking to me, then I have no choice but to defend myself and bring both you and Braden into custody. I told you to stay out of this."

I gave Braden one of those psychologically intimidating staredowns that Mama used to give me and my sisters and then I grounded my feet. Before he could warn his woman, I spun around, zapped three million volts into her neck, and watched her fold to her knees. She made a buzzing noise with her mouth as she gritted her teeth. The jolts from the stun gun ran its course through her body, while Braden screamed for her. The noise from it all began to make my head ache, until I saw a body on the floor in the foyer.

25

What in the world? I squinted. "Braden, don't move unless you want me to kill you."

"I won't, but I'm not going to jail for this. I didn't hurt anyone," he said.

"Shut up," I said as I stepped around Allison's body.

My heart pounded. Both Frisco and Maxim had the same build. I had spent so much time studying their faces that I hadn't recognized the shoes on their feet. Therefore, I had no clue who was knocked out in the foyer. However, I didn't think I had the heart to see Maxim sprawled out again, and if Maxim was down, then I was without another heavy. Honestly, I was tired of men falling at my feet, not the kind of words a woman liked to hear.

I stepped a little closer and peeked, then gasped. It was Frisco. He was knocked out, apparently by the baseball bat that was on the other side of Allison's twitchy right leg. My hands coiled into fists, but I couldn't hit Allison again. She was already knocked out.

I turned my attention back to Braden Logan and then pointed at a space near the foyer. "In that corner, on the ground, butt on floor, then eyes on me, *now*."

Braden immediately complied with my orders and didn't open his mouth.

I leaned down to check Frisco's vitals. He had a heartbeat and he was breathing, but his pulse was weak and thready. Judging by the bruise on his noggin, he would be a very rich man. Who knew Allison's golf swing would pay off for him?

"Where's the other guy?" I asked Braden.

"I don't know. I've been with you. I don't remember another guy."

Since Maxim was nowhere to be found, I assumed Allison had cracked her bat on him, too.

"Oh no." I began to pace. I looked around the foyer, behind the staircase, the foyer restroom . . . "Oh Lord, where did she put him?"

I heard sirens from a distance. My phone rang. It was Mom. I sent her call to voicemail.

Crap! I cut my eyes at Braden and wanted to kick him in his little boys. I flipped my phone open and dialed Fulton County EMS. I had no choice but to call their emergency call center. Frisco needed medical attention and Allison needed someone here to keep me from killing her when she woke up. That call for help would be broadcast throughout the county and online for everyone to hear. Anybody who wanted to find Braden Logan was about to know exactly where he was.

What made matters even worse, Maxim's miraculous recovery and return to work was about to be exposed, too. I could forget the commission on this, because once Fulton County Marshals arrived, they would transport Braden to

DeKalb. Bond forfeited. Tiger would have a fit and Riddick Avery would get a belly roll of a laugh at my expense. The only consolations I had were that Sanchez's fake death hadn't been uncovered by this fiasco and I had some alone time with Braden.

I flipped the phone closed and put it back into my pocket. I decided to have a chat with a friend of a friend before the EMTs found us.

I walked over to where he knelt and stood over him, then pulled out my Glock. I placed the barrel on his sweaty nose tip. "Braden, you better hope Frisco and the lost U.S. marshal didn't die, because then I've got to kill you and your girl, or kill your girl and blame the whole thing on you."

I removed the gun from his nose and tapped him on the top of his cranium with the gun barrel.

Braden rubbed his head and began to whimper. "I told you that I would tell you who the dirty cop is, but you don't care. So what else do you want from me?"

I heard something: a woman's voice. I looked down at Allison, but it wasn't her. She was still unconscious.

I turned to Braden; he shrugged. "What?"

"Did you hear that?" I whispered.

Braden tilted his chin up. "Check your phone."

I reached for the phone and pulled it out of my pocket. Sure enough, someone was talking in it. I lifted it to my ear and listened. I must have butt-redialed Fulton County. Another 911 dispatcher was on the other end of the call. She was calling my name repeatedly.

"Yes. My name is Angel Crawford. I'm a licensed bail recovery agent in your county. I just called a few minutes ago. There is a U.S. marshal possibly wounded somewhere on the grounds. I have a recovery agent down and a citizen's arrest on his female attacker. She's tased and on the ground beside him, and I have a fugitive in my custody"—I muted my phone—"who may become dangerous now that he knows there will be more charges attached to his prior."

Braden winced at me.

"I dare you to get froggy with me. I double dare you," I threatened Braden.

"Are you calling from the same number as before? Is the number . . ." I heard the dispatcher's words, but my mind was still stuck on Braden's plea. "Ma'am?"

Then my phone double vibrated. I'd set my mobile to do that when I had an important call coming through. I reserved the service for only Mama, Whitney, and Justus.

I unmuted the phone. "Yes, this is my number. However, I can't stay on the phone. My mom's calling."

"Ma'am, please hang on until EMS or the first responding officer arrives."

My phone buzzed again. My nose twitched. Mama wasn't the kind of woman who understood why her children didn't answer her calls on the first ring, so I was in another pickle.

"Miss Police Dispatch Woman, my mom's on the other line. Please get here else I'm a dead woman."

I ended the call and crouched down toward him so he could get a good look at me. "I don't look familiar to you?"

He shook his head. "No."

"Maybe if I say Gabriel Hwang, will that ring a bell for you?"

For a few seconds he shook his head and then his eyes widened. He sat back with a big surprised look on his face. "No way."

"Way."

"I thought you were a reporter?"

"I thought you were an accountant."

"Like I said, I'm good with numbers in a bad way."

I chuckled. "Sounds like you do more than just simple accounting."

"I have a lifestyle to maintain."

"Seems like Allison was doing all the maintenance."

"Do you think a woman like that would deal with a man who didn't have bank?"

"Honey, you would be surprised," I scoffed.

He looked over at Allison. She was still knocked out. "Will she be all right?"

I nodded. "Her heart's still beating, but if she comes to, I'm knocking her out again."

He smirked and looked down.

"I don't see anything funny about this situation," I said.

"I'm not laughing. It's just looking at you here holding a gun and acting badass is a trip. This isn't you."

"This wasn't me then, but it is now."

"What happened to you?" he asked. "Hwang couldn't stop gushing about you, how you were this intelligent, good girl that had her head on straight. He was cleaning up because of you. He cleaned up because of you. Now . . ."

I looked out the window. "Now what?"

He looked up at me. "You're not here to take me in, are you?"

"Why would you think that? Why do you think I'm here?"

"The way you're looking at me." His cuffed hands trembled in his lap. "You're making me nervous."

"I'm gonna make you dead, if you don't explain yourself."

"I don't know what happened. Something went wrong. You weren't supposed to kill him."

"What did you just say?!" I stumbled back.

I couldn't breathe, but I couldn't stop myself from releasing the chamber in my Kahr either. Braden cowered in the corner with his cuffed hands hiding his face. My hands were steady, but I still couldn't catch a breath.

If it weren't for the police lights twirling in my periphery, I would have blown his head off.

26

Thursday, 2:40 PM
Crabapple Orchard Country Club Community
Subdivision, Alpharetta, Georgia

Because we were in a country club in Alpharetta, the Fulton County marshals and EMS got there in under ten minutes and so did a white *Atlanta Sentinel* news van. Maxim's truck was gone, which was a good sign. He wasn't dead or dying somewhere on this property. Yet I didn't have the brainpower to figure out where he had run off to and I couldn't afford to waste my cell-phone battery on texting or calling him to find out where he was. Tiger said he was on his way. I didn't think he could help the situation, but I needed some support. I needed to convince these guys that Braden Logan was my fugitive and was leaving with me.

Most important, I needed Mom to stop blowing up my phone. She had called me again and this time I had to take her call.

"I don't care if the river turned red. It's no excuse for you to not answer your phone when I call," Mom berated me, while Alpharetta Police tagged every corner of Allison's property, including me. "So what's your excuse?"

I looked apologetically at the detective standing in front of me and shrugged. "Mom, you just wouldn't understand."

"We need to finalize reservations for Friday at Vinings Inn. Are you going to be there, and the answer better be 'yes' or I'll kill you," she said.

I sighed and lowered my head. Since Ava and I had reunited, everyone assumed that I would rejoin the Crawford Curtis family rituals: Mother's Day brunch at St. Regis Hotel, opening night of the Alvin Ailey Dance Company at the Fabulous Fox Theatre in February, Ballethnic's *Nutcracker*, and Vinings Inn on fourth Fridays. I wanted to ease back into the clan slowly and on my own terms, definitely not due to maternal death threats.

"Evangeline?" Mom squealed my name like a hog farmer.

I cupped the phone with my hands and looked at the detective. "Am I being arrested?"

She shook her head and mouthed, "No."

I smiled at her. "Are you sure, because I wouldn't mind a good excuse to be gone for a few days."

"No, but we do need to talk to you about Mr. Logan and Mrs. Kim." She looked ahead. "I'll be right back."

As she walked off, I turned my attention to Allison. She was still knocked out, lying sprawled across a stretcher. I wondered if she would have hit Braden with the baseball bat if she knew that what tipped us off was her boyfriend's booty call to his wife.

Mama kept yapping. "Evangeline, it's imperative. NO! It is your narrow behind in a sling, if you don't get here before our quiches are served tomorrow."

"Mama, relax . . ." I rolled my eyes, already tired of the melodrama with her. "I have too much going on today to think about tomorrow. Frisco has been injured, I have to take our fugitive to Tiger, locate a missing marshal, and get home before Bella ends her day without me. It may be hours before my feet touch home. Go ahead and make your reservation. One more thing to add to my 'to do' list."

I could hear Mama gasp after I said that.

When I was in my twenties, Mom's huffing and puffing would make me do miracles. I couldn't take her disappointment. But now, as a mother myself, I knew her tricks and I knew what worked with the Crawford Curtis women. She'd called me for more than just a reservation, but I didn't have the time today. I just didn't.

The phone was quiet. No one seemed to be breathing, not even her.

"Mama?" I whispered.

"Don't you 'Mama' me, Evangeline Crawford. In order for us to move forward, you must be here. It's the only way everything will work out for us."

"For us?" I frowned. "What are you talking about?"

"I'm talking about your life, your future life with Pastor Justus Morgan. He hasn't heard from you either."

My eyes were already rolled back, so they couldn't go any farther. "Mom, I need to keep this line clear. I'm on the job. My partner is down, multiple injuries, and cops are all over the place. I can't call him under these circumstances."

"And he's on God's errand every day," Mom said. "You know, Justus—your fiancé, or have you forgotten that, too?"

"That's impossible, because you're going to make sure that I remember that fact every day until we marry," I said, as I pulled my bail recovery paperwork out of my truck to take to the lady detective.

Braden sat in my plastic-covered backseat, handcuffed. Apparently he'd had an accident when we surprised him or when I pointed my gun at his nose. His cheeks were flushed and filled with shame. But I didn't feel sorry for him. Ty could have gotten me, Sanchez, and Maxim killed. For all I knew, Aunt Mary might have been right and he had Uncle Pete killed. Nothing was certain except I had the only clue to this puzzle stinking up my backseat. I should have used a car rental.

However, he couldn't get out of the back, because Bella had broken the door handles long ago. The child lock prevented the doors from being opened on the inside, so he was good and jailed inside. He would stay back there until Tiger arrived, if I only knew when that would be.

I checked my watch, while Mom ignored the fact that her daughter was involved at a crime scene.

"Evangeline, don't make me snatch your little neck through this phone receiver," she hissed.

"Yes, ma'am. I'm sure of that, too." I pointed my gun at Braden and placed my index finger over my mouth for him not to speak.

"And put your gun back in your pocket before you make that poor soul in your custody wet his pants. No grown man needs to go to jail with pissy drawers on."

"If Frisco doesn't wake up soon, the least of this guy's worries are pee pants."

Braden's blue eyes moistened. I think he was about to cry. He didn't need to worry. Tiger always provided clean clothes to any one of our convicts who needed it. As much of a hood as he claimed to be, Tiger was a caring man at heart. And late . . .

"Angel, what has gotten into you? Do you know how your engagement is? Are you aware that plans must be made?" I could hear a hint of desperation in her honey-drizzled voice.

Mom had a voice dripped in Southern elegance and charm. It kept her never lonely of male companionship and hid the terror that petite, wedding-eating dragon could unleash on her daughters.

"Mom, how did reservations for Vinings Inn turn into my wedding plans? Can I be engaged for a while? Can I just enjoy it? Can I do that? Can I?"

"You ought to be ashamed of yourself, talking to me like that."

I noticed the lady detective coming toward me. She was walking with a guy wearing a black golfer's tee and khaki pants. He looked like Alpharetta PD.

"Mom, I apologize if I offended you, but I have to go. They want me now. I need to get off the phone and take care of this. Like I said before, Frisco is hurt. I need to make sure he's okay."

"Make sure he's okay? What about your man?" Mom asked. "Honey, if you don't set a wedding date, you'll be without a mate. And will you be okay with that?"

My eyes rolled so far back, I think I saw my shirt tag.

"Gotta go, Mom." I ended the call, shut my door, and braced myself for the cops.

"I'm not going to take up much of your time, because I know you need to take this guy to DeKalb. But the lead detective has some questions from the statement you gave me earlier; he needs further clarification," she said.

The guy in the khakis didn't speak, but he smiled.

She touched his shoulder. "I'll leave you to it."

He flipped his notepad back and pulled a pen from behind his ear. "I want to make sure your statement is correct. You said that you and your partner, Frisco, came to Ms. Kim's home to apprehend Braden Logan and then all hell broke loose. Is that right?"

I wanted to respond, but I was preoccupied. Where we stood, I noticed Allison was now awake. She was sitting up in a wheelchair. Her hair was frazzled and her fake lashes had fallen off and mixed into the clumps of mascara streaking down her face. *Love will make a fool of you, if you let it.* EMS wheeled her out of the mansion and into an EMT van.

Frisco, on the other hand, had been taken away a few minutes ago. He was still unconscious. I overheard on my radio scanner that he was being taken to Saint Joseph's. Not good. Saint Joseph's was one of the best hospitals in the state. If he was being sent there, then his injury was more serious than a bump on the back of his head. I began to worry for my friend.

I turned my attention back to the detective. He had a boyish face and smiled when he talked. I'm sure his nature calmed most people, but it didn't charm me. The Knocker was charming and I killed him without batting an eye.

"I didn't use those exact words, detective. . . ." I studied his brown eyes.

He had long lashes. Cops with long lashes had crazy, jealous wives. I noticed the wedding band on his ring finger, too.

"I said that Frisco and I came to apprehend Braden Logan. He ran downstairs into Allison's wine cellar. Just when he was about to give himself up, Allison bludgeoned Frisco with a baseball bat. I tased her because she wouldn't stand down. And Braden . . . well, I made him pee in his pants." I looked over at Braden and shook my head. "I can't believe a grown man would do that."

The detective chuckled, then coughed. "Grown men scare easily, too, Angel."

"I bet they do." I smiled. "I don't want to sound rude,

but are we done here, detective? I really need to get out of here. I promised my pastor we would discuss wedding plans tonight or I may be in trouble."

"Congratulations on your engagement. I remember mine briefly, but my wife knows every detail." He closed his notebook and smiled again. "I think we're done here, and since we can't charge Mr. Logan with anything, he's free to go with you back to DeKalb County. However, if things change, I have your number."

He peered over my shoulder, noticed something behind my back, then returned his attention to me. He was still smiling. I found myself beginning to envy his inner peace.

"Something wrong?" I asked.

"You really should turn down the police scanner once the actual police arrive."

"Oh!" I slapped my hand over my forehead. "I apologize. I hope you don't think I stalk police chases."

"I don't know what to think. You're the first bail recovery agent I've met. We don't see them around here—at least, I haven't."

His phone buzzed. He looked down to read it.

"Yeah, I can imagine that you wouldn't. Most people who live here can afford to make their own bail. I overheard that my partner was taken to Saint Joseph's."

"Exactly." He nodded. "You're right, your friend was transported to Saint Joseph's. I'll give you the hospital number to check on his progress, and if you feel too uncomfortable, is there any family you would like to be called?"

I shook my head. "As far as I know, The Big Bad Boys and I are the only family he has, but I'll check."

"One more thing . . ." He placed the pen back behind his ear and the notepad under his arm before he folded his arms over his chest. "Your pastor shouldn't be rushing you.

A wedding is an event, but a marriage is a lifetime. Your pastor can wait, if you need more time. Trust me."

I touched his shoulder like the lady police officer had and smiled back. "If only my pastor wasn't my fiancé."

His eyes widened. "Then you better go."

I laughed. "I will as soon as I drop off my wet-pants fugitive."

27

When we arrived at Big Tiger's office, Maxim and Salvador stood in front of the entrance door, waiting on us. I was both surprised and angered to see Maxim there. Maxim opened the door for us, but I couldn't thank him or look at him. I wanted to wring his neck.

As soon as I chained Braden to a table, I was going home. This day had been too long for me and so any foul looks or actions just made it easier for me to leave.

Salvador, on the other hand, gave me the scariest look of the year. Why he gave me the mean mug was a mystery I really didn't have time to solve, but I would give it a shot.

"Why are you looking at me like I'm the one in trouble?" I asked him on the way inside the office. "I brought Braden to you, so what's the problem—besides that he needs a shower and fresh bottoms?"

"You'll know soon enough. Now follow me."

"Either tell me now or keep it to yourself, because I'm done for the day."

"Just give me a few minutes to get Logan processed."

"Salvador, the man needs a shower. It's going to take

more than a few minutes." I scoffed and patted his shoulders. "I have a family. Can it wait until tomorrow?"

Salvador huffed, then lifted my ring hand. My engagement ring shimmered in his eyes.

He looked at me and smiled. "It can't wait, but you're right. You have a family and that's more important than this. You did a good job. Now walk Mr. Logan back here with me. He'll get his shower after you leave."

"Thank you." I nodded.

Salvador led us to an empty room in the back of Tiger's mom's kitchen. The south wing of the office was Mama D's Soul Kitchen. I had been in here before, when Maxim and I met with Sean Graham. It was the last time I saw him alive.

Tiger wasn't here when we arrived, but I knew he was somewhere around. His car was still parked outside. He must have been hiding from me because he knew that I wanted to tell him off and make him pay for a nice steak dinner. He hadn't shown up like he said he would. No surprise there, but we had made a deal when we renewed our contract and then he'd promised me when we spoke on the phone earlier. He wasn't going to leave me in a lurch again or he would have to pay. It would be only fair if he paid twice.

"Tiger had to run to Saint Joseph's to square things away for our guy Frisco, but he's on his way back. He took his mother's car. She wanted to be there."

"That's cool Mama D will be there." I felt bad for not being there myself. "Any word on Frisco's prognosis?"

"Not yet, but if there was a problem we would have heard by now. Don't you think?"

"I'm sure." I cuffed Braden to the leg of Mama D's faucet. "In any case, I have to go. I can't wait any longer, and please wash down this area when you leave. Mama D don't play about her kitchen."

I waved good-bye to them and was heading down the corridor when Maxim hopped in front of me.

"Where are you going?" he asked.

"Why does it matter?" I walked around him and continued toward the door. "I did my job. Now hopefully you will do yours."

He caught my arm so tight it jerked me back. I grunted.

"What is wrong with you?" he hissed.

"I'm trying not to go to jail for bashing your head in with the fire extinguisher in my hand."

He looked down, then back at me with that Cheshire grin he wore so well. He removed his hands and threw his arms up. "I wouldn't want you to do that."

I placed the extinguisher back on the wall, then continued my walk.

"I can gather that you're mad at me, but I don't know what for."

"You know why I'm angry, Maxim." I frowned. "Where were you when we were fighting off Girlfriend Gone Gansta? One minute you're a part of our crew, then you run off. If you had stayed, Frisco might not have gotten injured in the first place."

"Frisco was down before I reached the foyer." His voice was now lower than before. "I'm sorry. If I had stayed, it would have blown the entire thing."

"But the security officers already knew that you were there. I assumed when you showed your badge, you were done with being in hiding."

"I paid them to keep their mouths shut about me being there, when I returned to their station. I had them call Fulton County to assist you."

"That answered the double call from 911, but your leaving me made me feel like a sitting duck. I never left you in danger. Never."

He looked in my eyes. I hoped he knew what I meant.

"Angel, come on . . ."

"What do you mean, come on?" His remark angered me. "I could have left you for dead in that swamp and gotten out of there, but I killed a madman to save you. I don't know what you marshals do. For a minute I thought you guys were better than me and the rest of us recovery agents, but you're not. You get a salary to capture a fugitive. I don't make paper until the guy is processed in. Maybe that's why you've got no loyalty. Your threshold for sacrifice isn't high enough."

"Angel, I knew you were safe. I didn't leave until I heard you tase Kim."

"And what about Logan? What if he would have hurt me?"

"Angel, I may not be great in math, but I can add two and two together. If Frisco was coming out, that meant you had captured Logan. When you subdued Allison, I knew you were fine." He placed his hands on his hips. "I knew that the security officers up front would call EMS and get Frisco some help. There was no need for me to be there with all those cops hanging around. Remember the reason we asked you to pick up Logan was so that I could stay incognito until we plug my leak."

"Your plan almost failed, because I almost plugged your leak with my bullet."

"Angel, I'm sorry. I should have texted you." He sighed. "I was trying to cover myself."

"Now you finally tell the truth." I folded my arms over my chest. "It's fine. I managed to get your boy here without you. Can I go now? I have to go spend some time with my daughter and my fiancé. You all can figure out my pay later."

"Angel," Braden shouted my name. "What's going on? You can't leave me here."

"Looks like you've made another fan." Maxim smirked.

I rolled my eyes at him and walked back to where I'd cuffed Braden. "You're fine. Just tell them the truth. Tell them what they want to hear and you're back in WITSEC."

"WITSEC?" He scoffed. "Ty said that's all you had for me and it isn't enough."

"You know what? I really don't care. I've done my job and did a really good job at not killing you." I leaned closer toward him. "We had a plan to pull you out without DeKalb County Police knowing you were in their custody, but your girlfriend went Arnold Palmer on my friend with a Chipper Jones autographed bat. I mean, who does that?"

He whispered, "So you know that there are people on the inside running things?"

I nodded. "That's why you're here instead of in County lockup. Like I said, Tiger's going to hook you up."

Maxim came over to where we were chatting. "She's right. Your charges will be dropped, but you have to leave this life behind. We will place you back into WITSEC. The good thing is that this isn't your first rodeo. You've done this before. And we won't hesitate to send you to County if you don't cooperate."

Braden's knee began to twitch. "I can't go back in there."

Maxim looked at me; I shrugged. I didn't want to know what was up with Braden. I wanted to go home.

"Why don't you tell these guys why you feel that way? They're smarter than they look." I touched his shoulder. "If you're still here in the morning, I'll call in and check on you."

I turned around to Maxim. "He's very afraid about going to County. He just needs some reassurance from you."

"Angel, do I look like a counselor? I need to check on Sanchez and find a way to take his statement without a paper trail. I don't have time for this."

"Then you have the perfect guy at your disposal to help with the paper trail." I looked at Braden. "I'm out."

Braden tugged my shirt sleeve. "Would you stay if I told you that the people who ordered the hit on Hwang are the same people who hired Ty, but I'm sure you figured that out by now?"

I gasped. "You're lying."

Justus had suggested it earlier today at our power break-fast with Salvador, but I thought it was a stretch. There were too many dots that needed to be connected in order for me to see patterns. I didn't believe in coincidences and I thought there was something fishy about this whole thing, but not that. I didn't believe in things tying up neatly in pretty bows.

"I can prove it, if you just don't let them take me back."

28

Thursday, 5:00 PM
BT Trusted Bail Bonds, Decatur, Georgia

"**W**hat is he talking about?" I shouted.

"Stop shouting . . ." Maxim took me by my elbow and pulled me toward the baker's rack. "He's just messing with you."

"No, he isn't!" I yanked my elbow back. "This is my last time warning you not to do that."

"I allowed you out of that hold because I suspected you were angry with me and had every right to be. But I'm not letting you go now until you hear my last orders for you. Are you ready to hear them?" He panted. I could nearly see his heartbeats puffing from under his shirt.

I nodded. "Yes, sir."

"Go home."

"Not until I get my answers."

"Listen to me." Maxim moved his hands from my elbows to my shoulders. "This case has nothing to do with your deceased fiancé's murder. Braden's trying to divert our attention by sending you on a wild-goose chase, so he can stall on telling us what he will eventually tell us: Who has been ratting us out to the Moonshine Syndicate?"

"I'm telling the truth, Angel!" Braden shouted.

"Shut him up, Tinsley." He looked behind me. "There's nowhere else for you to go but where I choose for you to go. If you want to join general population, keep talking to her," Maxim said. He turned back to me. "I'm sorry about that. You know how they get when they've experienced jail before. He'll do anything. If you want, I'll ask him some questions about his claim. After you've gone."

"He accused me of killing Gabe. I want to know why. Can you ask him that?"

His jaw tightened. "When did he do that?"

"When you ran off to save yourself." I scoffed.

"Sh . . ." He kicked his boot heel against a nearby stool. "Are we going to go through this again, Angel?"

I frowned in confusion. "What are you talking about?"

"You seem to have selective amnesia. The reason I was shot was because you were being hardheaded and stubborn when you snuck off without any backup."

"Sanchez did the same thing. What's the difference?"

"Sanchez is a marshal. She's trained to handle herself. What you seem to keep doing is making messes and then doing dangerous things in order to clean them up. I don't need you to make a mess right now. I need you to go home and plan your wedding with The Good Reverend."

"Let me remind you that you're still on medical leave, so if I deck you, you can't file worker's comp."

"Go home, Angel. Your threats aren't even sexy right now. Don't worry, you'll get paid."

"And I'm supposed to believe that?"

"What? Fed money is good, so what's the problem now?"

"Are you going to ask him who killed Gabe, who hired Ty? I won't sleep unless I know." I sighed, and sure enough, I began to cry.

Wow, this was embarrassing.

Maxim stepped toward me; I stepped back.

"Angel . . ." He spoke softly. "Go home and sleep. He's yanking your chain."

"Are you lying to me, Maxim?"

He shook his head slowly. "No. I'm a man of my word. You should know this."

"After the stunt you pulled today, how can I trust you?"

His brows furrowed and he looked over every inch of my face. His eyes rested on my lips. I gulped. He leaned toward my ear. My heartbeat sped up a bit. I exhaled to keep from getting mad at him for trying to use his chick-magnet tricks to calm me down.

"I remembered your kiss," he whispered.

I gasped. My heart almost leaped out of my chest. My legs trembled.

"Forget about it. Please," I whispered back as more tears came.

He stood straight and looked me in my blurry eyes. "I'll do whatever you want me to, as long as you trust me."

I bobbed my head so fast I thought my neck was going to fall off. "I trust you."

"Good. Now go home."

I stood there and didn't say anything as he walked back to Braden and Salvador. He was right. All I did was made my own messes and then cleaned them up. I had grown tired of me, too. I went home.

29

Friday, 9:00 AM
Saint Joseph's Hospital, Atlanta, Georgia

Frisco had become a brother to me in the short time I'd known him. His family was still in New York and I couldn't imagine living with family so far away. When he'd asked me if he could use me as next of kin for medical emergencies, I'd been honored. But as I watched this petite woman wearing Hello Kitty pink scrubs walk toward me, I didn't feel so well.

"Angel Crawford, I assume." The nurse smiled at me.

I nodded but didn't say anything back. My mouth felt like marbles were weighing down my tongue.

"Francisco has gotten an infection in his wound site."

I began to tremble. "How bad is it?"

"We're doing our best to clear it up, but right now everything is touch and go."

"And how long will it be touch and go?"

"Not sure, but if it doesn't improve by morning, then we may need to intubate him."

My knees buckled. She slid a chair under me before I fell.

"That's not going to happen," I whispered.

My breath was trying to leave me, but I believed that God would fix this, so I pulled myself together.

I stood up. "Can I see him now?"

The nurse frowned with worry. "I don't know if you can handle it."

"I can. I won't look bad in front of Frisco."

The intensive care unit was a huge room separated by glass walls and curtains. The nurses' station was housed in the middle of the room like an island. I guess it was good. They could all keep an eye on the patients. In order to enter Frisco's room, I entered through a different door from the nurse. The door led directly to Frisco's pod.

I expected the hospital room's mustardy smell, noisy machines, and wires on top of creepy wires polluting the white, pseudosterile decor, but I wasn't prepared for Frisco's appearance. It had only been four days since he was admitted and yet his massive, muscular frame had diminished. He didn't look like my big dough boy with a heart of gold. He looked like a sick man, hanging on a thin thread.

I gasped when I entered the room.

"Central line blood infection caused this?" I asked her.

She nodded. "It's common in hospital patients, but it was caught early, so his chances of recovery are good."

"And this is why he's in ICU?"

"No, his head injury put him in ICU. We had to put a PICC line in his jugular because we couldn't get an IV in his arms."

I touched my neck and felt my stomach drop. Frisco shouldn't be going through this.

Normally bail-recovery-agent work wasn't that violent. I've gotten myself into a few predicaments, but I wouldn't be doing this gig if I had to fight for my life after every hunt.

"Is there anything I can do?" I asked.

"You can come over here and let me look at you, bonita."

Frisco's husky Spanish-accented voice warmed the chill in the room.

Frisco lay on a blue thermal sand bed. Unlike the typical hospital mattress, it was designed to relieve pressure on the body and to act as a small form of therapy for the inactive muscles. I don't know what kind of therapy it was doing, but Frisco's ripped arms had whittled a little. But that was more than likely not the bed's fault. It was mine for not watching Allison Kim more closely.

I wiped back a tear and smiled. "Hi, my man."

"Did we get our boy?" he asked.

I nodded. "Of course we did and I tased the poop out of Allison."

"She didn't." He grinned.

"Yes, she did. When the cops and emergency services arrived, her white capri pants were khaki on the bottom."

"You are so wrong." He laughed.

"She was wrong for hitting you and not following our advice to stay out of it. So I beat the crap out of her, literally." I chuckled.

His laughs turned into coughs. The coughing got worse. I looked for the nurse call switch and hit the button. I cleared out of there so they could help Frisco. I had to call his family to let them know what was going on.

Friday, 10:15 AM
Vinings, Georgia

Every fourth Friday, Mom required Whitney, Ava, and now me to attend the Belle Brunch at the Vinings Inn. The Belle Brunch was a tradition as old as the Vinings Inn, the nineteenth-century general store turned Southern cuisine landmark. Our grandmother Lula Belle Johnson and her six sisters, who all had Belle as middle names, started the Belle

Brunch just after the restaurant opened its doors to black people. These women continued the tradition with their daughters, including Mom, who by the way had the good sense not to give any of us the Belle name stamp. I paid her back by naming Bella after the Belles. Nonetheless, once we became adults we were inducted into the fold. Now the Belle Brunch attendance was twenty-something strong, without me. I hadn't joined them since Bella was born. That was six years ago and no one seemed to care until now: Mom.

I was flying down to Vinings when she called.

"Mom, I'm almost there."

"You said that an hour ago, after you dropped off my grandbaby at school," she said.

"Well, I had a minor challenge."

"And what would that be?"

I gulped. "I couldn't find anything to wear."

I couldn't tell her the truth, that I had stopped by Saint Joseph's to visit Frisco. Before I left they had stabilized him, but he had to go to testing, so I would have to return later, if I could. However, it was going to be a challenge with Bella's school schedule. If he didn't come home today, I wouldn't see him until Saturday after Uncle Pete's funeral.

"Angel, stop lying. I know you're not late because of clothing. Whitney has been supplying you with fashionable clothes since that fiasco with you and that cupcake baker who had the warrant and the wheelbarrow."

"Mom, what are the travel plans for Uncle Pete's funeral? It's this weekend."

"I know that, and did you just change the subject?" she snapped at me.

"You were the one who said you would handle the arrangements, but I haven't heard from you when they will be."

"We'll discuss it once you get here. Now tell me, why are you really late?"

"First off, I'm not late. I'll get there in fifteen minutes." I merged onto the exit ramp I needed to get to the restaurant. "I'm just pressed for time because I stopped by to see how Frisco was doing at the hospital. I didn't get my answer, so I'll call later."

"I'm sorry for your friend, but I have to admit I'm glad it wasn't you who was cracked like an egg." She paused. "If I sound selfish, I have every right to sound that way."

"No, I don't think you're being selfish. I understand what you mean," I said.

"Good. Now, since you brought up the matter of clothes, what are you wearing?"

"Mom, was I supposed to get dolled up? Because I didn't have time to get girlied up and play pretty with my cousins."

"Play pretty with your cousins?" Mom scoffed. "That's not even in your vocabulary, but you do need to be dolled up or whatever the term is for looking like a woman raised by a Southern woman."

I rolled my eyes. Mom's Southern heritage shtick always got on my nerves. Sometimes I wondered if she thought regionalism was more important than race. Despite the Obama Age, we still had a large hill to climb. Brunching with silver-haired Old Atlanta socialites wouldn't change that fact.

"Mom, I'm not dressing up just to eat with some cousins who haven't said two good words to me since I left the *Sentinel*."

"Correct, you're dressing up to come to this brunch. No excuses."

"It's too late for that. I look fine."

"Since you thought it was more important to visit your friend than dress appropriately, stop at Francesca's and slip into something pretty. I will refund you the money."

I growled and pulled into Vinings Jubilee Shopping Center as my mom requested. "Sure, I'll do that, but let's be clear. No disrespect, but Frisco has been more of a relative to me than the sadity Belles. They didn't visit me one time when I was laid up or when I had Bella or when . . ." I huffed. "It's obvious they don't like me."

"And they could say the same about you." Mom paused, then cleared her throat. "Why do you have to be so difficult? Do this for me, Evangeline Grace."

I removed the phone from my ear and looked at it. She rarely called me by my full name. Something was up, but I wasn't quite sure if I wanted to know what it was.

"Mom, what's going on?"

"There is nothing wrong, and therefore, this is the perfect time to let bygones be bygones, for family to reconnect and to support each other again. They miss you, Angel, especially your Aunt Constance."

My heart fluttered at the thought of my aunt. "Aunt Connie will be there?"

"Honey, Aunt Connie has always been there."

I gulped. She did have a point. My pride and old schism with Ava had torn me away from my family. Now that we were back on good terms, I might as well fall on my sword or eat a rich plate of shrimp grits drizzled in wine butter sauce. Might as well . . .

"Okay, Mom. I'll be there in a spring dress. I want my money when I get there."

* * *

Friday, 10:20 AM
Vinings Jubilee, Vinings, Georgia

I'm not a shopper, but I knew how to obtain fine things. Vinings Jubilee was the spot to get them. I usually shopped through the twenty-five-year-old shopping district Web site. Although they had some of the same retailers as some high-end malls, they had the best selection of clothes, especially little-girl dresses. I had never driven this far out to see the place. When I hopped out of my truck, I couldn't help but marvel at it. It was gorgeous.

The property developers created the shopping center as an homage to turn-of-the-nineteenth-century Vinings, Georgia. It was designed to be a sort of neighborhood community center. They wanted it to look like a Victorian village with street lanterns, a big clock tower, and each shop resembling a Victorian house, each shop distinct from the other.

It was cute and efficient. I could hop into Francesca's and hop out without having to deal with the unnecessary foot traffic inside a mall. I spotted a blush-colored sheath dress with a lace embroidered neckline and a navy blue ribbon belt. It was cute, would make Mom happy, and the price wasn't bad at all.

After I bought it, I thanked my clerk for allowing me to change into it at the store, walked toward the exit, opened it, and bumped into Detective Francine Dixon. Un-freaking believable.

She looked at me like I stunk. I wanted to smack the stink off her, but the last thing I needed was to get arrested for assaulting an officer. Yesterday, Alpharetta let me off the hook for popping Allison Kim. No sense in chancing it in Vinings. Cobb County wasn't as forgiving as Fulton, or so I'd heard.

"Are you following me?" I asked her.

She batted her eyes and giggled. "Since I live here, I was going to ask the same thing about you."

I didn't return the laugh. I just kept watching her as she stepped into the boutique. She had on another finely tailored skirt suit. This one was gray. She also wore a pink and navy polka-dotted blouse that I had seen on Francesca's Collection Web site. It didn't take much to determine that she shopped here often, yet her timing didn't sit well with me. It never did.

"My mom lives in the area, too. In fact, I'm supposed to be meeting her as we speak. The women in our family have brunch at the Vinings Inn. I haven't been in a while, so I wanted to make a good impression."

"Hmm, and you definitely needed something less butch to wear to meet them." She nodded, while squinting her eyes and scrunching her nose. "I forgot that you belong to the black aristocracy here. That explains so much."

My neck jerked a little. "Explains what and how?"

"Since you and Justus got engaged, I've racked my brain with his decision, and seeing you here dressed like"—she smirked—"me, it now makes sense. This marriage will be quite advantageous for the both of you. Great power move on both parts."

"Dixon, how in the world you made detective being this long winded is a mystery to me, but I'm going to stop you before this conversation goes from nice to nasty."

She grinned. "I don't know what you mean. I think our conversation was quite pleasant."

"It was. I'm glad we ran into each other." I opened the door again, then stopped before I stepped out. "By the way, if you don't receive an invitation to our wedding, you don't have to rack your brain about it. You weren't invited."

Then I walked out.

30

I had texted Justus six times and left four messages on his voicemail before the Vining Inn's valet took my truck keys. Since I couldn't see Frisco, I had hoped Justus could check in on him for me. Justus never responded to my calls, however. And so now I was concerned. Where was he?

Before I could open the door of the restaurant, my question was answered. Justus Morgan's hand slid into mine, his arms wrapped around my waist, and his lips brushed against mine. They tasted like chocolate-covered strawberries and he smelled like a mint julep, hold the bourbon. I moaned. I was drunk in love with this man.

"Surprise," he said. His deep voice rumbled through my body in a good way.

I tried to pull away from him so that I could pull my wits together, but I couldn't. After a hard night and an even tougher morning, I needed someone grounded and good to hold on to. I buried my face in his strong chest and closed my eyes.

"If we linger in this doorway any longer than we already have . . ."

I looked up. "My bad."

"Don't apologize for loving me, woman." He kissed my forehead. "What I meant was if we held each other like this a minute longer, I would have to find a preacher in this place and marry you right now."

I felt my nose wrinkle. "Why right now?"

He lifted his eyebrow. "I may be celibate, Angel, but I'm no virgin."

For the first time in a long time, I blushed. I blushed hard.

Usually Mom reserved a room for the Belle Brunch. It was a smaller, private dining room. However, today Justus escorted me to the Main Room. It was a larger room with white linen-covered tables that sat adjacent to the patio. I should have known, right then, that something was up.

I stopped short of the dining room, then tugged Justus's arm. He turned toward me. I motioned for him to lean his head toward my ear. He was taller than me and my high heels had done enough damage to my burning calves. I couldn't tiptoe any farther than I already was.

I whispered, "What's going on?"

"I was going to ask you the same thing when I met you at the door, but you looked so kissable, I forgot."

I grabbed his arm tighter. "Then I'm afraid we're walking into an ambush."

"Why would you say that?" He chuckled.

"Because this is the Vinings Inn. Sherman's legendary burning of Atlanta still steams around here. We're walking into a trap; I can feel it in my calves."

"Should I carry you?" he asked.

I slapped his shoulder. "Stop being charming and peep game. This is a ladies' brunch, definitely not for a hot, scorching hot . . . not for guys like you."

"Well, maybe they need someone to pray over the dinner, especially since this is your first time back to the fold."

"How did you know that?"

"Ms. Virginia. She thought I would be a good surprise and good reason to keep your cousins and aunts off your case this time."

I shook my head and laughed. "I'm not calling my mom a liar, but she didn't tell you the whole story."

"A good mother never does," Mom said from behind Justus.

I would've stumbled out of my shoes, if Justus hadn't caught me.

Mom sashayed around Justus. Her hair held her signature golden-honey coif. She shared the same frame, bone structure, hair, and sense of style as timeless beauty Diahann Carroll. But her large Bambi brown eyes; that was her calling card. When she batted those beauties, grown men did things that amazed me. Never did I imagine she would use her powers to bait my boyfriend.

"See, I told you she would be much calmer if you accompanied her here today." Mom purred when she spoke to Justus.

"Mom, you didn't tell me that Justus would be here."

"I wanted to surprise you, darling." She ran her hands down my head, then placed a fresh white gardenia behind my ear. "I think your haircut has grown on me. I can see your pretty face."

I blushed again in a childlike awe sort of way until I remembered just who paid me the compliment.

"Mom, what have you done?" I asked.

She shook her head. "Just glad to see my baby. You do realize that every time you go on one of those manhunts, I don't breathe until you call. It really scares me. Doesn't it scare you, Justus?"

"Mama . . ." I called her that instead of giving her a side glance. That would be disrespectful. Although I hadn't seen my aunts yet, I knew they would have come out and slapped me from Mondays through Saturdays had they seen me cut my eyes at my mom. However, Mom was behaving more suspiciously by the minute. I wondered what she was up to.

"If you don't tell me what's going on, I'm walking out of here."

Mom smiled as if I hadn't just given her an ultimatum. "Mmm . . . I smell shrimp grits. Yum, yum, yum. I bet you're starving. Come on. We have special seating in the Main Room just for you two. You're going to love it."

She turned around and sashayed back toward the room. "Come on. My reservation doesn't last all day."

Justus caught my elbow, then kissed me on the cheek.

I jerked my neck and looked up at him. "What was that for?"

"I want to protect this moment before the bottom falls out."

I giggled. "So you do think something here is fishy, not just the fish tacos and shrimp grits enveloping the air?"

"I trust your gut, baby," he said.

When we entered the Main Room, our jaws dropped. All six of my aunts and my countless cousins stood up and clapped for us. I scanned the room for Whitney and Ava. I found them at the far left. They wouldn't look me in the eye, but it didn't matter. As long as Justus was with me, I could take whatever crap Mama was about to dish out.

Mom stood in the middle of the ladies. Her face glowed against the perfect blue day streaming from outside.

"Before we brunch I've been waiting to share my great news. Now that everyone is here, I can."

She extended her hand in the air toward me and Justus.

"Why do I feel like we're being led to slaughter?" Justus whispered.

I whispered back, "Because we are."

"As you well know, Angel and Brother Justus are engaged to be married. What you do not know is that the reason they haven't set a date is because they have been working so hard to save our streets and save our souls. . . . They need some time to focus on themselves. Wouldn't you agree?"

The Belles nodded their heads and applauded. I spotted Aunt Mary within the crowd.

I waved Mom's crazy notion off. "No, that's not the reason."

They were applauding so loudly they didn't pay me or Justus any attention.

Justus was looking at me. He mouthed, "So what is the reason?"

"I don't want to make a mistake," I finally admitted to him and myself. "I don't know how to do this. Ava planned her wedding to Devon when we were in high school, before she met him. I never thought I would be a bride."

"I never thought I would be a groom until you slid into that back pew." He smiled and, dagnabit, I blushed for the third time.

"When did you want to marry me?" I asked him.

"Last year," he said as he moved closer toward me. "When did you want to marry me?"

"The moment I kicked you out of my house for making Mickey Mouse pancakes in my kitchen." I giggled.

"So any time after that is good, then?" Mom interrupted us, but I didn't care. I hadn't realized that the Belles were silent and watching Justus and me through wet tissues in hand.

Justus nodded. "But the sooner the better would be nice."

"She needs at least six months if she's going to have a custom bridal gown," Aunt Mary said.

I smiled at her. It was great that Mom had invited her to be here, too. Since Uncle Pete's death, Mom and Aunt Mary had reunited. Mom was even helping her find a new home so she could live here permanently after the funeral.

"Oh, that's a must. . . ." Mom nodded. "But I could possibly speed the alterations on a gown if Ms. Angel picks a dress. So I could possibly shave off an extra month or two."

"Good, because surely she can't get married in the winter with that beautiful gardenia in her hair. It has to be a summer wedding. With a reception set open table on the floors of a vineyard." My Aunt Vivienne flayed her arms around after every sentence break. She was more dramatic than my mom, but she was the youngest, so I thought that played a part in it.

"Is a year too long, darling Justus?" Mama asked.

Justus's eyes were still on me, but I felt like I was floating on air. "I've waited this long. If she's sure that she will marry me, no matter what . . ."

"We don't have to extend this engagement that far away in order for me to have a tailored wedding gown. That's crazy."

"It would give me time to build a house for us," Justus said.

"A house . . ." I nodded and smiled. "It's enough time for me to get our houses in order and do all this overly Southern frilly stuff that would make my family happy."

"And make Bella mine." Justus took my hand.

I tilted my head. "I didn't understand what you just said."

He sighed. "I want to adopt Bella. I want her to be my daughter."

And then my feet touched the ground. Justus looked so lovingly at me. He said the words many single moms wished upon many stars for. But that was not what I wanted, because I had decided to reach out to Gabe's family after what had happened to Sean Graham. How could I tell that to Justus right now? It would embarrass him, so instead I smiled and cried. I had to protect the moment. We could discuss this adoption issue after the brunch.

Mom clinked her champagne flute with her unused butter knife. "Now that we've got that settled I can tell you why I brought you all here."

I sighed with relief. The sooner we could get off the subject of Bella's paternity, the better.

"So what's the big news, Mom?" Whitney asked.

"Carrolton and I have decided to take another honeymoon."

Whitney put her hands on her hips. "Is that it? My grits are getting cold for this?"

"Of course there is more." Ava turned to Mom. "There is more, right?"

"I wouldn't be me if there wasn't." She tossed her head back so her curls could sway as she laughed. I rolled my eyes as I remembered why I didn't miss coming to this spectacle. It was too flamboyant.

"We decided to cancel our plans for the French Riviera. Instead, we're taking the whole family to Turks and Caicos in two weeks."

Everyone gasped, then cheered. I glanced at Justus. He squeezed my hand and smiled. I looked away. There was no way I was going on a vacation until Maxim shared with me what Braden Logan meant by me being responsible for killing Gabe. I needed to get Big Tiger to fake a stakeout for me, to get me out of this family vacation nightmare.

Whitney's voice cut through the hoopla. "Stepdaddy got that kind of money to take all of us?"

"Well, not all of us are going," Mom said, then turned toward me and Justus.

The room grew quiet.

I stepped behind Justus. "What now?"

"My dear husband and I are gifting Justus and Angel a weekend stay at Château Élan in Braselton while we're gone. Let me tell you about this couple's package. Outside of them using this time to focus on their wedding plans, the couple will spend the evening with a master perfumer. He will help them create their own fragrance." She clapped her hands together in excitement.

"Ooh. Angel and Justus will have their own cologne. How cool," Whitney said.

"Even cooler is that they can give their cologne out as wedding favors." Ava nodded. "If I weren't blessed and highly favored, I would be jealous."

Everyone applauded.

I turned to Justus. He stood stoically, but I knew what he was thinking. *We can't spend three days and two nights alone in a romantic resort suite together. I couldn't be under that kind of pressure.*

"Justus, don't you worry," Mom shouted above the crowd. "You two will have adjoining rooms. We don't want anyone to question your faith and virtue."

The applause stopped and everyone's face had turned to me. If I could have fallen through the creaking hardwood floor, I would have.

"Thank you for the engagement gift, Mother Crawford. If you didn't have separate quarters for us, then I would have purchased an extra suite, because it is my job to protect Angel's virtue. She already entrusts me with shepherding her faith."

He kissed my palm, but I was furious with Mom. I stormed out and into the ladies' room.

31

Friday, Noon
Vinings Inn, Vinings, Georgia

Mom stormed in after me, of course.
"What has gotten into you?"

"Mom, are you serious? I can't . . ." I paused.

We stood in the ladies' room, away from the impromptu engagement party. It peeved me that she did what she wanted to do, despite how her children felt. I paced the bathroom floor asking God to keep me from shouting at her and saying something I would regret. I had been down that dark road of making Virginia Crawford Curtis Carter angry. It had taken her years to forgive me. I couldn't risk another six years without her overbearing, stubborn, flamboyant but kindhearted love.

"I can't believe you think it's okay to plan my life for me. I'm grown, why can't you see that?" I huffed.

"If you're grown, then stop being childish." She slammed her purse onto the vanity sink. "You have a grown, good man waiting for you to be the woman everyone knows you are, except you, and you have a seven-year-old daughter, waiting for you to step out of her daddy's grave."

"Mama, don't go there."

"Oh, I'm going there, because it ends today, Evangeline. Gabriel Hwang is dead and when he was alive he was bad for you. Why can't you see that?" She shook her head and threw her arms over her chest.

"He was not bad and it's not that simple, Mama."

"I don't care if it's a Rubik's Cube. When we leave out of this rest room, any talk about that man who almost killed you while you were carrying my grandbaby is out. Point blank. Period." She huffed. "I'm not going to let you make the biggest mistake of your life."

"Mistake? What are you talking about? Spending the week in Braselton doesn't qualify as a momentous occasion. You didn't even ask me if I wanted to get married there."

"You hadn't picked a date, so why would I assume that you picked a wedding venue. . . ." She checked her watch. "Look, before the Belles get more suspicious, if you don't want to marry there, fine, but at least use this great opportunity as a time to reconnect with Justus, to finalize your plans."

I sighed. "Yeah . . . I could do that."

"Good, and could you also take the tour of the grounds with the event planner while you're there?"

I put my hands on my hips. "Is this a condition for the free trip?"

"Honey, there wouldn't be a free trip if the walk-through wasn't included. We have money because we never look a gift horse in the mouth." She flipped her hair. "Let me tell you, your little trip with Justus cost more than sending all my sisters and their children on a cruise."

"Wow."

"So you better not mess this up. You hear me?"

Mom was back in rare form with the threats—all in the name of motherly love—again. I chuckled.

"Mom, what am I going to do with Justus for three days?"

Her left eyebrow rose.

"Mama . . ." I stamped my foot. "Get your head out of the gutter."

She waved her hands in the air. "I didn't say anything disrespectful about my soon-to-be-son-in-law."

"You didn't have to say it: You look it."

"I didn't say anything, but if I did, I have to say that the way he looks at you sometimes tells me that you may need to ditch the dress and up that wedding date."

"I don't care about a wedding dress. I was trying to make y'all happy. If it was left up to me, I would have married him after he kissed me downstairs."

Mom laughed. "Now you're beginning to sound like my daughter." She laughed some more.

"Now you see what I mean? This wedding planning stuff. It's not me; it's Ava's thing. I just want to show up."

"Stop being underdramatic. You do want this. This trip will give you the time and space for it. Besides, when the girls and I return, we're taking you to New York."

"For what?"

"Just like you said. We're ditching the old Belle way. We're not waiting for Filene's either. We're going to Amsale."

Ever since I'd helped Elaine's daughter, Lana, find the perfect wedding dress at Filene's, I'd fallen in love with wedding-gown fashion, especially designer Amsale. Until now, I thought my obsession with her elegant bridal gowns was a secret hobby. I should have known my nosy little sister, Whitney, had spilled the beans. If she kept this up, she might get thrown out of my house.

"You really booked an appointment at Amsale?"

"You may not believe this, but I've always wanted the

best for you." She hugged me, then kissed my cheek. "Justus is the best, and you and Bella deserve him."

"I know, Mama." I squeezed her tighter, because I wanted this to work. I really did, but I also feared the worst. "If I told you something, would you not panic and keep it a secret?"

"Angel, have I yet to tell Ava that you were the one who killed that story on Devon seven years ago?"

Ava and I had patched up most of our past catfights with each other. The real reason for our blowout was over a story I was working on with a team of other investigative journalists for the *Atlanta Sentinel*. Gabe was one of our contracted PIs/informants on that case. When my brother-in-law, Pastor Devon McArthur, became a new subject in the story, I was removed from the project. Conflict of interest. However, it was because of me and Gabe that Devon was cleared from further investigation. But I couldn't share Gabe's involvement. I had to protect his privacy. In retrospect, I wish I had broken the rules and told the truth. Perhaps Devon and Gabe would still be here.

"That's right, you did, but . . ." I said. "Gabe saved Devon from the IRS investigation."

She gasped and stepped back.

"There's more."

"No, I don't want to hear it."

"But then you would understand why I've been acting this way."

"Stop it, Angel. What you do, what you know: it hurts people, and I know you don't mean to. So, baby . . . I love you, but don't say another word about this. Let the dead bury the dead. Okay?"

I rolled my eyes again and sulked. "Yes, ma'am."

"Take two minutes to collect yourself, then come out and join your man, the right man."

I watched her close the door, but somehow I felt that things would never just be open and shut between us.

When I stepped outside, Justus was waiting for me. I could see his concern in his eyes.

"Are you okay?" he asked. "I'm sure you feel like you've been ambushed, but I promise I didn't know anything about this or the trip to Braselton. You do believe me, don't you?"

In the past year and a half, I had learned to trust Justus. The person I was concerned with was myself.

"I do, and although this may sound crazy coming from me, I want to go with you—in separate rooms, of course."

He took my hand and kissed it. "When do we leave?"

"Next weekend," I said. By then I would have gotten to the bottom of this news about Gabriel Hwang.

My phone buzzed. I looked down at my phone. There was an emergency call from Bella's school.

32

When I had dropped off Bella at school this morning, she didn't have a fever, and didn't complain of a tummy ache or a headache. In fact, she'd kissed my cheek, giggled, and said her good-byes as usual. But this was first grade. Kids catch viruses faster than a meth addict can catch a case. I shouldn't have been surprised.

My nemesis Mrs. Montgomery, the school office manager, stood at the front desk. She looked at me with a contempt I knew so well. The lady made it her mission in life to tell me how horrible a mother I was because I was a bail recovery agent. I didn't like her and secretly wished that whatever bug had attacked Bella would bite her in her dusty backside. And then I took it back. *Vengeance was the Lord's*, I said to myself. Then my eyes widened. When had I begun spouting Bible scriptures?

"Miss Crawford, Isabella is in the nurse's station to our left. Just sign her out here and you can pick her up."

I reached for one of the flowerpot pens the school kept on the desk and began adding my signature to the checkout clipboard. She caught my hand, then leaned forward.

She looked at me, back at the ring, then to me. "You're engaged?"

I nodded. "I am."

She scoffed. "Are you marrying that bail bondsman you've been dealing with in all the newspapers? Or is it that marshal that you almost got killed in South Georgia?"

"None of the above," I said. "I'm marrying Reverend Morgan of Sugar Hill Community Church. He's one of the community partners on the school council. You know him?"

"Justus?" She crooked her neck back. "I guess I didn't know him like I thought."

"He's full of surprises. Isn't he?" I gave her my best Cheshire grin and then walked out with my head held higher than before.

Like they say, "Revenge is a dish best served cold." It sure tasted wonderful in this unusually warm spring heat.

I knocked on the nurse's station door before I walked inside. Bella sat on a black leather bench in front of the school nurse's desk. I took a quick sweep of the room. It was a basic setup. Bare walls except for some "medicine for kids" poster attached to the wall.

The nurse waved me inside. She sat at a desk near the bench Bella sat on. I caressed Bella's back, then sat down in the chair in front of the nurse's desk.

"Bella has caught some twenty-four-hour stomach bug. It's been going around the school."

"Do I bring her back to school tomorrow or keep her out until the day after?"

"If she doesn't show any more symptoms or have a fever, then she can return to school tomorrow."

"All right." I stood up.

"Miss Crawford, one more thing. . . ."

I sat back down. "Okay."

She leaned forward. "I've been reading about you in the

papers and I overheard that you were engaged to Pastor Justus Morgan. . . ."

I sat back and sighed. If she was about to make me feel bad, like Mrs. Bitter out there loved to do, then we were going to have some problems.

"I want to offer you early congratulations. Bella talks about him all the time. I think it's wonderful."

"Oh." I wasn't prepared for her kind words. "Thank you. Thank you very much."

Friday, 5:30 PM
Home, Sugar Hill, Georgia

When I told Bella about her grandmother's plans to take her on an island vacation, she danced so hard that she danced herself into bed. I wanted to do a Happy Dance because she hadn't gone to bed on time since the time changed a few weeks ago, but I had other things to think about.

Justus, for one. He'd had a long night with his sister Trish and her family. Trish was definitely pregnant and tortured by morning sickness. Unfortunately, her family couldn't scramble eggs without her help. Therefore, I knew I wouldn't see him tonight, so that gave me a little time to figure some things out.

Whitney was here. Perhaps I could run some things by her. She stood at the kitchen sink. She was putting up the silverware and plates while I packed away tonight's leftovers into the fridge.

"I'm going to miss this," she said.

I closed the refrigerator door, turned around, and looked at her. "Miss what?"

"Me, you, and Bella together for dinner."

I leaned against the refrigerator and looked at her more closely. Whitney was Mom's spitting image and the glue that really kept us together. When Ava and I hadn't been speaking to each other, Whitney was our Switzerland. She never took sides, and wanted world peace. As I watched her, I realized that world peace for her was peace in our family. Knowing that tugged at my heart a little bit.

"Girl, are you planning on going somewhere?" I asked. "Unless we all decide to go on a hunger strike, I don't know why we wouldn't continue eating together."

"Because I'll be a third wheel once you and Justus marry."

"Technically you'll be a fourth wheel, which will actually make us a wagon," I joked. "So what's your point?"

She flung the dish towel across her shoulder. "Maybe it's time I get my own place."

"In this economy, Whitney, why would you want to ruin your credit history? No one is making you leave. In fact, Justus is working on floor plans for our new house that have a separate bathroom and bedroom for you."

Her eyes brightened. "Really?"

"Yes, so you're not going anywhere except for on that vacation with Mama."

"I can't wait to go to Turks and Caicos. It's going to be off the chain." She clapped and laughed, then she stopped and danced over to where I stood. "So you and Justus are going to be alone together in one of the most romantic places in Georgia. How are you going to keep from trying to jump his bones?"

"Stop," I ribbed her. "Even if I wanted to entertain the thought, Justus will make sure to knock it down and I'm fine with that. I want to do this thing right. I can wait for him. I've been waiting for him my whole life."

"Child, please. You're saying that because you know there will be separate rooms." She chuckled.

"What do separate rooms have to do with it? If I was my

old self and if he was somebody else, we would test every bed, every floor, every place we could without tearing the place up."

"Ooh, I'm telling. . . ." Whitney snapped me with the towel. "You're so bad."

"That's what they tell me, but Justus is different. He is a man, a real God-breathed-air-into-his-lungs man, and I like that. I respect it."

She caught my hand. "You want me to live with you for real?"

"Don't make me say it twice." I nodded. "We're family. I love you and I need you."

"To help with Bella?"

"No, to help with me." I sighed. "I don't want to ruin it with Justus. Bella loves him so much. He's the only father figure she's accepted. But you know me. You know my past. I'll mess this up, if I get too far into my head."

"Right. . . ." She nodded.

"I need your dumb butt around because I don't know who I would be without you near me. You keep me real, so let's not talk about you moving again."

"I won't." She squeezed my hand tighter. "But what if I get married? Can he live with us, too?"

"Now I know you're talking crazy, because a man who wants you for his wife wants to provide." I shook my head. "I know it now with everything in me, but I wish I knew it a few years ago."

"Why?" she asked. "Are you thinking about Gabe again?"

"I need to stop thinking about Gabe, but I can't. Every time I think I'm moving on, there he is."

"What's happening now?"

"You know the skip we brought in for Salvador and Maxim? He tells me that the same people who hired Ty to spy on the task force are the same people who hired a hit on Gabe. But check this out. He also said that Gabe's death was my fault."

She sucked her teeth. "Sounds like I need to clock this fool."

"Whitney, no, you don't."

"What did Maxim and Salvador say?"

"I didn't say anything to Salvador about it, but Maxim told me that Braden was playing with my emotions. He knows my history and he's trying to cut a deal with me."

"What kind of deal does he think you can give him?"

I shook my head. "I don't know. I told him I'm just a bail recovery agent."

"That's weird."

"Yeah. After all, the reason for me and not Alpharetta PD picking him up was to keep him from going into County lockup, but somehow he thinks that he's going anyway."

"He's that afraid to go to County?"

"He wasn't the only one. Ty killed himself in the DeKalb County police station instead of telling Maxim who the mole was. This person must be pretty bad."

"Angel, stay away from this." She clutched my hand. "It's crazy, and too many people around us are dying. Tomorrow we have to go to Valdosta to bury Uncle Pete, and I think you have hit your threshold for deaths in the springtime. Stay out of that mess. Prepare for your wedding. That's something nice and happy."

"So you agree with Maxim?"

"Yes, I do. I don't know this Logan guy outside of the stuff we found trying to track him down, but his tie to Gabe . . . man, that's some bull. Logan is a geek who knew who you were when he chose to go through BT Trusted Bail Bonds to get bonded out of jail. He thinks he's smarter than you because he Googled you. That's all. He ain't nobody and he don't know nothing 'bout Gabe."

"You're right." I took a deep breath and exhaled. "He pegged me good."

She took her hands and gripped both my arms, then shook me. "It's a good thing that I keep it 100, then?"

I giggled. "Yes, ma'am. It is."

"So what's next? What are we doing this week? A new skip?"

"Nope, I'm going to chill after we return from Uncle Pete's funeral. I'm going to spend time with Bella. Go buy an armful of expensive bridal magazines and figure out what I want for my wedding before Mama and the Belles take it over."

"Without Mama's approval?" She snickered. "I think that's the best plan you've made yet. But you might need to reconsider you and Justus sleeping in separate bedrooms when you two go to the Château. Something tells me that one of those rooms will be wasted."

"That's because your mind is in the gutter." I giggled.

A little after midnight my phone buzzed. I was in the bed lost in a great dream when it woke me up. I grumbled until I saw who was calling. Justus. He was downstairs.

I tiptoed from my room through downstairs so that I wouldn't wake anyone and I could have some alone time with him.

When I let him inside the house, he lifted me in his arms and held me close to him.

"Is something wrong?" I whispered.

"I can't go to sleep without seeing your face."

He smiled, then kissed me. He didn't go too far, because he didn't want to compromise my position. I won't lie. If he wanted to go upstairs, I would have let him.

I lowered my head to his neck. "I have to go home for the funeral tomorrow."

"I can't come." He put me down.

"I know. Don't worry. The funeral won't be long and we're flying with Mom. Even the trip will be short. I'll be back by noon. Will you be able to do the Château Élan weekend trip with me? I'm beginning to warm up to the idea of us having some alone time together to iron out how we will bring our lives together."

"Don't be mad, Babe . . ." He lowered his head. "I don't know if I can leave Trish."

"She's that sick?"

"Her pregnancy has complications. This afternoon I had to take her to Maternal Fetal. She's going to need some help, and right now I'm all she has."

"I should have known. . . . That explains why you're here." I folded my arms over my chest and slumped back against my foyer wall. "I'm too sleepy to argue with you and I don't want to wake the girls if I yelled, so . . . this is the best time to tell me that our engage-cation is off."

He sighed. "Angel, if I didn't have to watch the kids, I would go, but my sister's on bed rest."

"It's a good thing that the wedding isn't until next year. When's her due date?"

"Angel, you're not being fair."

"You said you took me as I was and I've never been fair. I mean, think about it. In my line of work, being fair doesn't get me far." I tightened my arms around my chest. I could feel that my bottom lip was poking out into a little-girl pout.

"You're being selfish."

"No matter how selfish I sound, you've made your decision, so let me be pissy about it. Can I at least have that?"

"That's not a healthy way of dealing with disappointment," he said.

"And your coming over here at dark forty in the morning isn't a healthy way of giving me bad news."

"You're right."

"I know I am," I scoffed.

"Angel, you're everything to me. I tried to call in a few favors, but it's too short notice. I have one of our members, a registered nurse, who will check on her in the daytime next Friday; the ladies will prepare some meals for them; but that's all I could get right now." He walked toward where I stood. I turned away from standing in front of him. He took his hands and turned me back around. "If there was another way, if I had more help, I would be with you in a heartbeat."

"You're going to regret saying that."

He frowned. "Why would you say that?"

"Because I have a way. Let's see if Trish will okay it."

He smirked. "But you haven't run it by me first."

"Do you want to go with me to Château Élan to plan our wedding together or what?"

"I'll go to the ends of the Earth with you."

"Then prove it. I'm not doing any hard work this week. Let me take care of Trish while you prepare for next Friday at the Château."

"I want you to know this is hard for me," he said.

"What's hard? Letting me do what a good wifey does?" I batted my eyes at "good wifey."

He laughed so hard I had to cup his mouth. Justus grabbed my waist and pulled me closer into him.

"Shh . . . you're going to wake them up." I began to kiss him just to shut him up.

I needed sleep, because first thing in the morning, before we flew to South Georgia, I would have to go beg my mom to add three more kids to the island getaway and see if Mrs. Loretta meant what she said about helping me become a good wife.

33

Saturday, 8:30 AM
McCollum Airport, Kennesaw, Georgia

The best time for me to do my job was on Saturday mornings. Most skips didn't bail themselves out of jail. A family member or loved one would. Therefore, if a skip tried to leave the county, state, or country, oftentimes someone else had to fund his getaway. Usually this benefactor was his jail wifey, sister, or mother, and usually this person got paid on Fridays, but couldn't cash her check until Saturday. For some odd reason, the skip would forget that he was supposed to be in hiding. He would be so anxious to get out of town that he would tag along with his benefactor to the bank or neighborhood Western Union. I can't tell you how many skips I've picked up in a Western Union or a Walmart parking lot.

Moreover, most skips didn't do bold things to out themselves like visit the Atlanta Motor Speedway for NASCAR or tailgate an Atlanta Falcon's Game under the bridge near the Georgia Dome. But they would hang out at the Greyhound or Megabus terminal, stop at a gas station and take a smoke, eat at Waffle House—the kind of careless activities they do on Saturdays that are like Hansel and Gretel bread crumbs to bail recovery agents.

The other reason . . . my mind just worked better. It has always been that way.

Because most of the adults in Bella's world would be with me in South Georgia, Bella had to come with us. Ava didn't agree with the decision.

"You need a nanny," she said after we'd boarded Mom's Cessna.

Bella had headsets on. I hoped she didn't hear us.

"I know I need a nanny, but even if I had one, Bella was coming with me this morning," I said. "I'm surprised you didn't bring Taylor and Lil' D. I know you weren't ready to pay any respects to Uncle Pete. However, I thought this would be a good time to introduce her to our father's side of the family. How many times do they get to see family other than us and their father's family?"

"Has it ever dawned on you that I don't want my children to get attached to that side of our family?" she asked.

My jaw dropped. I looked at Mom. "Say what?"

"Don't act surprised. Dad's side of the family got drama and too many jailbirds flying in and flying out. If they know too much about what you do and how much money I have now, we'd both have to change our telephone numbers and addresses."

I gasped and threw my hands over my mouth.

Ava put her index finger in the air and waved it around in a slow zero. "Don't even try to judge me for being bourgie while you're sitting with me on this private plane. That would be bourghetto."

"Forget that, Ava." I flipped her off with my wrist. "What I was thinking about has nothing to do with you being out of touch with regular folk and the fact that you've learned some new words from Whitney. My mind is on something more important."

"Like what, baby?" Aunt Mary asked.

She sat next to Bella. I hadn't had time to talk with her since Maxim brought her to Mom's, after she was released from South Georgia Medical Center. She still hadn't decided whether she would move here after the craziness died down after Uncle Pete's funeral. I didn't know why she would stay.

"Ma'am, I'm just thinking about this guy I had to drag back to jail this week. He said something to me that I didn't understand, but now I think I do."

Whitney, who sat near Mom, dropped the newspaper she was reading and leaned forward. "I thought I told you to let it go," she hissed.

"But I think I know what Braden Logan meant by me helping him not go to County." I whispered to her. "The leak is someone who spends a lot of time in booking at County."

"Sounds like someone that works at the jail."

"No. A prison worker wouldn't scare an ATF agent into committing suicide. It's someone who either works in law enforcement who has to be there or someone who works around jails, someone coming in and out of jails, probably more than one."

"A police officer, a recovery agent, an attorney, a minister . . ." Whitney shook her head. She had a confused look on her face. "You're giving me a headache."

"I'm giving myself one, too, but I'm thinking it's a DeKalb County sheriff, which means that Salvador was right by meeting at Tiger's yesterday instead of police headquarters."

"Are you really asking for my input or brainstorming?"

"A little of both." I pulled a small notepad out of my purse and jotted down points of my new theory.

Whitney placed her hand over the notepad. "You've done your job, Big Sis. If Braden wouldn't tell you who he was afraid of, then it's his butt. A1 Recovery Agents can't investigate without a name, so . . ."

I nodded. "But what if I could get Braden to talk to me?"

"And how do you plan to do that?" she asked. "We're about to take off."

"You're not leaving this plane, Evangeline Grace Crawford soon-to-be Morgan," Mama said through gritted teeth.

"I'm not leaving. I just need to make a phone call."

One great thing about being a bail recovery agent is having a lot of interesting people in my back pocket, who will do what I ask, no matter how farfetched. Since I've been doing this, I've worked with a teenage dumpster diver, a former madam, a bootlegger, and tons of jail wifeys.

Jail wifeys were women who were girlfriends, baby mamas, or wives of habitual jail inmates. They accepted their troubled man and knew the caged drill of incarceration. Sometimes they paid bail and sometimes they paid commissary. Whatever he wanted, they did—until they got fed up, caught cases of their own, or died.

There was a particular jail wifey who was pretty good to me. Deja Jackson was her name. She was a twentyish, freckle-faced woman with a golden-honey complexion. She had light brown eyes and sandy brown–colored hair. She was a pretty girl who didn't look like the mom of three ladder kids, children who were born so close together that they were a slight step ahead in height. Her kids were two, three, and four, respectively. They lived in a three-bedroom, brick, classic ranch in Clarkston, a block from my favorite Vietnamese restaurant and that pawnshop off Ponce, which had trouble with buying hot jewelry.

Deja's man, Izzy, vacationed at her home. He lived half of the year at DeKalb County and the other half at Fulton County Jail. This time he was at DeKalb, which meant she would visit him and bring him commissary. If he had gone to Fulton, she would have called Big Tiger in a heartbeat. The jail has a contagion and HIV problem that was just too risky even for her.

But don't be alarmed; her man was taken care of as well as any convict could be. He was the unofficial leader of the Blacks inside. He had his own cell phone and a constant supply of long johns, cigarettes, soap, food, and toothbrushes, courtesy of debts that needed to be paid by other inmates. Moreover, Deja and their three kids were taken good care of by other inmates with bigger debts, who usually had to have someone reliable to make good on the payment and the men who worked for him.

However, there was one thing Deja's man and his band of brothers couldn't do for her. Bail his punk butt out when he caught a case, and always seemed to catch one, at Atlanta Fulton County. So in exchange for her man not doing some real hard time, she did favors for me.

Right now I needed her to pay up.

She picked up on the first ring.

"Angel, is that you?" Her voice was a mixture of joy and worry.

"It is. I need a favor."

"Whatever you need I'll do my best for ya," she said. "You know you're my girl."

"I need you to talk to Izzy for me today. I have some questions only he can answer and I promise to keep it on the hush."

It would seem easier if I went to the jail and visited Deja's Izzy, but it wasn't. Male detention centers had different rules and unspoken codes from the world outside. The culture in there was turf driven and built on an intricate system where snitching wasn't allowed. Inmates found sharing too much information sat on the bottom rung of prison life. Izzy currently stood king. He wasn't changing that for nobody, especially me. So my best bet was to relay my questions through Deja. No one would think Deja's calls or visits would be suspicious.

"When do you want the answers?" she asked.

"I'll call you later tonight when I return to Atlanta."

"Girl, where you at?"

"On my way to a funeral."

"Oh yeah. Sorry about your friend. I didn't know his funeral was going to be that fast. But he's not Black. Right? They don't wait for a week like we do. Shoot. If Izzy die, I'm not waiting a week to bury him."

I frowned. "What friend? Who are you talking about?"

"Your boy Frisco. It was on the news a few minutes ago that he died."

"You must be mistaken. Frisco isn't dead."

Ava placed her arms around my shoulders. I jerked until I saw her face. She had tears in her eyes.

I lowered my phone. "Why are you crying? You never liked Uncle Pete."

"It's Tiger on the other line. . . ." Her mouth quivered. "Frisco is gone."

I gripped the phone. My heart pounded so hard I couldn't see straight. "Deja, actually I'm on my way to my uncle's funeral. But I need to call into Tiger about what you just said. I'll text you my questions. If you can get them answered for me, it will really . . . I have to go."

I ended the call, then turned again to Ava, snatched her phone out of her hand, and lifted her phone to my ear. "What in the world are you talking about, Tiger?"

I could hear Tiger blowing his nose on the other end of the phone. He cleared his throat. "Frisco had a blood clot on his brain. The doctor said the strike on his skull from the bat must have torn a blood vessel. The clot put too much pressure on his brain."

"No, no, no. He was talking last night. How could he talk last night if all that was going on?"

"Angel Soft . . . this isn't an investigation. Frisco is dead. I'm sorry."

I looked around me. Everyone sat still in their seats. Everyone's eyes, except Bella's, were on mine. If I got off the airplane, there was still time to drop her off to school. She would be considered tardy but would be present in attendance. And I could see for myself whether Frisco was dead.

I lifted the phone back to my ear. "Where are you now?"

"I'm in the hospital lobby. I've seen enough in my life, but I can't watch my boy being folded away like a deck of cards. I really wish you were here." He began to cry.

I'd never heard him cry before. It brought me back to tears.

I pulled the phone back from my face. "Stop the plane. I need to get out. Now!"

34

Saturday, 9:00 AM
McCollum Airport, Kennesaw, Georgia

"Have you lost the last bit of your good mind?!" Mom shouted at me. "Mary, get up. Angel, sit down next to your daughter until you've come back to your good senses."

"No." I huffed. "I need to see Frisco."

"Frisco's gone, Angel." Ava clutched my arm, then leaned to my ear. "We're not going to talk about this in front of the baby."

I looked down at Bella. Her attention was still focused on the movie she was watching.

"Virginia, you know I have a fear of flying on planes. I'm staying in this chair beside you," Aunt Mary said. "Angel, baby?"

I looked up. "Yes, ma'am?"

Aunt Mary no longer looked like a shell of a woman wearing foam pink rollers and a seersucker bathrobe. Today she wore a navy skirt suit and red wedged pumps Mom had bought her for the funeral. Ava brought us all a red rose to pin onto our clothes. Aunt Mary's was pinned to her lapel. Her rollers were gone and replaced with her beautiful brown hair that hinted of silver where she had begun to gray. Unlike Mom, she had refused to color her hair. Mom had adorned her with silver jewelry to balance the look. As good as she looked, the sad reality was Uncle Pete wouldn't have treated her better. Aunt Mary understood that fact. Her eyes were now at peace. I could see it written on her face.

"I need you to help me say good-bye to your uncle. I told the undertaker I didn't want no repast. There isn't nothing worth celebrating down here. So that leaves you plenty of time to say your good-byes to your friend when we return to Atlanta."

Ava gasped, then clapped. "Aunt Mary, you're coming back with us?"

"Yes, baby." She nodded. "I might be old, but it's time I get to be me."

I plopped down feeling great loss and great joy at the same time. Bittersweet. "I'm sorry, guys. I get selfish sometimes. I forget everyone has their own problems."

Mom patted my leg. "I'm sorry about Frisco. I really am. We're going to get through this day together, because that's what we Crawford women do. Whitney, put your name in that fishbowl, too."

"Thanks, Mom." Whitney wiped her eyes. She was still crying. "Angel, can I come with you when you visit Frisco's family this evening?"

"Of course you can, but I'm going to park at Tiger's. We will drive up together."

" 'K." She could barely spit that out.

I turned to Whitney. Her body trembled. She had her arms wrapped around her body. The tears were still coming. She kept her head hung low. Tears ran down her arms and dripped off her elbows.

I couldn't believe she would be more emotional about this than me.

I took a handkerchief from my purse and wiped her elbow. "Are you all right?"

"I was in love with him," she whispered.

Saturday, 5:00 PM
BT Trusted Bail Bonds, Decatur, Georgia

Whitney and I arrived at Tiger's an hour after we returned to Atlanta, thanks to Mom's chauffeur, JJ. Justus would meet us at Saint Monica's and take us home. Ava agreed to keep Bella with her for the night. I would pick her up after church. Whitney was still a blubbering mess. I convinced her to have a seat in the lounge, while I went to Tiger's office.

I burst through the door. "Tiger, what happened?"

Tiger turned around. He wasn't alone. Someone was standing behind him. A man wearing a black suit, white button-down shirt, and a Fulton County Police badge dangling around his neck.

"This is Detective Phillips." Tiger widened his eyes, then narrowed, then widened again, as if he was warning me about something. "Phillips stopped by to ask you some questions about what happened with Frisco."

"I know this is tough, but I need to talk to you," Phillips said.

"Did Mr. Jones inform you that we're going to a special homegoing service in a few hours?" I asked. "This might not be a good time. Perhaps you can leave your card and I will call you and set an appointment."

"I can do that. I also wanted to let you know what will happen with Allison Kim."

I pointed to the pair of empty armchairs in front of Tiger's desk. "Have a seat and start with the latter."

"Wait." Tiger stuck his hand in the air. "I want Phillips

to tell you what he told me about what happened with Frisco before he gets to that. Have a seat, Angel."

I sat down.

Detective Phillips nodded. "Frisco Cabral died from blunt-force trauma to the back of his head with Allison Kim's bat, but I don't have to tell you that. You saw him. You knew he wouldn't make it shortly after that."

Tiger grunted. "I thought he was going to be okay. In our line of work getting hit by a baseball bat is a walk in the park."

"Deep inside I think I thought he wouldn't make it, but I was hoping." I nodded while a tear trickled down my cheek. "When I touched him in Allison's foyer, I felt him leaving me."

Phillips touched my hand. "I could tell he was a great friend to you."

"I hate to burst your bubble, but I didn't know him long. He was new here, but I liked him very much. He was the perfect partner for me in this game."

"I bet he was." He looked up at Tiger, then to me. "For the sake of time, let me say this in the nicest way I can. What I'm about to tell you is going to be uncomfortable for me and difficult for the both of you to hear."

I looked up at him. "My mom is pissed with me because I haven't set a wedding date yet or prepared for my engagement party. So understand that whatever you're holding back from me will pale in comparison to that woman's wrath."

He chuckled dryly, then paused. "Allison will not do jail time for Frisco's death."

Phillips's words sliced the air into silence. My mouth opened but wouldn't close. His eyes were locked on his Fulton County Police Department–approved rubber shoes, so he didn't see my hands ball into fists.

Tiger touched my shoulder. I saw him do it, but I couldn't feel it. I was trying not to boil over in anger. My coiled fingers dug into my palms.

"Angel, did you hear what I just said?" Phillips asked me.

Frisco's bright smile flashed across my face. I trembled. *How could I tell this to Whitney?*

"Come on, say something, Crawford. You're scaring me," Detective Phillips said. "Do you think she's okay?" he asked Tiger.

"I'm fine." I turned toward him. "If I had drop-kicked Allison into a dirt nap instead of a KO, what would be my charges?"

Phillips cleared his throat. "That's not the same and you know it."

"Not the same how?" I bolted off the couch so fast he hopped back a few steps. I scoffed at his fear of me.

"I can understand you being upset about this," he said. "That's why I wanted to tell you before you heard it from someone else."

"Nope, that's not why you're here." I walked toward him slowly with my eyes locked on him, making him sweat. My fists were tighter than the muscle T-shirts Big Tiger often wore. "You came here because you thought I wouldn't slap the taste out of your mouth."

"I'm going to act like you didn't just threaten a police officer." Phillips lifted his arms to his waist. A sunbeam shimmered over his detective's badge.

"You can't be an officer, because you didn't do your job." The words gritted through my clenched teeth. "If the shoe was on the other foot and Frisco had pushed that woman on her fresh fanny, he would have been charged. Now what?"

"Angel, I'm not here to arrest you."

"But you're here. . . ."

He lowered his arms. "What do you want me to do?"

"I want you to tell me that the DA will at least charge Allison for involuntary manslaughter for Frisco's death."

He shook his head. "We were looking at assault, but . . ."

"Assault?" I shouted. "How could the DA's office be so stupid? Something's not right. There's no way the ME could have ruled on his death so fast."

He clenched his jaw, then sighed. "Allison's lawyer made a deal. Manslaughter. Ten years probation. . . ."

I heard Phillips's explanations but couldn't believe my ears. Allison's lawyers had convinced the District Attorney's office that when Allison cracked Frisco's skull with her baseball bat, she was acting in self-defense. When both Frisco and I had pulled our guns on Braden, she panicked. Since Frisco was dead and Braden was licking his wounds back in jail, Braden would do nothing more than make me suffer because of his situation. Therefore, his and Allison's tainted testimonies were two words against mine, even when my account was the truth.

In my years as an investigative journalist, I had become jaded by the unfairness that enveloped my fair city. If I hadn't known any better, Phillips would have easily made me believe that if I had a lot of money I could get away with almost anything. Except lonely Allison couldn't have Braden back in her bed tonight. Money couldn't change everything.

My old frenemy Sean Graham had learned that lesson a few months ago. He had bought himself a new identity, which landed him the coveted assistant position with my old mentor, Congresswoman Elaine Turner. But his well-paid lie had caught up to him and unfortunately, many others died with him because of it.

"How much is she paying the courts in probation?"

"Angel, it's not special treatment."

This horrid economy and its effects on Atlanta had turned bad people into devils. Home invasions, bank robberies, theft: all the worst kind of bailed-out offenders. It baffled me that they didn't have enough money to have a pot to piss in but could always make bail.

But it shouldn't have been a surprise to me, because I was a woman who remembered wanting to be loved by a man. I knew what it meant to miss feeling like a woman. Unfortunately, many of us Southern girls were brought up to believe that our womanhood rested on the affections of a man.

And so we would do anything, even if it meant bailing out our sorry sons, having a kept man, or living with our private demon who couldn't keep his fist out of our faces. Sometimes we women did bad things for good reasons. However, I would never empathize with the Allison Kims of the world. I would take her down.

"Get out," I mumbled.

"I'm sorry. I couldn't hear you." Phillips stepped closer toward me. "Could you repeat that?"

I felt my lips prune like they did when I used to bite on a lime before I took a tequila shot. There was a fury in my spirit that reminded me of the day I'd shot The Knocker down in his front yard. I couldn't still myself in front of Detective Phillips. All I could do, in order to keep myself from imploding, was to release my frustration with it all.

"Get out!" I shouted. "Get your inefficient, Johnny-come-lately behind out my face."

"I can't."

"Brother . . ." I said through gritted teeth. "I don't want to go to jail today and you don't want to be on the other side of my round kick. Table your discussion with me for another day. How about another ninety days? Maybe by then I will want to hear your side."

"But I can't . . . wait." He stepped back some more. This time his hands were up, as if he was pleading for me to give him a reprieve. "I didn't just come here to talk to you about Frisco."

"Please don't tell me you came here to talk to me about helping you bring in some skip that Riddick Avery or any of his cronies can't do, because you're dumber than I thought."

"Allison Kim is considering pressing charges against you."

My nose wrinkled. "Then you need to go back and inform her that the only way I'm leaving my child to serve time is for murder. Does she want to be my victim, because I'll oblige her."

He huffed. "Crawford, I can't tell her that."

"Well, that's on your head, because she has been warned."

35

Whitney and Tiger lit a candle for Frisco, while I sat on the back pew. Frisco's body was at Hartsfield-Jackson Airport. His family was flying him back to New York. He belonged to a large Nuyorican community in South Bronx. To say our good-byes, we attended Mass at his local church, Saint Patrick's. His parents were there. I was afraid to meet them.

I was hoping Maxim and Salvador would come, but I assumed Braden hadn't revealed the mole, since I hadn't seen anything about Sanchez's miraculous rise from the grave on the local news. They had to be poker faced about Frisco's death. However, Salvador called me on the way there with his condolences. Maxim hadn't spoken to me since he chewed me out for wanting to talk with Braden Logan about Gabe's murder. I suddenly felt better about him not being there.

Justus sat beside me. He rubbed my shoulders. I'm sure he could feel my tension.

"It's okay to stay right here with me," he said under his breath.

I took his hand and squeezed it. I felt so guilty and shameful about Frisco's death.

Uncle Pete's funeral, on the other hand, had been nicer than I had expected. No one was mean to Aunty Mary. In fact, they celebrated her life more than they did Uncle Pete's. I guess it was a cautionary tale. If you live your life full of selfishness and strife, folks will dance at your funeral—not for you, but because the removal of your presence in this world made the world better. That's not good, and the sun shone.

But here in Atlanta, the sky poured tears for Frisco. We arrived later than usual because the plane had to circle above the city until the storms subsided enough for us to have a safe landing.

"Angelina?" A woman's voice startled me from behind. I jumped.

Justus stood, then helped me up. I hadn't let go of his hand, but I didn't want to let go of that seat, either.

A woman, who appeared to be a few years younger than Mom and had Frisco's pretty eyes and long lashes smiled back at me, I couldn't smile back. I cried.

I felt her arms around me. "Don't cry, Angelina."

"I feel so bad." I sobbed.

"No, no, no. Don't do that." She lifted my head with her cupped hands. "Frisco loved what he did and that's all we wanted for him, to know his purpose and live it. No cries for that."

"What can I do, then?" I asked.

"Finish what you two started. Get the bad guys." She emphasized the last words with a heavy whisper.

I nodded. "I promise."

*   *   *

Saturday, 8:00 PM
Mi Pilón, Norcross, Georgia

"So what's the plan, Angel Soft?" Big Tiger asked.

After Mass, and after we'd said our good-byes to Mrs. Cabral and the rest of Frisco's family, we decided to have dinner together at Frisco's favorite eatery, Mi Pilón. Mi Pilón on Buford Highway was the Dominican/Puerto Rican version of Matthews Cafeteria in Tucker: hometown feel, banquet buffet, with a Latin flavor, and Spanglish with a twang. The thing I loved most about Atlanta was that no matter how diverse it had become, Southern child seeped into everything, even here.

I placed my fork down and wiped my mouth. I'd been plowing through grilled lobster when Tiger asked the question. My mind had been on Whitney and Frisco's crazy-fast, secret love; Ty committing suicide to save face with his about-to-walk-out-the-door wife; and Aunt Mary's self-actualization after killing Uncle Pete. I felt they all were puzzle pieces to a cautionary tale the world was trying to teach me, except I couldn't see the big picture. The only thing that made sense was that I needed to get my life right. I had done what Salvador and Maxim asked. I'd found Braden Logan for them. That was the plan. Now I had to trust that Frisco's life hadn't been taken in vain.

"There is no plan," I said. "Frisco and I did our job. There's nothing else for us to do. Tiger, you'll send his parents his take of the bail recovery money, or should I?"

"Money?" Whitney cut her eyes at me. "I thought you promised Frisco's mom you would get the bad guys. What happened with that?"

"I said that to her so she would feel good. What was I supposed to say? 'Gee, Mrs. Cabral, Allison Kim, Frisco's assailant, paid for her own bail and more than likely has paid good money to keep the DEA's office from charging her with manslaughter. So your best bet is to sue her on civil charges with hopes to settle out of court for a couple of mil,' which she'll probably send the Cabrals anyway to appease her guilty conscience, because that's the truth. Money is sometimes the only justice you can get."

"I don't buy it." Whitney pushed away from her plate. "You're not doing anything because you don't want to."

I frowned. "Like what? I have done the job Tiger hired me to do. We got Braden back."

"No, you know what I'm talking about. You used to run your own investigation in secret in tandem with whatever Salvador was doing, just to beef up your byline at the *Sentinel*, and then last year, you did it again to save Ava's life. Why can't you do that now? Why can't you find out why Braden Logan was more important than Frisco's life? Why is Maxim in hiding? Why is the U.S. Marshal's office turned upside down?"

Tiger leaned across the table. "She has a point. Why are you backing down so easily?"

I turned to Justus, who sat beside me.

He shrugged. "This doesn't seem like you to back off so quickly, especially when someone you loved is involved."

"Now you know you need to do this if I'm agreeing with Justus," Tiger said.

Ava joined us. She'd checked on our kids and left instructions with her nanny. Aunt Mary had invited herself to spend the night at her place and to keep the kids company. I really liked that idea. She made the house feel like one of those warm and fuzzy romantic comedy movies on television.

I looked to her. "What about you, Ava? You're the voice of reason. What do you think?"

She looked around the table. "I'm not a fan of your meddling, but you saved my life. It's too late to save Frisco, but can you really sit well with not closing this book yourself?"

"Are you kidding me? Now you guys want me to play dirty?" I shook my head and scoffed. "Now, that's rich."

Justus touched my arm. "No, that's not what we're saying."

"I know what you guys mean, but really, there is nothing more I can do except to solve the bigger case on my own." I sighed. "I can't . . . I don't know where to begin or even have the resources."

"You have me, Angel Soft," Tiger said.

"Me, too." Ava, Whitney, and the entire table said one by one.

"Frisco risked his life for whoever that is," Whitney snapped.

"You're right." I sighed. "Whitney, you're right. I just . . . I have only one lead right now."

"Okay, let's start with that," Justus said.

"I need to call my source at the Decatur Hotel" (slang for DeKalb County Jail). "I'm hoping to get a clue about why Braden stayed inside for two extra weeks, although a reluctant informant had given him the money to bail himself out. I also want to know if he had any outside pressure on him that would keep him in Atlanta when he clearly could have left town and disappeared from the world." I still didn't feel cool about sharing Ty's name to the group.

"He wasn't disappearing from nothing until he met his court date." Tiger sneered. "That's why he couldn't leave on time. I might look like this big, black, Decatur-licious thug, but I'm not stupid. I had a lock on every out in this city: bus, plane, train, rental, troopers clocking the highways. White bread wasn't leaving here without me knowing about it."

"That's why I love ya." I smiled at him and glanced at Ava.

Ava sitting next to Big Tiger didn't make me feel warm and fuzzy. I couldn't pinpoint one emotion that would describe it, because I had other more pressing concerns on my mind. Like Whitney . . .

Whitney was still a ball of mess, but she had pulled herself together enough to be a part of this conversation. Yet she didn't look too good. Something else was up.

"Are you sure you're up for this?" I asked her.

"Why would you think I wouldn't be?" she snapped at me and flipped her hair to stress the point.

"By the way you're acting." Ava completed my sentence before I could. "You're young and you're not used to all this violence and all that comes with it. You've been spending your good time in an ivory-tower law school class after law school class has been studying the world you now live in. That's a lot to deal with."

"Who do you think you are, Ava?" Whitney glared at Ava. "You don't know anything about anything. Don't get it twisted. Dating Tiger don't automatically make you the Rule Keeper of The Game. Why don't you go back to your kids or make them armor-bearers run hoops around your unnecessary flash. My eyes are wide open, thank you very much."

"Enough." Justus cleared his throat. "Please don't take this the wrong way, Whitney. When you lit that candle for Frisco, that was your moment to let him rest in peace. You know he wouldn't want you sad like this."

"Right, baby girl," Tiger said. "Everybody loves you. We all love Frisco. No doubt. But check this. Everyone here wants to make Frisco proud. Everyone. So let's get a dog-gone move on."

She cut her eyes at Tiger. I studied her face and squinted. Something was up.

I said, "Whit, we're all fam. We know about your feelings for him. I'm sad for you. I know what you're going through. I've been there. My only consolation for you right now is that you're not left with a baby to parent without him."

"I hate to disappoint you, but: I'm pregnant." She stood up and walked out.

36

Sunday, 11:00 AM
Sugar Hill Community Church, Sugar Hill, Georgia

Usually I completed Friday manhunts in enough time to make the Sunday services at Sugar Hill Community Church. In fact, Justus had noticed me out of a sea of eligible single women in church because I often arrived late and sat on the church's back pew. Before he met me and became a part of my life, he thought I was an enigma, an attractive mystery. Now I assumed he thought I was selfish. I sighed.

When I pulled up to Sugar Hill, all eyes were on me. I gulped and hopped out of my truck. My friends from the Ladies of Sugar Hill Communion and Brunch smiled at me and patted my shoulder, but they didn't give me their usual cheerleader-like pep talk. I hoped I wasn't in any hot water, because then I would have had to add to today's prayer that water didn't scald. They probably blamed me for Whitney's premarital pregnancy. I blamed myself. I should get an award for Worst Role Model of the Year.

Justus stood at the top of the stairs, smiling and waving good-bye at his congregation. When he saw me, his eyes lit up. I exhaled and ran up to meet him.

He grabbed me up and held me tight. I melted and didn't want to do anything else today.

"I love you," he whispered and kissed my neck.

"I don't deserve you," I said back. "And I'm so sorry for missing your communion today. My house is a madhouse after Whitney threw that pregnancy bombshell at us. Mom won't answer her phone, so she must be furious with me. You know she'll blame me and she has every right to."

He released his hold of me and then took his finger and lifted my chin until my eyes met his. "No, she doesn't, and don't ever say that you don't deserve to be my wife."

"But come on. I'm a mess. Maxim was right. . . ." I sighed.

"Maxim?" He frowned. "Did you talk to him last night?"

"No, he said that the other day, after I took Braden Logan to him. We got into an argument when I shot him a theory. It was a stupid theory about Gabe. Maxim dismissed the idea and told me what everyone has told me for the past seven years, to let Gabe's murder go." I paused and closed my eyes. "That's when he said that I make messes."

"I see. I can't agree or disagree about that. I don't know that part of your life, and every time I think that I should be a part of it, our happiness is in jeopardy."

"Right, more mess," I grumbled.

"No." He chuckled and kissed my forehead. "You're not a mess and Whitney is old enough to make her own messes. Don't worry about today's brunch. I'll share it with you in private tonight after you have dinner with your mother and sisters. I believe a communion is in order for us all, including my family. So the dinner will be at Trish's."

"Now I know why she hasn't answered her cell." I felt my lips purse. "Mom called you. Didn't she?"

He nodded. "But it's not what you think. She didn't mention Whitney at all."

"Really?" I was stunned.

"No. I don't think she knows. She only stressed that it was imperative that we meet them tonight. She said it was for our benefit."

"For our benefit? Yeah, right." I sucked my teeth. "She's trying to force me into setting a wedding date, but that's not her decision to make. It's ours."

He smiled brighter. "Yes, it is, and what have we decided?"

I looked at him and knew he wasn't asking on behalf of my mother but for himself. I also knew that he wasn't pushing me or giving me an ultimatum. He just wanted me.

I smiled back. "I've kept you waiting so long, I've decided to let you set the date. Whatever you decide . . ."

"Pastor, can I have a moment? I'm sorry. This can't be helped." Regina Mitchell interrupted our conversation, something I had grown accustomed to since I'd decided to surrender my heart to Justus.

I needed to practice my "I don't care if you interrupt me" face anyway.

Justus grabbed my hand. "Stay here."

I nodded before he walked a few steps away with Regina. My phone buzzed. I looked at it. It was Deja.

I suddenly remembered I hadn't called her back yet. I answered.

"Tell me something good, because I sure do need it," I said.

"Oh, it's good, real good, but um . . . Ang, I don't feel good about talking about this on the phone. Maybe you can meet me at The Spot tomorrow."

Meet her at The Spot? She was referring to the Vietnamese restaurant down the corner from her house. Real talk. That restaurant rarely served food. It made its money by being a dropoff/pickup for trafficking illegal activities too numerous to list. The biggies were: drugs, cigarettes, shine, guns . . . I'd overheard that escorts went on dates there, too. So you know I wasn't going there by myself, even in the daylight.

"What are you doing there? You're not Vietnamese."

"So? Bich and nem like me. Izzy took care of their boy, Cam, when he popped a case a while back for joyriding in a stolen car. I don't even know why he did that, because he got his own ride." She smacked. "But anyway . . . As a favor to Izzy, now I do a little bookkeeping for Pho and nem. It's good work experience for me. Who knows? I might become a CPA and stuff. Today's my day to pick up the receipts. That's why I was calling. Tomorrow we can lunch and chat. You know how we do."

I chuckled and shook my head. "Let me think about it."

"All right." She smacked her lips again. I wanted to smack her for sounding so nauseating.

I didn't know how I was going to see her, because I couldn't think of anyone to go with me. Well . . . anyone who knew how to use a gun properly, that is. Frisco was my new ride-or-die and he was literally dead. Big Tiger was at a lunch mixer at Atlanta Station, so he wasn't available either.

In fact, he had turned a 360 since he'd begun seeing Ava. She had convinced him that since he contracted bail recovery agents to pick up fugitives, he no longer had to. It was time for him to look like the businessman that he was. I agreed with that, but I needed him, nonetheless. Unfortunately, if Tiger rolled up in there, someone might add two and two together and connect Izzy to this.

I sighed. Working in bail recovery had more covert activity going on than a spy novel.

"Deja, I don't know if I can meet you and lunch, too. My family is still mourning my uncle and then this news about Frisco . . . I don't have much of an appetite. I need to just calm my nerves and let all this settle in, so I'm probably eating soup."

I didn't want any soup and Deja didn't work for a Vietnamese restaurant owner named Bich. She was being funny, probably got a private chuckle every time she said the name that sounded like a name of a female dog, a name that would get you cut if you said it around me and her, as a matter of fact. I had to hand it to her, though: she was slaying me with those names.

The big reason why Deja was my girl was because she was a master at making ciphers on the quick. She knew how to hide information and play dumb. Deja had gotten her MBA in accounting before she met Izzy. He convinced her to choose the dumb and rich life over something more stable and safe. I couldn't argue with her too much about her decision, because I did the same thing. I just did mine on the other side of the law.

"Yeah, you need to do that, girl. Dat's so important. Maybe some other time."

I sighed. "Yeah . . . It'll be soon, though, after I'm feeling better. It'll be good to see you and the kids."

"How 'bout this?" She paused. "Bich has a really good *Pho Ga* noodle soup. He told me the recipe. I took notes when I was invited to join him and his family at his home yesterday for dinner. I wrote the recipe down because I didn't want to mess it up. You know I'm not good around the kitchen. You ought to see the chicken legs on my kids."

In her words, she was telling me that she wrote down

Izzy's answers to my questions and she was going to give them to me. I needed for her to tell me how.

"Your kids are healthy, so stop it. They probably think they have Vietnamese grandparents, though." I chuckled. "So will you text me this recipe?"

"No. I got this new smartphone and I don't know what to do with it. But I can get you the recipe. I was going to give it to you after we caught up with some vermicelli and ginger ale at The Spot. I thought your daughter would like the noodles. I know my kids do."

"Good looking out for me, Sis. I appreciate it."

"We mothers have to stick together, you know . . . but I feel you, so what I can do is have my little brother Corey drop off the recipe. We don't live far from you now and I'll even have Bich throw in a special order of spring rolls for the baby, some house Pho, vermicelli, and a sweet treat on me. I'll have him drop it off in time for dinner."

She didn't have a brother named Corey. She was having the notes couriered to me, probably by some drop-boy lackey of Izzy's. Now, all that food she was talking about I had no clue, but I hoped she was sending me some. My stomach grumbled.

"What do you mean, you live nearby?"

"Oh, that's right. We haven't talked in a while. Guurl, you got to do better." She smacked those lips again. I wondered what kind of lip gloss she used. It must taste awesome. "That's not my area anymore. Izzy upgraded me."

I felt my neck roll in that way when I become both shocked and amazed at the foolery I have heard. My neck almost rolled off its socket, if there was such a thing.

"Upgraded you where?"

"Dunwoody." She smacked her lips harder now. "In the good part, ITP, not far from John's Creek and your neck of the woods."

She's dumber than a bag of barber hair. I shook my head. It didn't take much to ask the Lord to have mercy on her dumb-bunny behind. I might as well have used the first name that came to mind, because, to tell the truth, Dunwoody, Georgia, inside the perimeter (ITP) was the worst place for a Black, Grady baby, petty drug dealer, his wifey, kids and nem to move to. They might as well have put a big bull's-eye on their house.

That area, alone, had the potential to make a bail recovery agent rich, ergo Riddick Avery. It didn't look like it from the outside: suburbs, boutique shopping centers, cute private schools, sidewalks, and playgrounds. However, after you'd lived there for a few months, the mirage faded and you realized you had moved into a den of Dirty Birds about to go to war.

The Asian gangs circled North Atlanta suburbs like Georgia turkey vultures.

And there were the Cuban marijuana house growers living deep in the heart of Norcross, which was a stone's throw from Dunwoody. I didn't want to mention the New Orleans robbing crews that came after Hurricane Katrina, who were so bad that Atlanta PD had to hire NOLA's police chief to take some of those bad boys down. The Korean mafia numbers had grown since the white flight of middle Gwinnett, thanks to the Mexican cartels, who were offended by all those criminal copycatters moving onto their turf. But none of them, not one of them, could hold a candle to the hillbilly church cookers riding up and down Blue Ridge Mountain and into Peachtree Industrial Boulevard, waiting for the opportunity to sling a Molotov cocktail through the window of anyone who had the nerve to run shine or meth in the land their forefathers bled and died on. So if you had good sense and looked beyond the peacock feathers, you left them birds where they nested.

It's like small-gang world over there. I hoped "up-graded" was code for "I live in Johns Creek" or "Suwa-nee."

"Could you send it over for lunch tomorrow, because tonight won't be good for me?" I tried to smack my lips, but I didn't think I positioned my lips correctly. "I hope the recipe hits the spot."

"Girl, all I can say on this phone is that the soup will knock your socks off."

I observed Justus walking toward me. "I'm sure it will."

"Feeling better?" Justus asked after I hung up.

I nodded. "I will soon."

37

Sunday, 4:00 PM
Canoe Restaurant, Vinings, Georgia

As Southern traditional as my mom worked hard to be, she never slaved over a stove. Therefore, Sunday dinners happened at the choicest Southern cuisine restaurants in Atlanta. This week she chose Canoe. Canoe was located in the Vinings area, not far from the Vinings Inn, where the Belle Brunch was hosted. All of these places were within walking distance of Mom's other house.

Since we were this close, I hoped to see my new stepdad. "El Capitán" was my nickname for him. I've met him about three times in total: at Devon's funeral, at Christmastime, and at Lana's wedding reception. He was about six feet, tan colored, bald head, and with brown freckles across his upper cheeks. He was quiet and taking his retirement from the Atlanta Police Department and marriage with my mom very nicely. When I first met him, he seemed tired and grumpy. Now his eyes looked refreshed, there was a little sun in his cheeks, and he was rocking the trendiest golf-inspired loungewear for a man his age. No wonder Mom kept him away from us: he was a Connery Cutie. A "Connery

Cutie" was my term for an older man who looked better with age, like actor Sean Connery.

El Capitán stood in the lobby. I assumed he was waiting for the rest of us to join the dinner party, since we'd arrived about the same time. Whitney, Bella, Aunt Mary, Justus, and I arrived together. Ava, Taylor, and Lil' D came without Tiger. We'd spotted them in the parking lot and decided to come in together.

"Hi, Cap. Where's Mom?" I hugged him as everyone said their hellos and continued to follow the hostess toward our dining table.

Justus stood by my side.

I released my hold of El Capitán. He smiled at me and then shook Justus's hand. "She's in the ladies' room, but I would like to speak to you two for a minute."

Justus's right eyebrow rose into his forehead. "What can we do for you?"

"I know I've only been Angel's stepdad for about a year, but it seems fitting that I'll be the one giving her away at your wedding, so Justus, I think you and I need to have a talk."

"Giving me away?" I giggled. "Are you serious? I'm grown, Cap."

"And I'm dead serious, and my name isn't Cap," Cap said with a smile in his eyes. "I gave my daughters away and I'm giving you away. You're not that grown. I don't know what the problem is."

"It's no problem, sir," Justus said. "When do you want to talk?"

"Before you and Angel go to Château Élan for the weekend by yourselves."

The way he said "by yourselves" made me blush in a

teenaged embarrassed kind of way. If I could have fallen through the lobby floor, I would have.

After the brunch I couldn't wait to talk to Justus about how ridiculous Cap was this evening.

"Justus, you do not have to meet that man," I said.

We were parked inside my garage. Whitney, Bella, and Aunt Mary had gone inside the house.

Justus ran his hand through my hair while I was trying to talk to him, which was so distracting.

"Are you going to say something?" I asked, trying very hard not to moan. His hands felt incredible.

"When I learned that there were a lot of men in your life who cared about you, it opened my eyes. You're precious, and to have you as mine is like finding a treasure. I don't care what I have to do, in order to have you. I don't care how many men I have to get through."

I moved his hand from my head. "Justus, are you going to talk like this for the rest of our lives?"

He chuckled. "No, not when you make me mad—I'm sure of it—but between those times, and I don't think there will be many, I will talk like this. You know you're the only person I talk to like this."

"Oh my goodness." My heart began to beat so fast. I began to feel anxious and guilty and then more anxious. I had to catch my breath to keep from hyperventilating.

"Angel, are you okay? What's happening?"

"Yes and no. . . . I need to tell you something," I started.

"No, it'll have to wait, because you're shaking. I need to get you into the house. Your aunt is a nurse. Right?"

"Justus. No." I panted. "I don't need a nurse. I just need to get something off my chest."

He cupped my face in his hands. "I already know about Maxim and the kiss."

"How long have you known?" I whimpered.

"Does it matter, if I'm sitting here holding you and telling you that I'm ready to marry you?"

"You can't be real?"

"I know about the kiss because you can't keep a secret in your sleep." He grinned. "But I need to know some things from you."

"You have me literally in the palm of your hands."

"Clever . . ." He paused. "Do you still want to marry me?"

"I do."

"Do I kiss better?"

"He was semiconscious, so I don't think it's fair to judge, and it wasn't that kind of kiss, so I can't compare the two."

"It wasn't that kind of kiss . . . Clever." He cleared his throat and lowered his hands from my face. "Are you keeping anything else from me?"

"No, and I won't keep another secret from you."

"Can you do me a favor? Call it an engagement gift?" he asked.

I nodded. I tried hard not to cry. "Anything you want."

"Since you've completed your assignment with Maxim, I want you to not work with him until after we're married. Will that be a problem for you?"

"I'm not going to lie. It'll be difficult." I thought about our meeting tomorrow.

"Knowing all this time that you kissed him has been difficult."

"So why do you want to marry me, then?"

"Because you're the only woman I've ever prayed for, ever wanted, ever loved. I still want you," he said.

"I want you, too. Look, I'm not going to leave you for him, so why make this demand?" I asked.

"Because although you accepted my proposal after you kissed him, I'm a man, Angel. I'm not going to put myself in a position to be angry with him for something you did out of curiosity." He lifted my chin with his hand. "I can't do me knowing you're spending your day with a guy that you kissed because he saved your life or you're ruled by self-condemnation. What will happen the next time?"

"Can we go back to your old request to tag along with us?"

"I'm a minister, not a marshal." He shook his head. "No, Tiger has plenty of skips for you to pick up that don't involve Marshall Maxim West. If that's not enough work, then how about you help me plan our wedding."

"Okay, but can I start boycotting Maxim after we return from Château Élan?"

"You mean not see him again after this weekend?"

"No, he doesn't want to see me now. But I'm waiting on some very important information that could benefit his current operation."

"Angel, he's a U.S. marshal, a federal fugitive recovery agent, who happens to also be your PI instructor. There will always be very important information to give him and vice versa."

"Give me this week to tie things up. Like you said, it's not his fault that I have issues, and I promised Frisco's parents that I would find justice for them."

"Angel!" His face puffed up. "What about your promise to me?"

I lowered my head. "I told you I wasn't good at this."

"Fine. . . . I'll give you until Thursday, because I don't want him or his case following us to Château Élan this weekend. Can you promise me that?" he asked.

"I'm so sorry. I will make it up to you."

"Let's just not talk about this again." He popped the door and hopped outside.

But I will somehow. I promise. I rubbed the baby hairs on my nape until he opened my door, helped me out of the car, and escorted me into my house.

38

Monday, 10:30 AM
Home, Sugar Hill, Georgia

It was a good thing I'd asked Deja to send what I asked for to my home. After that conversation with Justus, I could barely get out of bed. Whitney dropped Bella off to school for me. She assumed I had caught some kind of bug. I hadn't. I was embarrassed, ashamed, and couldn't hold my head up. Allison Kim wanted to press charges against me for tasing her bat-crap crazy behind, Frisco was really dead, and Justus had forgiven me for kissing Maxim but then demanded I end our working relationship by the end of this week. As bad as I wanted to blame someone for all of this drama, there was no one. Again Maxim's last words to me haunted me. I made messes and then did dangerous things in order to clean them up. I don't know what Justus thought of me now, but I didn't want that to be it. So I was going to do what I hadn't thought I would do. I was going to take this information to Tiger and wash my hands clean of it.

I needed Ms. Loretta. I called her home.

"It's about time you called." Her voice was certain, confident, and hinted that she knew all things. "Last time you called me, it was for me to look after your soon-to-be-sister-in-law."

"Yes, ma'am. Will you still be able to do that?"

"I said I would. Didn't I? Now, why are you really calling?"

"I don't know what I can share with you about me and Justus and what I'm supposed to keep between us."

"Must be bad, if you're calling me to share a secret."

"It's not a secret. He knows and he's forgiven me. But . . ."

"You haven't forgiven yourself."

"Yes, ma'am."

"Let me ask you a more important question." She took a breath. "Have you ever forgiven yourself for making a mistake?"

I thought for a moment before I answered. "No, I guess not."

"Well, now I know what your first assignment to becoming a Good Wife is."

"And what's that?"

"Angel, you need to get over yourself. There are too many people depending on you to do what they can't. Whatever you did is forgiven. Move on."

"But I don't understand that kind of forgiveness," I admitted. "Who does that?"

"We mothers do it for our kids all the time. We do it for our sisters. It's unconditional love. Now pay it forward."

"How do I do that?"

"Forgive someone who doesn't deserve it."

"Who? Uncle Pete?"

"Isn't he dead? No. It's too late for that. I don't know who the person is. I'm just saying drop your pity party, move on with your life, and when the time comes share the gift."

"All right."

"Feel better?" she asked softly.

"I think so."

"Good. Now I have to go. My stories are about to come on. You know they're on the Internet now."

Monday, Noon
Home, Sugar Hill, Georgia

Deja had my recipe and my lunch delivered shortly before noon. I didn't read the recipe packet, because Justus was here. I was afraid that the sour look on his face, if he knew what I read, might give me indigestion and I didn't want that. I wanted to enjoy his company.

Whitney was roaming around in her room. She was avoiding me, which was stupid. I left a bowl of *bún bò Huế* at her door. She would need the energy before we met Mom for dinner tonight. It was apparent that Mom didn't know anything about Whitney's baby announcement. I didn't know why I was surprised. Ava kept secrets better than the CIA, and I didn't tell Mom because I just wasn't up for the death threats. She might have followed through this time.

I knocked on Whitney's door and then spoke to her through it. "I'm downstairs with Justus for lunch. There is soup for you on a tray outside this door. After he leaves, you and I will talk before I pick up Bella from school. And don't worry about this. I'm not putting you out. You're still coming with us, you and the baby. Okay?"

She cracked the door. "Can I not tell Mom about this until after the cruise?"

I bent back down, lifted the tray, and handed it to her. "Whatever you need to do, but next week you must let the cruise medical staff know that you're expecting when you're on board."

She nodded. "Thanks."

"Don't thank me yet. We haven't had that talk." I smiled.

I returned back downstairs. Justus had moved to my unused dining room, taken the food out of its containers, and plated them on my grandmother's old china.

"I've never eaten Vietnamese food on fine china, but it makes sense," I said.

He looked up at me and grinned. "Just like *we* make sense."

My heart pounded at the sight of him. After Justus had confessed his feelings for me, I'd tried not to fawn over him like I had done before, while sitting on the back pew at church most Sundays. If he saw me staring in amazement at the way his lids creased around his eyes in such a way that they reminded me of perfect rainbows, he would know that I bent to his will more times than I cared to admit.

"You still think we make sense?" I asked.

He walked from where he stood on the other side of the dining room table toward where I stood. He pulled out the chair closest to me for me to sit on. "I believe that we do."

I sat down with my eyes on him. "How can you be so sure?"

"That's easy." He smiled and placed Deja's packet labeled "recipes" on the other side of my plate. "I have faith in us."

"So is this how our arguments will go? I do something stupid and you forgive it?"

He kissed my forehead. "Didn't you forgive me for going to Francine Dixon about your sister when you were trying to gain her freedom?"

Mrs. Loretta's words enveloped me and I understood what she'd meant. Justus had forgiven my mistake like she had forgiven mine. I wasn't going to do anything else without being completely honest with him.

"Let's not talk about that again." I pulled him closer and kissed him.

"Wow." He smiled. "You know I'll do anything for you?"

I noticed the packet, then looked back to Justus. "Could you pray with me about this package before you say grace?"

He frowned slightly. "I assume it's not recipes."

I shook my head. "But it may be the answer to my prayers."

39

Monday, 2:00 PM
Sugar Hill, Georgia

After Justus left, I decided to not open the packet until after I had that talk with Whitney. I hopped up the stairs and knocked on her door. She didn't answer. I checked my watch. I had to pick up Bella in thirty minutes. I was hoping Whitney would ride with me and we could talk on the drive there. I knocked again.

Nothing. I touched the doorknob. It was locked.

"Whitney?" I raised my voice, thinking she might have fallen asleep.

Then I heard a slight whimper. I leaned into the door to determine if the noise was coming from her or her television.

I couldn't tell. After what had happened to Frisco and what Ty had done to himself, I didn't want to take any chances. I went to my room and pulled a contractor's universal door key out of my dresser drawer and returned to her room. The key popped the door open and I went inside. Whitney wasn't in her bed. I heard water running in her bathroom.

"Whitney?" I called her name again as I approached the bathroom.

The whimpering noise became louder. The door was cracked open, but I didn't feel good about stepping in there unannounced.

"Whitney, this is Angel. Can I come in?" I asked.

"Yes," she whispered.

I slowly pulled the door open, to find her in the bath. She had her legs curled up toward her chest and her arms wrapped around them tight. Her hair was wet and she had been crying.

"Whitney, you don't look okay. What's going on?" I asked.

"There's no need for you to worry about how Ma will take the news about me being pregnant, because I think I just lost the baby." She lowered her head to her knees and cried.

I looked around the room. I didn't see anything out of place, any blood or foul stench anywhere.

"Are you sure? Let me just call Mary Margaret across the street. She's an RN and doesn't go to work until tonight. Let me have her look at you to be safe. Who's your obstetrician?"

Angel pointed at the closed lid toilet. "The baby is gone."

My legs began to twitch again. I refused to open that and be grossed out or worse in front of my distraught little sister. She gave me no choice. I called Mary Margaret, Ava, and Mom. I'd take getting my head chewed off, because as supportive of a big sister I was to Whitney, she needed our mother.

After that, I called Bella's school to tell her teacher that I would be late picking her up because of a family emergency.

I would pick her up as soon as Mary Margaret knocked on my front door. Then I called Justus to reschedule the family dinner at his sister's home.

When I returned home with Bella, there wasn't space for me to park in my own garage or driveway. We entered the house through the back door. I let Bella hang out in her dollhouse while I went inside to see if the worst was true for Whitney.

Mom was the first to greet me when I peeked inside. She caught the skin on my elbow and tugged. I didn't feel a thing. She had numbed that spot for me about twenty years ago.

"Ma, I don't hurt there anymore," I confessed.

"I knew that. That's why I did it." She pointed for me to follow her into my pantry.

I switched the light on; she switched it off.

"Evangeline Grace Crawford, explain to me how your sisters have gotten themselves carried away by your band of brothers in the hoodies."

"Since I turned good, no one listens to me."

"Are you mocking me?" She pointed her index finger in my face.

The tip of her French manicured nail hung just above the tip of my nose. I didn't know if she was going to thump it or gouge my eyes out.

I shuddered. "No, ma'am. That was the best explanation I could come up with."

"I don't need you to come up with an explanation. I need you to give me your answer. What in hell has been going on over here? I thought you were searching for a fugitive, not playing matchmaker."

"With all due respect, Ava had become friendly with Tiberius"—Mom didn't like when I called him Big Tiger—"before I did my PI training."

Mom's chest rose higher. My mouth was getting me nowhere. "I didn't know there was anything going on between Whitney and Frisco. It popped out of the blue and happened way too fast, unless she had also been seeing him before Lana's wedding."

She leaned her body against my deep freezer. "I never had children out of wedlock. . . ."

I lowered my head and prepared for her to drop the ax on my neck.

". . . but I lost a child before I married your and Ava's father."

I looked up while keeping my head hung low. "You did?"

"Yes. That's why your father and I married." She took her ivory-shell glasses off her face and placed them on the freezer. "He had wanted to marry me the moment he saw me, but I wanted a bigger life. I had come to Valdosta for an internship. One of the first women attorneys in the state, who hired black women as law clerks, had an office there. I had heard rumors about the sleepy, very segregated town, but I wanted to take that opportunity. Three months later, I lost my first child after learning that my boss's gardener's son, whom I loved, had drowned in Ocean Pond. He was a champion swimmer, who drowned. Law school doesn't teach you how to deal with that."

"So the baby wasn't Daddy's?"

"No, I met your father at my lover's funeral. Your father converted me to Christianity that day. If it weren't for my faith, I wouldn't have been able to find meaning for life again."

"Does Whitney know about this?" I asked.

"Some of it." Mom checked her watch. "She's too broken to see the pieces to her puzzle."

"Was she right? Did she lose the baby?"

Mom nodded. She reached into my back pocket and pulled out one of my collectible lace handkerchiefs, then dabbed her eyes with it. "I hope you never feel the pain of reliving heartache through your children's lives. Déjà vu has nothing on this."

"If you and Capitán want to call off Turks and Caicos next weekend, everyone would understand. I'll stay here with Whitney if she's still feeling bad."

"No, dear. These girls need this vacation more than anything now. Whitney wasn't far enough along to have any serious medical complications. Her doctor is upstairs with her right now." She patted my hands. "I had my honey invite him over for a house call and he obliged."

I smiled despite the mood. "Mom, you know a lot of people."

"I do. Maybe you should sit down with me once in a while before you traipse all over town to talk to someone about the darkness in this city."

I cut my eye at her and smiled. "What do you know about the city?"

"I know that Château Élan is enchanting this time of year. I don't know; instead of you and Justus having adjoining rooms, it might be best that you have separate rooms at the end of both halls."

I frowned. "Why?"

"Because I had a dream about fish last night and I didn't think the dream was about my baby." She sniffled, as she referred to Whitney. She looked at me. "Life is short, Angel. You know that. I love my girls. Although you have a daughter of your own, you will never feel the depth of the love that I have in my heart for you. I love you. I will get Whitney through this hurt. However, it will give me great comfort to know that you are ready to live outside of the shadows with a man who adores you."

"I'm ready, Mama."

"Good. Now, how long will you make this man wait for the honeymoon, because I don't like dreaming about fish every night. There are far better thoughts in my mind."

"He won't wait long." I chuckled. "Did you find a nurse to care for Justus's sister, Trish, while we're gone to the Château?"

"I just did. Your neighbor next door is a gem and her rates are great, too."

I harrumphed. "I could have asked her myself."

"But you didn't, and you know why? Because I know the answers that I seek are always right in front of my face. As soon as I stop making things seem so complicated, the answer is always staring right back at me."

I remembered Deja's recipe packet. It was still sitting on the dining room table. I hoped.

I went to the dining room and found it under a box of fried chicken. I looked around the table. It looked like the entire neighborhood had dropped off fried chicken. I decided not to take this sweet gesture as some hidden racial agenda. White folks like fried chicken, too.

When I pulled the packet from under the box, I ripped it open. No need to put it off any longer. I read what was inside and then plopped in the closest seat to me. Things were beginning to make sense, but I needed further confirmation from a reliable expert.

40

Since I became a mom, I rarely saw the inside of my bed sheets until sometime after midnight. I couldn't blame my insomnia on my life as a bail recovery agent. Big Tiger would debunk that myth anyway. I'd called him two hours ago; he was asleep in bed. When he tapped on my front door, I dared not ask whose bed he was sleeping in.

We greeted each other quietly and then I led him into my home office and showed him a chair. Although the bungalow in the back served as my office, my in-home office was the place I worked at night when everyone was asleep in the house and when I met with my private-investigation clients. This office looked more professional, feminine, and marketable, according to Ava, my official meddler. However, the clientele was still just trickling in, so I didn't use the office much.

Tiger rubbed the arms of my walnut wing chair. I turned on a lamp and sat on the edge of my desk. There was some weird tension between us that needed to be removed before we could get started.

"How's Baby Sister?" he asked.

"She's scaring the bejesus out of me." I walked him through the foyer. "I was shocked enough about her and Frisco as an item, then that she was pregnant, too . . . How did I miss all this?"

"You've been busy with your new life."

"Ain't nothing new, just more of the same old drama." I scoffed. "You warned me."

"And you never listen."

"I'm listening now; that's why I called you."

"We haven't met in the middle of the night like this in months," he said, while taking off his leather jacket. "It feels different."

"That's because before, we met downtown in the back of some strip club or night club, not in my home with me dressed in pajamas."

"True. I do miss the bustier and miniskirts. " He chuckled. "But that's not what I meant by different."

"I know what you meant. We both have been busy."

"No. We used to be busy together. That's what I meant and that's the difference," he scoffed.

"Well, we can't do everything together, now can we?" I huffed and folded my arms over my chest.

"We could have, but you're hardheaded about Justus, so . . ." He rubbed the back of his head. "And I take it you and Black Maverick still ain't speaking to each other."

"Who told you that?"

"The Big Bad Boys, of course. They said that you and the marshal got into it when Mama D and I were at the hospital with Frisco. I wasn't expecting to see him at Saint Monica's, but I saw you roaming Mass for him."

I looked away. "No, I wasn't."

"Yes, you were. You can't lie to me." He grinned, then

leaned forward toward me. "So what happened? Why is Black Mav mad with you?" He kicked his boots up on top of my table near where I stood.

I pushed his feet off of my nice mahogany desk. "He's not mad with me, and it's not relevant to why I called you here tonight."

"Fine. You'll tell me eventually anyway. You always do."

"Whatever. . . ." I threw him the courier envelope from Deja. "I had Izzy's girlfriend, Deja, get me some information about what went down inside lockup when Braden Logan was at DeKalb. These are the answers."

He pulled the sheets of paper out of the folder and cleared his throat. " 'Braden needed protection from the Koreans. He paid Izzy's crew from his commissary and had to make some outside payments.' "

"That's probably how Deja could move to Dunwoody so fast," I said. "But I'm curious as to why the Koreans wanted to hurt Braden."

"First off, does Izzy know he just gave you information to keep his butt behind bars longer?" Tiger asked.

"I promised Deja I wouldn't tell his business and I know you won't either, since Izzy's mom is one of your best clients."

"She sure is." He shook his head. "As hard as that woman works to keep her son out of jail . . . Sometimes when she calls me in the middle of the night for me to pick his butt up, I want to take him for a long drive, yank him out the car, and knock the sense back into him."

I chuckled slightly. "I had been wondering how you really felt about this work."

"Don't get me wrong. I love what I do, because I've been there." He sighed. "You catch a case . . . sometimes it's your fault and sometimes it's not. Either way, case you need a lawyer, you need to keep paying your bills, and you'll have to spend a whole lot of cheddar to take care of this situation. Bail helps you take care of things."

"That's why I couldn't understand why Braden didn't come out the minute Ty gave him money. Why would he sit there and keep paying Izzy? And get in more hot water with the Koreans?"

Tiger looked down at the paper in his hand, squinted, and then looked at me with a puzzled look on his face.

His expression sent a chill down my spine. "What? Why are you looking at me like that?" I asked.

"The questions you asked him. It's like you're a psychic."

"No, that's my experience at the *Sentinel*, coupled with the tools Deacon West and Maxim had taught me in the state private investigations course, and a little mother's wit thrown in for good measure. Why? Am I on to something?"

"Yeah." He handed me the note that was in Deja's handwriting, but written in Izzy's voice. "Your next question. 'Did the molester who Braden was protecting have any victims' parents inside?

" 'The pastor he was charged with abetting volunteered as a teacher for the adult Korean ESOL program for Gwinnett Head Start and Pre-K programs back in the '90s. One of the guys inside was one of his victims.' "

I gasped. "No wonder Ty was putting so much commissary money on his books. Ty's wife probably threatened to leave him, if something bad happened to her brother."

"Sounds like this Braden dude is a first-class idiot."

"I don't think he knew the man was a pedophile. However, I agree. He seems very sheltered, like he's never been outside of a country club, but I don't feel sorry for him."

"I'm thinking his family was fed up with him, because they could have put up a cash bond to bail him out instead of going through Riddick."

"Again, I think that was some of Ty's doing," I said. "Although he had protection inside the jail, he didn't have enough on the outside. When Ty gave him that money it was for him to leave town, but we kept him from getting out and that's why he doesn't want to go back to DeKalb. Now that Ty is dead, he doesn't have the clout or money to be protected in the same way again."

"Ty sure did his best to take care of him. I wouldn't do that for my brother-in-law."

"You will do anything for love, Tiger."

"Girl, you're good." Tiger clapped.

"Sh . . . You'll wake up the house."

"So what's next?" Tiger's cell phone buzzed. He looked at it. "It's a text. Keep going."

"I don't know. If Braden's afraid to go back to DeKalb, which he seemed very much so on the night I brought him to your office, he'll tell Maxim what he wants. He'll tell him who else is leaking federal investigation's information to those being investigated. He'll take the deal with the FBI and go into WITSEC, if he has good sense."

Tiger cursed. "Speak of the dadgum devil . . ."

"What? Who is it?"

"It's Max."

"He lets you call him Max? So you two are best friends now?"

"No, but since you and he fell out, he's been blowing up my phone. If I didn't know you, I'd think something was going on between you two."

"I'm glad you know better." I shrugged.

I tried to appear smug when the truth was that I was still upset about what Maxim had said to me.

Tiger's eyes were on me. "Nothing happened between the both of you, right?"

"Tiger, come on now . . ." I blew his question off without telling him the truth. I've never lied to Tiger before, but I agreed with Ms. Loretta. The kiss was a mistake, and I didn't need to let it have any more power over me. "I'm getting married, and you know how hard that is for me. Getting myself involved with two people . . . That's your thing, not mine."

"That's not my thing anymore. I'm changed."

"Please don't start telling me how my sister has changed you."

"Why can't I talk about this with you, Angel Soft? That ain't right. I know way too much about Justus than I asked for, because of your fat mouth."

"Stop it right there. I didn't tell you anything you didn't want to know, and whatever Ava told you, that's on you."

He responded to another text. "Max again, and this time he mentioned you."

"I can guess what he said." I rolled my eyes. "Tell Angel not to snoop around."

"Well, there goes my psychic theory about you, because you were wrong. He told me to tell you that he needed to see you today."

I stood up. "Really? Where?"

"At the Waffle House in Duluth off Boggs Road. Around ten. Do you need me to come with?"

"No. Actually, yes. I need you to go with me because you'll keep me focused. I need to prepare for my weekend trip and I may need to talk to a lawyer about this issue with Allison Kim."

"Don't worry about Allison. I had a chat with Phillips. She backed off that stupid idea."

"Thanks. I appreciate it, because after this weekend I'm out. I'm going to stick to my side of the fence and focus on those jackets you have on my desk. I hope this information will help Maxim and Sanchez, because I've hit my threshold."

"It should, which reminds me . . ." He folded his arms over his chest and grinned. "You never answered my question."

I stiffened. "What question?"

"Me and your sister. Has she said anything about me?"

"Yeah, she did." I wiped my brow in relief, because I'd thought he was going to ask about Maxim and me again. "It's hot in here. I think it's time to turn the air-conditioning back on. I usually don't do that until May."

"Angel, please quit playing with my emotions," he grumbled.

I giggled. "She hasn't said much because she knows better. As you know, I don't approve of your crush on her, but I saw her for Sunday supper with Mom and she was beaming. I hadn't seen her that happy since before Devon died."

"Hold on. You went to Canoe? You haven't been there since you had to give Charlotte Lewis the bad news about Rachel. Did you run into her?"

Rachel had been a person of interest in Ava and Devon's murder case. She later suffered the same fate as Devon. Charlotte was Rachel's mom.

"No, but I should have called her long before now, just to check in on her."

"I hope she's doing well. Now, that woman's life is full of secrets."

I nodded. "It sure is."

"Ava told me about you coming to the Belle Brunch/engagement party the other day."

"Mhmm . . ." I nodded. "I'm trying to weed out whom I should add to my wedding invitation list."

"I get it. Your Mom's side of the family is bank like

Hank and you need to get back into their good graces for a fancy toaster."

"Not just that. I don't want them to miss the opportunity to meet Justus. He's a really good guy. He deserves to marry a woman who is humble enough to admit she was wrong and to also show the family she's changed."

"I only want what's best for you," Tiger said. He opened his mouth to say more but seemed stuck for words.

"Are you going to speak before I nod off and fall asleep in here or what?"

"I take back what I said when I asked you to investigate Frisco's death," he said. "You were right to stand down and move away from this. Frisco wouldn't want you putting yourself out there like this."

"I'm confused." I really was.

"I'm concerned for you." He stood up. "The way this thing is going down, whoever shot Braden and possibly hired Ty to out Sean Graham is the same person or runs with the same person. This sounds like organized crime, Angel Soft.

"Follow me. I need to get home." He walked toward my front door. "You did the right thing not telling Maxim. I'll get this info to him. Let him and Tinsley figure it out. Too many people are dropping like flies. I don't know what I'd do if I saw your name floating across my scanner app."

"Do you think the person who shot Braden knows that I was the last person he talked to?"

"Who else was in the room with you, while I was gone?"

"Just me and Salvador."

"Then you should be good." He checked his watch. "Angel Soft, we've talked for about three hours. The rooster is about to crow. I can't believe we talked that long."

"I guess we had a lot to talk about."

He turned around, snatched my hand, and swooped me

up in one of his famous bear hugs. "Don't you ever wait this long to talk to me again."

I hugged him tighter. "I won't, because I'll see you at the Waffle House."

"You know what I'm talking about." He released his hold.

"Are you going to lay off Ava?"

"She hadn't let me on her, yet." He smirked.

I elbowed him in the gut.

He bent over and grunted. "Angel Soft."

I opened the door and pointed with a grin. "Get out of here before I do much worse."

41

After I'd dropped Bella off at school, I drove to the Waffle House to meet with Tiger and Maxim, as planned, but neither were there yet. Tiger had called me on the cell phone and told me he was running late. I took that time to read every item on the menu and case the place. For those of us who spent considerable nights on stakeouts and chasing down bad boys, we became Waffle House connoisseurs. We knew which locations had the best steak and eggs, the worst bathrooms, and the snitches in rare form, at our disposal. The Satellite Boulevard location, however, was the best cooking, hands down. It was also one of the cleanest, and that's important for women like me.

I was glad that Maxim wanted us to meet here. It was closer to my home than travelling back to DeKalb County. Salvador walked through the door. I hadn't expected him, but I took out my folder on Braden. Maybe I should give it to him and break out of here before Maxim got here. That way I would have today and tomorrow to get myself together before Justus and I headed off to make our own wedding cologne. At first I'd thought the idea was cheesy, but I was looking forward to it now.

Twenty minutes later, Salvador and I were enjoying our breakfasts. "So you and Maxim have kissed and made up?" Salvador asked me between slurping a big bowl of buttered grits and scrambled eggs.

I shrugged. "What's that supposed to mean?"

Salvador shook his head and chuckled.

I frowned. "What's so funny? Didn't he want me here?"

"You'll know soon enough." He wiped his mouth, sat up, and looked toward the front door.

I followed his gaze and turned around. Maxim glided into the diner like a cool October wind. His arms looked more ripped than the last time I'd seen him and he had begun to grow a goatee, which made his cane-syrup brown eyes draw you in before you could catch yourself.

A lot had happened in the past few days. But I had been privy to his charm, so I knew how to shake it off. Maxim wasn't a bad guy, by any means. He was just the right guy at the wrong time in my life, which made my unease with him sitting directly across from me incredibly intense. Salvador chuckled some more before he poured himself another cup of coffee.

Maxim kept his gaze on me. I wanted to eat my hash browns in peace, but they kept spilling off my fork. I could hear Justus's voice in the back of my head. *I'm a man, Angel.*

"Don't ruin that pretty trigger finger on food meant to eat with your hands." Maxim smiled.

He referred to the incident that almost got us both killed on a red Georgia clay road near the Okefenokee Swamp.

"I guess it wasn't meant to be. . . ." I placed my fork down and wiped my mouth with my napkin. "I'm satisfied."

". . . for now." He smirked.

"Are you going to order something to eat?" I asked.

"I can take care of myself, thanks for asking." He picked up a menu, glanced at it, and then placed it back down.

I rolled my eyes toward Salvador. He tilted his head at me. I could tell he was warning me not to push it. But that was hard. Maxim was acting like a spoiled kindergartner who hadn't gotten chocolate milk for lunch, although no one else could have chocolate milk either. I didn't understand why he was acting this way. Why had he asked me to come? I looked away.

"Thank you for meeting with us, Angel. I know you're a busy woman," Salvador said.

I let him stroke Maxim's ego for a few minutes and texted Big Tiger. Tiger told me that when Maxim had requested for me to meet him today, he hadn't seemed angry. Either something had happened in the past twenty-four hours or I was being set up for the okey doke.

"Actually, guys, I need to go, so can we get on with it?"

"One minute you're concerned about me ordering a decent breakfast, now you want me to rush our meeting and drop the breakfast all together." He scoffed. "You can't have it both ways. Tell her, Tinsley."

Salvador looked at me and smiled. "Max has been on a stakeout for a few days, so he's a little grumpy."

"Seems more than grumpy to me, but let me remind you that I don't have all day, gentlemen. Did Braden give you the information you wanted? Is Sanchez still in hiding?"

"I'll answer all that once I finish chewing," Maxim said.

I rolled my eyes at him and texted Justus. Since I was washing myself from this case as soon as Maxim stopped eating, I had time to bring dinner to Trish and the kids tonight. Bella and I would hop on over. I could share with Trish the itinerary for the kids, who were going with Mom and the family to Turks and Caicos. I knew Whitney needed her space. She was still in mourning for Frisco and their baby. I didn't know how to comfort her. I hoped Whitney went with the family this weekend to the excursion, because I was afraid to let her be home alone feeling the way she did.

"You've set the wedding date. Haven't you?" Maxim asked.

I looked up from my phone briefly and kept typing. He was done eating but looking at me like he wasn't satiated.

"Not yet, but we're going to Château Élan for the weekend to discuss it."

"Château Élan." He nodded. "This is a great time of year to go, rain or shine."

My texting fingers stopped in midair. I looked up at him. I couldn't tell if he was hurt, pissed, or just being his old arrogant self. Either way, I had to keep calm. Although I haven't caught every skip on Tiger's books, I didn't like to lose and I didn't want to let Frisco's parents down. More important, I hoped that helping Maxim and Salvador would help Whitney heal. I would do anything to get her smiling and wisecracking again.

"So you've been there before?" I asked.

"I married my ex-wife there."

Salvador coughed.

"Oh. I'm sorry. I keep putting my foot in my mouth," I said.

Maxim grinned. "I'll forgive it if you send me a wedding invitation. When's the date?"

"Stop." I chuckled. "Men don't care about wedding dates, especially men like you."

"Come on, I was just trying to clear the air. There was enough tension in here you could cut it with one of your daggers." He sipped his coffee, then leaned back in his chair.

"Please tell me you didn't think I called you here to help you come up with a wedding date."

"No, but I was going to ask you to be my maid of honor until I remembered you look better than me in pumps." I snapped my fingers.

Salvador waved his white napkin in the air. "Can we get back to why we're really here? I have a staff meeting to get to."

"Finally transferring Dixon to a department more suitable for her? Like larceny and theft? Oh wait. She's not good at that either." I giggled.

"Glad to see you're in a good mood, but I'm not happy with the way things are going." Salvador poured another cup of coffee. "We're not any further to finding the mole than we were before we picked up Logan."

"And on top of that, I have a dead recovery agent to add to the growing body count," I said.

"My condolences again, Angel," Salvador said.

"Well, if there is anything I can do . . ." Maxim mumbled.

"You can get Allison Kim off my back. She wants to press charges. Tiger says he's handling it, but this woman has a lot of important people in her corner."

"Yeah, and some of them will be in the same place as you and Reverend Romance this weekend."

"What do you mean?"

"Allison Kim's ex-hubby hosts his annual Supper Club and Night Golfing Fund-raiser at the Château this Saturday. I can get you and Justus in, if you want."

I cringed and smiled. "Can you do that without Justus knowing about it?"

Maxim grunted. "You told him?"

"Told him what?" Salvador asked.

I shrugged. "Apparently I talk in my sleep."

"I thought you knew that," Maxim said.

"Whoa, whoa. TMI. Too much information." Salvador raised his voice and straightened his tie. "I don't want to ask what you two are talking about, because it isn't my business. But this golf thing . . . Angel, it wouldn't hurt to cozy up to some of those political wives, and not for nothing Justus is a great dime piece on your arm. I'll talk to the authorities on my end, but can we focus on the special case at hand."

"My fiancé is not a dime piece." I pushed the folder over to Maxim. "I assumed Braden is why you called me down here."

"No, I called you here for this." He reached into his jacket, pulled out an envelope, and placed it on the table. "Answer this question for me? Why were you snooping into Braden Logan's inmate file after you had completed your assignment with us?"

"What's in that envelope?"

"Nothing important like whether or not Gabriel Hwang is still alive; just answer the question."

I took a calming breath. "I don't have to answer that, because just like you said I have completed my assignment to bring in Braden Logan for BT Trusted Bail Bonds and A1 Recovery Agents, neither of which have anything to do with you."

"It does have to do with me," Salvador said.

"Okay. Fine." I snatched my envelope off the table and handed it to Salvador. "Braden is afraid of a Korean gang inside your jail and operating OTP. Throw these names around and Braden will take that protective custody deal with the FBI. It'll keep you from having to place him in lockup before you reach your holding deadline today. I think I'm done."

I stood up.

Maxim caught my hand. "Angel, stop being bratty about it. I was trying to help you out."

"Help me out how?"

"You were not answering your number when I called you."

"You told me to my face I was a mess. You wouldn't listen to Braden about what he knew about Gabe."

"Angel, Gabe is dead. If he's dead he's dead and if he's alive, then he is dead to you. It is for your benefit that you let this go and plan your wedding like you should be doing. Like I said, the invitation still stands for you to attend the Supper Club and Night Golf Fund-raiser. I can make the call right now."

I folded my arms over my chest.

"You're going to have to trust my expertise as a U.S. marshal, that I know what I'm saying." Maxim nursed his coffee cup. "Besides, I can't tell you much."

"You don't have the clearance to find out much or you don't know much?"

"Government clearance much." He looked at me when he said it.

His gaze made me feel a little uneasy. I looked away again.

"Well, what can you tell us?" Salvador asked.

"Not much right now. Not until I get back in the office. And I can't go into that office right now until I know who's sharing what I do with criminals in the state."

"Whatever . . . what was I thinking, to ask you."

I looked down at Salvador and he smiled in that way that made me feel like everything would work out. "I'll take this to Braden as soon as we leave here. Go on and enjoy your engagement getaway."

"And I'll get to the bottom of Logan's claim," Maxim said. "I owe you that much."

"Thanks, guys." I sighed, then smiled. "Any more pre-marital advice?"

"Take it from an old, happily married man: honesty is the glue to a successful marriage." Salvador stood up and gave me a hug.

"Tell that to my mom...." I scoffed and looked at Maxim. "A woman can't afford to show all her cards."

42

Tuesday, 11:00 AM
Waffle House, Duluth, Georgia

"**B**efore I get out of here, I need to go to the grown-man's room," Salvador said. He walked away from the table toward the men's room; I reached into my purse to get my share of the bill.

"Angel, I need to ask you one more question before you disappear from my life forever."

"Now who's sounding melodramatic?"

"You said Justus knows. If he was the kind of man I think he is, he's not going to be amused with me calling you on assignments from time to time."

"But you pay well." I chuckled.

"I'm sure his paycheck will catch the shortfall, but then again, Gabriel Hwang made sure you were taken care of before he died. Isn't that why you have this big tie to him after all these years?"

"Is that the question you wanted me to answer?"

"No." He pointed at my ring finger. "Is that the reason why you didn't visit me in the hospital?"

"No." I shook my head. "I didn't visit you because you told me not to."

"I was semiconscious. You knew I was out of my mind."

"I didn't know you enough to know when you were telling me the truth."

He frowned. "So you're blaming your decision to settle with preacher man on me being hemmed up in the hospital?"

"Do I look like the kind of woman who would settle?" It wasn't a question.

"No, you don't. I'm just glad I could help you make the best choice." He grinned, but his eyes didn't look very happy.

Salvador returned just before I was about to speak.

He stared at the both of us. "Should I go back until you finish whatever you two started, back in the swamps?"

"Nothing happened in the swamps. The ring on her finger's proof of that." Maxim sipped his coffee. "When you arrive at the Château, your concierge will have your invitation, so pack accordingly; just not that blue dress you seduced me with. Reverend Romance isn't as strong as me."

I wanted to slap the taste out of his mouth, but I was the only non-LE at the table. There was no way I could explain to Justus why I was in jail this time.

I picked up my things and tried my best to ignore Maxim's bitterness with my decision to marry Justus.

"I have to meet with Tiger and I don't think there is much more to say except how is Sanchez doing?"

"She's doing well. She's keeping Logan company," Maxim said.

"Well, I've been down that dark road." I chuckled. My phone buzzed. I observed it. Big Tiger was texting me. It said two words:

call now

He didn't have to state anything else.

"I'm sorry, guys. There is an emergency at BT Trusted Bail Bonds."

"I can take you there," Maxim said.

"Thanks, but I drove. There's nothing wrong with my truck." I grabbed my purse. "But thanks for offering."

Maxim caught my arm. "I can get you there much faster and I'll cut the lights on."

"So your government protocol can't tell me if my daughter's dead father is really alive, but it could clear me through Atlanta traffic. . . ." I snatched my hand back. "No, thank you."

I stormed out of the Waffle House. Maxim's insolence better not give me indigestion.

"Hey!" Maxim shouted after me.

I picked up my pace, but Maxim's long legs caught up with me before I could break into a sprint.

"Don't be like this, Angel." He huffed. "I wasn't trying to rub you the wrong way. Let me drive you. It'll give me a chance to explain."

"Explain what? Why you've been such a jerk for the past week? There's no need to explain, because that's exactly who you were when I met you. A jerk." I unlocked my door and grabbed the door handle.

"You changed me, Angel, and I don't know what to do with myself now." His voice cracked when he said those words.

My heart warmed up to him. I felt bad. Although I hadn't known Maxim long, I did know that being vulnerable wasn't his normal M.O.

"Maxim, let me be honest. I almost didn't come here. I wouldn't be here if Tiger hadn't agreed to show up. After what you admitted to me, I think it's best that we not spend so much time together anymore."

"Forget that. Let me drive you."

"And like I said before, I can drive myself."

"I'm not talking about that kind of help."

I looked up and frowned. "What?"

"I'm talking about Gabriel Hwang. Let me drive you and I'll tell you what you need to know."

I gasped at his proposition. "Are you kidding me?"

He observed his watch. "Time's a-wasting."

I slammed the door. "I hate you. Don't you know that?"

"That engagement ring on your finger is proof enough."

He walked me toward his Mustang. As we drove off, I saw the concerned look on Salvador's face. It didn't come close to how I felt.

43

I texted Justus, to let him know where I was and whom I was with. Then I texted Whitney to make sure she was up for picking Bella up from school for me. Maxim hadn't said a word.

"Are you going to tell me what you know or what?" I asked while I texted my assistant, Cathy Blair, to see if I had received any client calls.

"I was being thoughtful and waiting until you completed your call."

"It was just texts."

"Sex?"

"That's it." I put the phone down. "Pull over and let me out."

He chuckled. "Stop being dramatic. I was just breaking the ice."

"You're about to get a broken lip if you don't grow up real quick, Maximus West."

"Wow. The whole name, huh?" He chuckled as he sped through Interstate 85 toward Atlanta. "I guess I better come clean, then."

" 'Better come clean'? Maxim, I knew you weren't going

to tell me anything about Gabe when we stepped into the Waffle House."

"So why are you riding with me?"

"Because I still hope that you're a better man than you think you are."

He sighed. "I never thanked you for saving my life."

"Yes, you did at Lana's wedding, or did you forget that, too?"

"I deserve that." He nodded. "I'm not good at this."

"You definitely aren't, but bribing me to ride with you was low. And you may be a lot of things, but this isn't you."

"As always, you're right." He veered into the HOV lane.

These lanes were created for vehicles that carried more than one passenger. I didn't like them, because they were too close to the shoulder for me. I sucked in my breath as he rounded each shoulder's curve.

After a few seconds, Maxim glanced at me. "What's wrong?"

"Highway shoulders don't like me."

He got the hint and moved back into regular traffic. "Sorry, I didn't mean to scare you."

"But you meant to cause me discomfort." I folded my arms over my chest. "Maxim, you can't possibly like me this much after spending only a few days together."

"I know that. Don't you think I know that?"

"Then what's with the big chip on your shoulder? You're acting like I chose Justus over you, and that wasn't the case. There was no choice and you know this."

"I do, but it doesn't mean I have to like it," he said. "You of all people should understand that."

He reminded me of some of the things I'd told him about my sister Ava's and my relationship. He had a point and I didn't like that.

I shook my head. "You're right."

"I'm right?!" He guffawed. "Now, that's a first, coming from you."

"It doesn't have to be, Maxim," I said. I hoped he would have a change of heart about helping me. "You and I are the only ones who know that there was more than one shooter in that parking garage where Gabe was murdered."

"In my line of work, when two mysteries are intertwined, the one you want to solve may cost you everything," he said.

I could see Tiger's office a few blocks ahead.

"What you need to ask yourself is will finding this matter out help your upcoming marriage? Will it help your daughter? How will it benefit you, because the truth is Frisco is dead. He's not coming back, and that ghost of a deadbeat dad haunting you can't hold a candle to me."

My nose twitched. "You always find a way to put yourself in the mix."

"I'm just saying. If you need a reason to back off this wedding, then let it be a real man. Let it be me."

I laughed. "Now, that was funny."

"And it's the truth." He hopped out of the car and opened the car door for me. "All my records show that one Gabriel Hwang of Dacula, Georgia, is dead. When I said I didn't have much, that's all I had."

I thought my heart would leap, but it didn't. I felt numb. "So what does this mean?"

"It means there's nothing stopping you from marrying the preacher"—he leaned toward my face and kissed my cheek—"unless you want there to be."

Then I slapped him good. I hopped out of his car and went inside.

I slammed the door. "Tiger, what was so urgent that you called me?"

"Surprise," Ava cooed, as she walked from behind the receptionist desk.

She carried a huge cupcake on a platter.

"What is this?" I smiled.

"The armor-bearers and I agreed that it would be pulling teeth to get you to come to the church this week."

"Mr. Jones said how busy you were, completing cases before you go on your engagement excursion with good pastor Morgan," Mrs. Loretta said. She held a white gift box covered in a pink satin bow.

"So we thought of meeting you here for a working engagement brunch."

I looked around. "Where's Justus?"

Then I felt Justus's hands wrap themselves around my eyes. I placed my hand on his.

"You're not getting rid of me that easy," I heard Maxim shout. He must have just come inside.

I shuddered.

"What's going on here?" Justus asked.

Justus and I were in Tiger's office. It was supposed to be so that we could have some privacy while I explained why Maxim had driven me to Tiger's. But I didn't feel like I needed to explain. After all, I'd promised to not work with him after this weekend. It was only Wednesday.

"Tiger texted me. He made it sound like a big emergency, so Maxim offered to escort me through the city so I could get here fast. Now what's your problem?"

"My problem? This is our engagement party?"

"No, it is not. I didn't plan it. Did you? Nothing that has happened lately has been what we planned or I wanted? I didn't ask for Château Élan and I definitely didn't ask for—"

"You don't want to go?"

"That's not what I said. Don't you dare put words in my mouth."

"You know what. I didn't walk out of war-torn countries to come here and be stuck in a roller-coaster ride with someone who is clearly not ready to be married."

"Again you're putting words in my mouth. I want to marry you. I want to drop all this frou-frou crap and marry you. I want you in my bed, in my shower, flipping those silly pancakes right now, but I have a whackadoo family and I work with a lot of hot men. Take it or leave it!"

He walked toward the door; I felt my heart sliding down to the floor. I couldn't breathe.

"If I was the kind of man who didn't have great self-control, I think I could impregnate you in this room. I love you, but I need to rethink our future. I'll see you tonight," he said before he walked out Tiger's door.

"Tonight?" I followed him outside and looked at Ava. "What's happening tonight?"

"This is what happens when you don't answer your phone. The Captain is barbecuing for all of us, including Justus and his sister's family."

I shook my head. *I seriously think we should have eloped.*

44

"So what did you do?" Whitney asked.

We sat at a patio table on Mom's deck, watching our stepdad try to grill catfish in the dark. I had missed Sunday Brunch, but had arrived in time for Fish Taco Tuesday, another family obligation I was expected to meet. The kids were hidden somewhere away from adult conversation. Mom and Ava had Justus hemmed up in the kitchen.

Part of the reason I was out here, besides laughing at the Capitán catch a hot charcoal with his foot, was that I didn't know what to say to Justus.

"What I usually do: make dumb decisions." I sighed. "I thought that, after all I had been through lately, I had learned from them."

"You have been shooting bad lately in the men department." Whitney frowned, then shook her head. "Have you heard from Maxim since you got him in trouble this afternoon?"

"He's working on his case."

"Good," Whitney scoffed. "At least we don't have to deal with that drama."

I frowned at her. "What drama?"

She leaned forward and whispered, "Don't act like you didn't catch feelings for that man when y'all were hiding out in the GA swamps."

My frown turned into a full-blown scowl. I kicked her leg as hard as I could. She screamed. I hoped it bruised. Then I clutched her shirt sleeve and pulled her chair toward me. It clanked when it hit my armchair.

She gasped. "I'm still a little sore."

"Oh gosh. I forgot." I sighed.

"I'll forgive you. If you tell me the truth about what happened."

"Sure. We camped inside a bed-and-breakfast on the outskirts of the swamps, which was off limits because of a fire, you fool. But look"—I gritted through clenched teeth—"nothing happened between me and Maxim, and if I hear that crap come out your mouth again I'm going to butt-kick you to the Okefenokee Swamp. You got me?"

Tiger's domineering catchphrase oozed out of me like it had always been there. My heart raced as I stared back at my sister. I didn't know where that anger came from; I thought I'd buried it long ago. The revelation that I had let it return scared me. I didn't want to be that bad Angel again, not when I'm supposed to be marrying the closest thing to an angel, especially when I was raising the sweetest child on the planet.

Whitney bobbled her head. Her eyes were wider than the full moon behind her head. I loosened my grip on her shirt, then pushed her and the chair away from me.

She caught her arm and hopped away from the table toward the screen door. I thought she was going inside, but then she turned around. "I was just being curious, since you hadn't said one thing about him since you came back from South Georgia. You can't be mad at me for asking."

"Change the subject, Whit," I said. "And I'm glad you're back."

I heard the screen door slam and assumed Whitney had gone inside to join Justus and Mom.

"Are you planning on avoiding me all night or are we going to talk?"

Justus's voice made me shudder.

I turned around to face him. Justus Morgan stood before me, but didn't look like the man he was a year and a half ago. Back then, I'd thought he was a beyond-my-reach, super-handsome, incredibly intelligent, illuminating shepherd of my church, Sugar Hill Community.

Back then he wore sun-kissed twists that hung below his shoulders. He'd reminded me of one of those Black Jesus paintings that hung on Big Tiger's war-room wall. Now he rocked a dark brown Caesar cut that made the dimples in both his cheeks hard to resist staring at for an embarrassingly long time. He was taller than me by at least one full foot. At night, when he stood in front of me, his shadow covered me and made me feel safe, even when he was mad at me like he was now. And his eyes, honey colored, with brows that made me weak in the knees when he lifted one, charmed me.

I gave Justus a hard time because he gave me an even harder one. Men weren't supposed to be this captivating to me anymore. I begged God to not let this happen to me again. Yet here I was, stuck as if a statue, yet pliable like Silly Putty. My only saving grace was that he didn't know how much power he had over me. Well, at least I hoped . . .

"I was hiding from you because I know what you came here to say." I lowered my head and mumbled, "You're breaking the engagement off."

"Isn't that what you've been trying to do since you said 'yes'?" he asked.

I shook my head. "No, it's just . . . I didn't know things would get this crazy."

"You mean that I wouldn't learn about your bachelorette kiss with Maxim?"

"You're right, but . . ." I sniffled. "I don't want to end . . ."

"End what?"

"Us. I don't want to end us. I love you. Gosh," I spat out. I was trying too hard to hold back from crying to answer. It felt like I was drowning inside.

He lifted my chin with his finger. I tried to push my chin down to fight him off, but I began to cry.

"Stop crying and fighting me." He pulled me into his arms. "You know I'll do whatever you want."

"So you're not breaking up with me?" I asked between sniffles.

"I'm not breaking up with you, but I do have two conditions, which I think I rightfully deserve to have."

I looked up. "Anything . . ."

"I want us to agree on a wedding date this weekend, and next week I want to begin completing papers to adopt Bella."

I gulped over the latter.

45

After I dropped Bella off at school, I ran back to my bed.
Ava was coming over to help me shop for the weekend.
Whitney would be back from her internship with Roger
Willis to tag along, too. That gave me a good hour to nap.

And then my doorbell rang. I would have ignored it had
the person not lain their hands on the doorbell. That was
the kind of thing I did when I knew a skip was hiding inside
his parents' home. The noise would aggravate them so that
the skip would either peep out a window or try to make a
run for it, because they didn't want the cops to come. They
didn't want to get picked up for an FTA.

It had to be Tiger.

I stumped down the steps.

"Why didn't you call me? I'm tired." I opened the door.

My best friend, Charlie, stood on the opposite side of the
door with her gloved hand on her hip and her Tiffany blue
Burberry suitcase propped up against my porch pillar. It
was a good thing that designs from the 1940s and 1950s
had become fashionable again, because now she didn't
stand out so much. Today she was dressed in her favorite

periwinkle floral-print halter swing dress and nude stilettos that were too high for an executive administrative assistant of a German and Japanese engineering company to wear on any given day. But that was Charlie. She looked like a bronze Gene Tierney: shoulder-length sandy brown hair that was pin curled and expertly framed around her oval face. Her big, wide, long-lashed, doelike emerald eyes put all our friends to shame and kept Ava in Halle's salon chair too many times to make good Christian sense. However, she wasn't arrogant, vapid, or obnoxious. She was sweet and hilarious, and had this knack of saying whatever was on her mind.

"I can see you didn't miss me much. You look like a big ol' hangover." She left the suitcase and sashayed over to me.

I smiled. "I had to do something with my time, while you were jet setting with your boss."

"Well, you picked a fine time to get engaged." She cradled my arm under hers and helped me toward the living room. "Now, what am I going to do with all this illegally transported food I brought for you to gag over?"

"Put it in the freezer or give it to Mom. She's been starving herself to enjoy her honeymoon." I chuckled. "I'm sure she'll be ravenous when she returns."

"Honey, please. By the time Ms. Virginia came back from the islands, she would rip up your mandelhornchen. Almond and chocolate would be everywhere. Her infamous gold belts would pop off and cause one of y'all to lose an eye." She giggled. "It would be brutal for her new hubby to see that. He might change his mind and get an annulment."

"Then you're right. She can't have any, because a married Mommy is a nicer Mommy."

"I bet she is. Speaking of marriage . . ." Charlie unzipped the front pocket of her suitcase, pulled a newspaper article out of it, and then placed it on my lap.

It was a photo of Justus holding me in his arms. The caption read: "When a Minister Loves a Bounty Hunter."

I lowered my face in my hands. *Got to be more careful.*

"Girl . . . what in the world have you gotten yourself into, and with my pastor, at that?"

I looked up. "Charlie, you've only been to Sugar Hill twice, so how is that your church?"

"Exactly." She nodded. "That's the only church I've returned to, and now that you and Reverend Justus 'Too Hot to Be Holy' Morgan are an item, I'll be coming again."

"Please don't call him that. He wouldn't like that."

"Wow." She smiled wide and big. "You're really into Brother Morgan, aren't you? This is good, really good for you."

Charlie had a PhD in comparative German literature from Brown University, and had studied German printmaking as an undergrad. She wasn't Southern like me, but she was just as smart. We met during the Atlanta Summer Olympics and became roommates, and then fast friends.

I once ridiculed her for becoming an admin for Obi & Junger. I thought it was beneath her and that she was copping out for married life. She was engaged to an Army guy stationed in Germany at the time. I thought he was a jerk. But she got the chance to travel the world on Obi & Junger's dime and meet some of the most interesting people. It gave her the confidence to ditch that joker and live the glamorous life.

Her job wasn't taxing, because she was so dadgum proficient. She was off on the weekends, had two vacations a year, full benefits, and I'm pretty sure she had Mr. Junger when he visited the Atlanta plant.

She'd never married and hadn't had a child. Yet she was happy with her life and very self-aware. As I marveled over my friend, I envied how together she looked.

I'm a mom of a young girl. It was my duty to have it together. I thought about Ava's offer to get me PI training. Perhaps I should take her up on that offer, since I have all this time on my hands.

"Penny for your thoughts," Charlie said.

"You're going to think I'm crazy, Charlie. But remember when I called you about those flowers that were sent to me a few months ago? I found out who sent them to me. He said he sent them for a friend. I think Gabe is that friend."

"Did he confirm or deny?"

"He said that Gabe was dead."

"I agree dead men can't send flowers, doll," she said. "It's a prank from one of your many enemies who more than likely read the same article I did. I told you your job had residual danger. How many people do you know like to go back to jail?"

I chuckled. "No one."

"Now, see . . . that's why I'm here. Laughter is good for the heart and soul."

I kissed her cheek. "I'm glad you're here, but I'm leaving tomorrow. Justus and I are going to Château Élan. It's a gift from Mom."

"Well, I'll hang with Whitney and the baby, then."

"Whitney and Bella are going to the islands with Mom."

"Well, dang. This is what I get for not answering my phone while midair on a continental flight."

"Do you still have your condo in Buckhead?"

"I do, but I don't want to go there yet. I'm trying to stick to my plan."

"What plan?"

She teared up. "I don't want to be the mistress anymore."

"Then don't. You can stay here while we're gone. There's plenty of room."

She hugged me. "Thank you, girl. How is Whitney?"

"She's wilder than the last time you were here."

"Well, she's been through a lot, and so have you." She sat back on the sofa. "What will you do once she's completed law school?"

"That's another problem I can't solve right now." I sighed. "Whitney is falling apart. I don't want to tell her business, but she is falling apart."

I reached for a tissue box.

Charlie snatched the box out of my hand. "You stop that crying. Stop it right now."

I grabbed it back. "What are you talking about? I need this cry. I've been waiting for this cry. I deserve this cry."

"No, honey. You deserve this time to recharge and get back to being your fabulous, hard-as-nails self. You can't do that watching sappy movies and crying. We're not built like that and you know it."

I frowned. "But you cry all the time."

"Yeah, over stupid stuff like men and men and men. I don't cry over something I can't control and I don't cry when I know the solution."

"Ava and Whitney will be here at noon to go shopping with me."

She slipped her gloves off her hands. "When does the baby get out of school?"

"It doesn't matter today. Justus will be picking her up for me. He's taking the kids over to Mom's to get ready for the trip."

"Well, that settles it. I'm transferring back to Atlanta, because I deserve a Justus, too."

46

I spent the day packing and shopping with Charlie, Ava, and Whitney. Charlie would be house-sitting for me, which was great. She decided that quiet life in my empty house was far better than checking in at the Omni Hotel downtown or going to her condo. I promised to bring her back a bottle of wine.

During our outing, I bought cute clothes for Bella to wear on the trip and a vintage 1930s peach flapper dress for Château Élan's Supper Club and Night Golfing event. I also went to the spa for a facial and a haircut. Although the Château had a great spa package, I didn't want to come there looking like I looked yesterday. I was exhausted, but when Justus called with an invite to dinner, I perked up.

He met me at the front door, but he wasn't alone. Bella, whom I had dropped off with Ava earlier today, was with him. She ran toward me. I lifted her in my arms and squeezed her tight.

"Mommy, we're taking you out to dinner," she said. I could hear the wind whistling between her missing two front teeth. She sounded adorable.

"Where are we going to eat?" I asked.

"The best place in the world," she said. "Chuck E. Cheese's."

I smiled at Justus, but he wasn't smiling.

"What's wrong?" I whispered.

He nodded toward something behind me. I turned around with Bella in my arms and saw Maxim in his car, watching us, more like watching me. My chest tightened. I felt hot. I was going to have to find him a girlfriend stat. Since he claimed to be so attracted to me, maybe I should hook him up with Ava. Then I thought about it and chuckled to myself. They had nothing in common. If those were the last two people on the planet, mankind would be doomed. But it would fix my Tiger problem. . . .

"Why is he here?" Justus asked.

I sighed. "I have no idea, but I'm sure he will tell us."

"I hope he's not here to ask you to join another one of his dangerous manhunts," he said. "The last one scared me into asking you to marry me."

I gave him the side eye. He chuckled.

I shook my head and smiled. "Let's get out of here."

I could feel Maxim's eyes on the back of my head. I knew he wasn't through with me and neither was I with him, but I agreed with Justus. We needed some time apart from each other.

Dinner with Bella and Justus was perfect and just what I needed. I had a lot of apprehension about Bella traveling without me. Although my job took me out at creepy hours of the night, I never was more than a short drive away from her. As excited as she was about this trip, I was scared. They were flying out and then taking a ship. Who would I be without her?

* * *

Friday, 7:00 AM
Mom's home, Marietta, Georgia

"Don't you forget to call me every night before you go to bed. Use your grandmother's phone," I said to Bella between kisses.

"I will." She giggled and tried to squeeze me tight with her little arms.

"You act like she's going away with strangers," Whitney scoffed.

"I'll miss your snarky mouth." I walked toward Whitney and extended my arms to her until she took the hint and let me hug her. "I hope you have a great trip. When we get back, you and I need to have some big sister/little sister bonding time."

"We can do that when we get to New York for your dress fitting," she said.

"No, I mean me and you go on a trip together. Just us."

She leaned back from our embrace. Her eyes were lit up like Christmas lights. "For real?"

"No, for play. Of course, for real. I feel like you're slipping away from me. I had that with Ava; I don't want that with you."

"But how are you going to do that and plan for your wedding?"

"Fool, Mom is planning this wedding. I'm just showing up, looking crazy as I want to be. Ava is helping me prepare for the wedding. I need you to help me get ready for the bachelorette party. Most think Vegas is the spot to be, but I think Biloxi is underrated. What do you think?"

She chuckled briefly, then cleared her throat. "Ang, I know what you're doing and you don't have to do that."

"What am I doing?"

"Trying to make sure I'm okay about you marrying Justus. I'm glad for you. Shoot, I'm the one who hooked you up."

"And I owe you."

"Hmm . . ." She tilted her head and looked up as if she was thinking very hard. "You're right. You do owe me."

I chuckled. "And I'm still serious about you staying here."

Her face relaxed. She hugged me again. "You can't get rid of me."

"Why would I want to?" I kissed her head. "Take care of Bella for me and make sure she eats something fun. Ava treats her kids like a piece of candy is the devil."

"Gurrl, she is going to be a hot mess on this trip. Look at her."

We both still held each other, but turned in the direction where Ava stood. She had Burberry luggage for her and the kids. She was dressed in head-to-toe khaki, including the Panama Jack Hat, as if she were going on a safari instead of the most fun theme park in the world. I wanted to laugh at her, but a twinge in me felt bad for her instead. She was still mourning Devon's death.

I knew what that felt like.

"Maybe I need to include her on our sister getaway," I said to Whitney.

"She would spoil it. Kill it dead, Angel. Do you want that?"

"I want her to be happy."

"Don't worry about that. Your little sister is on the case."

I turned to her. "What have you done now?"

She rubbed her hands together. "Was I wrong about you and Justus?"

"Oh, Lord." I sighed. "Please tell me . . ."

"I invited your buddy Maximus to see us off."

I frowned. "You what?"

"Look. He's been coming around the office a lot lately."

"Whose office?"

"Mr. Willis's, or have you forgotten that I work for him, too. They've been catching up and talking about some old cases. But I hear your name come up every now and then. I hear Ava's name come up, too. Something about that investigation where you and she fell out about years ago."

"And what did you say?"

She shrugged. "I didn't say anything, because I didn't want Mr. Willis to know I was eavesdropping on them."

"Did Maxim say anything to you?"

"No, he just smiled and smelled real good."

"Sounds like you have a crush."

"Sounds like you're jealous."

I shook my head. "Why can't that bad time just die?"

"Because it's not resolved. You saved her from being charged for Devon's murder, but she's still gun shy around you."

"But I didn't do anything."

"I know that, but she still doesn't," she said. "But Marshal 'Mouthwatering Hot' Maxim could make her see things straight."

"Don't do this, Whitney."

"Why? She needs somebody and he's single. If he can't be with you, then—"

"What did you say?"

"Come on . . . I know you love Justus. I know you wouldn't be unfaithful to him, but there's a thing between you and Maxim. I wonder if it's misguided attention. Maybe if he could take his eyes off you for a minute and see Ava, then he would see the right person for him."

"And you know that our stiff-lipped, sanctified, and highly favored sister is a match for Maxim?! Ha!!" I guffawed.

Whitney threw her hands on her hips. "You'll see. I know what I'm talking about."

She didn't have a clue, I thought. I couldn't care less about Whitney's screwball attempt to match Maxim and Ava together. My attention was still focused on Whitney's comments about Maxim hanging out with Roger Willis. What had they been talking about and why was my name mixed in it?

Justus had some work to complete at the church office, so he didn't come with me to say good-bye to the family. However, we were to meet at noon and then head to Château Élan. It was nine. Mom and the gang would push off within the hour. They were taking a charter bus to Florida to catch the boat to Turks and Caicos. Mom and El Capitán, of course, didn't rent an ordinary charter bus. This thing clogging up the front yard was a celebrity rocker band's bus. It had bathrooms, plush bedding, a living room . . . posh.

"There was no need for Maxim to be here," I said under my breath.

"And yet, I'm here." His voice made me jump.

I turned around. Maxim stood in front of me. His tall body towered over me, but I wasn't intimidated. Actually, I had hoped that by now we would be friends. Instead, he felt like this new thorn in my side. I didn't like it.

I folded my arms over my chest. "Why are you here?"

"Your little sister invited me."

"She invited you to come on the trip? I don't think so."

He grinned. "What if she did?"

"I already know that she didn't."

"If you know why I'm here, then why did you ask?"

"Because I know her reasons for asking you and I'm sure they don't match yours." I leaned closer. "Why *are* you here?"

"Are you going to rough me up if I don't tell you?" he scoffed.

"I'm out of here. Do whatever . . ." I spun around and headed toward my car.

"I offered your family a safe escort to Florida. So I made a few calls to my buddies at the Georgia and Florida State Troopers' offices."

I turned back around.

He handed me a piece of notebook paper, then put his hands in his jean pockets. "The troopers who will be looking out for your family are on this paper, along with the car numbers. If anything happens on the road, the driver can contact these guys."

I observed the words jotted on the paper. He was telling the truth, but I didn't feel bad for my reservations.

"Thank you," I said.

"That's all?" He chuckled. "That's all you have to say?"

"That's all you'll want to hear from me."

"Is that right?"

I nodded.

"I don't understand you." He took off his hat. "You've made it clear that my attraction to you isn't reciprocated. Yet you come at me like a moth to a flame."

If I could've slapped him in front of my family without them noticing, I would have. Instead I gave him my classic blank stare and then walked away.

As I was about to get into my car for the second time that morning, Ava called after me. I sighed and turned back to see what she wanted.

"Were you going to say good-bye to me?" she asked.

My twin was sweet and salty. I never knew which kind on which day.

"Sorry." I hugged her. "You were so busy with the kids, then the Belles. I did say good-bye to Taylor and Lil' D, though."

Ava rolled her eyes when I said "The Belles," then she leaned toward me and whispered, "What was Mama thinking inviting all of them?"

I snapped my neck back, surprised. "I'm shocked. You don't want them here?"

"Angel, they never invite us to anything. They weren't there for me when Devon died and I was accused of his murder, and they didn't come by and do any baby-sitting duty for you a few months ago when you had that concussion. Yet they're partying on our good blessing. I don't like it. I wish you were coming."

I chuckled. "Yeah, I would clear all of them off that bus."

"I know." She laughed. "But I'm glad for you. I'm glad you're putting yourself first for a change. You deserve it."

We grabbed each other's hands.

"Hey, let the Belles watch Lil' D and Taylor, while you dip out and get a massage."

"Oh, you know it." She smiled, then looked behind us. "So Marshal West is here."

"Oh! I forgot." I handed her his notepaper. "He has contacted both of the state troopers' offices to watch out for you guys on the road. Here is their contact information."

She smirked. "Really?"

I nodded. "Why don't you go over there and thank him?"

She smirked. "Why would I do that?"

"I think he may find you attractive."

She giggled. "In what world. That man doesn't know me."

"Well, he's here and he's not here for me."

I kissed her cheek and blew a kiss at Bella. Mom had her seated on the bus. I could see her through the window. And then I bounced before Ava got a clue.

47

Friday, 8:00 AM
Home, Sugar Hill, Georgia

It rained on my drive home from Mom's, but it didn't matter. Justus and I had weathered the storm. When I got home, I pulled my suitcases to the garage door, then decided to surprise Justus with some send-off pancakes. I couldn't flip them and make cute faces out of them like he did, but I knew how to use a skillet. Plus, Aunt Mary had taught me a secret to the batter yesterday that I wanted to try. I thought it would be a great surprise.

Someone knocked on my patio door just as I laid the last cake onto my bread warmer.

Justus must have run through the backyard gate instead of the front door like usual. Maybe he smelled my cooking from down near Trish's house. He had spent the night there after he dropped the kids off at Mom's. By the end of the week, we had an army of women church groups, girl scouts, neighbors, and military wives taking turns watching over Trish while Justus and I were gone. Trish couldn't believe how supportive everyone was, but that's why I moved out here.

"Hold on. I'm coming." I removed my apron from around my neck, walked to the door, and opened it.

Gabriel Hwang stood on the opposite side of my patio door threshold. I didn't gasp, because I had suspected he wasn't dead despite all the foolery from Maxim. Yet, I wanted to kill him now if he took one step over my door threshold. He must have sensed my resolve, because he didn't move.

"I guess I'm not the man you were waiting for," he said to me, while he stared at the sapphires and diamonds wrapped around my ring finger.

My home security alarm shrilled around us and the thunder rolled underneath our feet. Yet I heard every note in his words. Gabriel's voice held hints of snarl and rejection that almost made me chuckle, were it not for the fact that he had deceived me for the past seven years.

Come to think of it . . . I left my old, good life because of his lie. I've almost died three times because of his faked death. I've killed two people because I thought I was avenging his murder. And yet he stood on the other end of my back door, pissed-off with me for loving someone else, someone who hadn't lied to me, ever. Someone who had helped me raise *his* child, while he hid under my hydrangeas or whatever part of hell he'd just crawled out of.

Before I could curse him out, my landline rang. It sat on an end table in the great room near my bay windows. I gave Gabe my "don't come in my house" death stare, stepped away from the opened door, and went to answer the phone. I didn't read the caller ID because I knew it was the security call center. Everyone else called my cell phone.

I was right. It was my emergency services representative for today. Her very Southern voice trembled. After I gave her the pass code, I reassured her that I wasn't being attacked, and apologized for my blunder, then returned to my patio door and slammed it shut in Gabe's face.

But I didn't walk away from the door. I stood at my kitchen island clutching my chest. I was getting emotional. My six-year-broken heart quaked. I didn't know where to go. I couldn't go back upstairs and pretend that my dead fiancé/baby daddy wasn't standing outside my door looking even more handsome than the day he'd died in my arms. I hated him. I loved him. I couldn't move, because I was losing my mind.

"Evangeline, let me in. I know you're here alone and I'm not leaving until I know you and Bella are safe," he said.

Safe? I wiped my eyes with my sleeve and cracked the door open.

"You can beat me up from inside your house, if that will make you happy. But you have to consider that I wouldn't be standing outside The Bounty Huntress of the South's house during an electrical storm if it weren't gravely important."

"You still use too many adjectives," I mumbled.

"Angel . . ." He purred my name like a happy lion lying back-up in the grass.

The trouble with that visual was that I glared at him like a lioness prepared to defend her cubs. What had scared him out of Zombieland? Why was he back and begging for me, to start with?

Thunder clapped so hard my windows rattled. I grabbed Gabe's sweater and yanked him inside.

He stood over me, but somehow felt much closer. His hands were wrapped around my waist and his cinnamon scent made me hungry.

"Let go of me," I growled.

"You first." He smiled.

"I don't do what you ask of me anymore, because you're

dead," I said before I clutched his shirt tighter and then decked him with my right fist.

I hopped back when he dropped to his knees and fell over.

Then my cell phone buzzed. Justus was on his way. I had to get Gabe out of here.

"Charlie!" I screamed.

"Are you kidding me? Is that who I think it is?" Charlie threw her hands on her hips.

"It is, and Justus is on his way to pick me up."

Her eyes widened. "Are you serious?"

"As a quadruple heart attack." My heart raced. "I need you to hide him."

She shrugged and looked confused. "Hide him where?"

"Anywhere but the foyer, the kitchen . . . Take him upstairs."

"Do I look like I can carry a very built Asian man upstairs?"

The doorbell rang. "Help me put him in the pantry."

"I might can slide him in there."

"No 'might.' Do this for me and I will owe you big." I ran toward the foyer.

"Like maid of honor big," she shouted.

I stopped in my tracks. "Like I won't tell your boss's wife about you."

"Now, that ain't even right," she mumbled.

I continued toward the door and opened it. Justus stood on the other side looking better than the breakfast I had made for us. He walked inside and kissed my cheek.

He sniffed. "Did you make breakfast?"

I cringed.

"No, darling. I made breakfast for me," Charlie said from behind us.

"Um . . . Charlie has come to town."

Justus face lit up. "What a blessing. I'm so glad to meet you."

"Well, we've met before. I'm a member of your church."

He squinted and then turned to me. "She is?"

"She's one of our members who shows up for the holidays."

"I watch the service on the Internet, but really, I live in another time zone. That's not completely fair."

I chuckled. "I'm just playing with you. Justus knows all about you."

"Good. Now, I apologize, Reverend, but those pancakes are for my boyfriend. He's coming over in a few." She smiled sheepishly. "I thought you two would be gone by now."

He nodded. "That's my fault. I had to stop off to pray for a member who passed this morning."

He looked at me. I knew who he was talking about and felt bad.

"We can go to Cracker Barrel on the way there," I said.

"Sure. Where's your luggage? Near the garage door?" He walked toward the kitchen.

My legs began to wobble.

Charlie pulled me up. "He's not in there," she whispered.

"Where is he?"

"I don't know, but don't you worry. I'll find him. Now go."

"Call me when you do. I'm serious."

48

Friday, 1:00 PM
Château Élan, Braselton, Georgia

Château Élan looked like a sixteenth-century European castle set on Georgia soil. It had opened a little over twenty-five years ago as a winery but had become a premier golf resort and the largest winery in the state. It was comprised of an inn, where we would stay; a golf club; spa; seven restaurants; and an art gallery. Mom had had her eye on wedding one of her daughters there since it gained luxury status. Ava and Devon hadn't married there, because Devon's parents wanted him to marry in the church his great-grandparents founded. So if we got married there, it would be Mom's dream come true. That was the real reason she was treating me like a twenty-something virgin bride.

"When your mom suggested we get married here, I thought she was being overbearing, but look at this place. . . ." he said as we drove up to the valet. "This place is incredible."

I nodded. I was still numb over the fact of Gabe being alive and hiding somewhere in my house. I needed to call Maxim as soon as I could get some time away from Justus. I needed Gabe out of my house.

After we checked in and were shown our rooms, the first thing I did was call Charlie.

"Did you find him?"

"She found me," Gabe said.

"What are you doing with her phone?" I hissed.

"Tell me where you are. I need to talk to you."

"Are you crazy?!" I stomped my feet. "I can't do that."

"I need to talk to you about Braden Logan and who's after him."

There was a knock on my door.

"Can you tell me now?" I whispered.

"Not until I explain myself."

I held the phone away from my face and screamed silently. "Sure. How do you want to meet?"

Someone knocked on the door again.

"I'm coming!" I shouted.

"Sounds like you have to go."

"I do. Now, how will we meet?"

"Angelina, I was pretending before. I already know where you are, and we're here." He hung up.

"What?"

The bamming on the door got louder.

I opened the door. Justus stood in front of me. He had changed into knee-length shorts and a golf tee. He looked amazing. I exhaled, then dragged him inside the room.

"I can't be in here." Justus stayed near the door.

"Yes, you can. Nothing is going to happen. Trust me."

"I came in here because the concierge said he had called your room but you hadn't answered."

"I was on the phone."

He sighed. "Babe, I didn't want to suggest this, but maybe we should turn our phones off so we can enjoy this weekend."

"I want to do that, but something has come up that I need to share with you."

"Is something wrong with the family? Bella?"

"No, it's a different issue."

"Then I don't want to hear it." He stretched his hand out. "Hand me your phone."

"Huh?" I asked.

"For the next three days and two nights, we aren't answering these phones. If it's an emergency, your mom and your sisters can handle it and your mom knows how to get in touch with the concierge."

"Justus, I'm serious. I'm trying to tell you—"

"I know, and no way, not today. No . . ." He took a breath. "Evangeline, I love you, honey. Now hand me your phone."

I handed him the phone. What else could I do?

He smiled, then kissed my forehead. "Now let's get out of here, before I carry you to that bed behind us."

49

Saturday, 7:30 PM
In the vineyard, Château Élan, Braselton, Georgia

I hate to admit that Justus was right, but he was right. If Gabe was on the premises, I didn't see him yesterday or last night. So far Justus and I had had a wonderful time. We made a cologne that smells more like him than me, but that's how I liked it. He smells yummy to me.

During the day we checked out the different venues where we could have our wedding or reception. He played a round of golf with some of the people who had arrived for tonight's fund-raiser, while I had a massage and tried some of the spa packages.

No Gabe. Total bliss. Tomorrow, when I got my phone back, I would tell Justus about Gabe's resurrection. I didn't know how he would react, but I suspected there would be a little egg on his face. The good thing was that the egg wouldn't be on my face.

My hotel room phone rang. I picked it up.

"Are you dressed or have you been trying to make outside phone calls?" It was Justus.

I chuckled. "I had all day to make those calls, but the concierge kept me busy."

"Good. Now, are you ready, because I want to kiss you."

I giggled, then opened the door.

Justus looked at me, then down me slowly. His mouth dropped.

"Do you like?" I twirled around so he could see me dressed to the nines. "The concierge brought in a makeup artist and hair stylist to make me fit the dress."

"You are making it real hard for me to want to take you outside this room," he said.

"If you don't, then I will make a phone call." I shut the door behind me and wrapped my arm under his.

The Supper Club dined on two long tables in a spot inside the vineyard. It was the only lit area on the grounds. We had to follow tea lights to get to it. The tables were decorated in votive candles and white magnolia blossoms from the greenery. The storm from yesterday had cleared. Above us were dancing stars and a gorgeous full moon.

We were walking toward the first hole in the dark when I stopped Justus. "This is breathtaking."

"You're breathtaking." Justus took my hand and kissed it. "If we married tonight, would anyone mind?"

I shook my head. "You're asking the wrong woman, because I don't give a . . . I don't care."

He leaned down and kissed me. We held each other close until I felt something cold touching my back.

"Don't turn around, lover." I heard a familiar voice in my ear. "I don't want to tip off my employers."

"Detective Dixon?" Justus removed his hands from around my waist. "Are you here for the fund-raiser, too?"

I then realized the cold thing in my back wasn't her hand but the tip of a silencer. "No, honey. She's here to kill us."

"Maybe just you," she said.

"What do you want?" Justus asked.

"It's not *what* I want, it's *whom* do I want. Isn't that right, Angel?"

I stood stiffly. "I don't know what you're talking about. Justus and I are here to plan our wedding."

"And it happens to fall on the night of the Supper Club and Night Golf Fund-raiser? I don't think so."

"It's the truth. Her mom set this up as a gift to us."

"I bet she did. Did she also pay for Gabriel Hwang to be here, too?" Dixon asked.

Justus's brow furrowed. "What are you talking about?" He looked at me. "What is she talking about?"

My knee twitched. "I was trying to tell you yesterday. Gabe is alive."

Justus's face dropped. My eyes began to well up. I knew right then that as soon as I got the chance, I was killing Dixon for messing up my life.

"Oh, you didn't know." Dixon smirked. "I told you, Pastor, that I thought you weren't making the best choice. Now you know. Your lovely bride to be can't be engaged to two men. She's going to have to pick—or do you want me to pick for you, Angel? Just tell me where Hwang is and I'll leave you to your miserable life."

"She didn't know I was here," a voice said somewhere in the darkness.

Dixon spun around. "Who's that?"

"It's who you're looking for, and if you want me, you're going to have to come after me."

"I don't have to do anything, because I have your woman."

Maxim stepped from behind a shadow. "But I'm single, baby."

"Marshal!" she hissed.

I lunged for Justus and threw him on the ground before

bullets whistled through the air, and then I heard footsteps patter off toward the direction of the supper-club attendants.

Justus grunted under me. "Are you all right?"

"I've got to take her down or she's going to kill someone," I said to Justus.

"I'm sorry again," he said. "My heroic timing is always bad when it comes to you."

"Hush or you'll get us killed." I pulled him quietly.

I reached in my brassiere and pulled out my mini night goggles. I put them on and whispered, "Come with me."

"You can see in this darkness?" he asked.

"You can't whisper properly, so hush," I said, as I moved us toward one of the green rooms.

The door was locked, but I unlocked it with a gadget Tiger had bought me for Christmas. I hoped the place had some kind of trip alarm, so that it could alert the authorities we needed help.

"*Now* talk," I said to Justus.

He panted. "Did you know Maxim was here?"

"I don't need my phone to get in touch with a U.S. marshal."

"Charlie called him," Justus concluded.

"I think so." I nodded.

"And where is Gabe?"

We heard people screaming.

"I have to go. Don't you leave this room."

"I can't let you go out there and get hurt," he said.

"If you don't stay in here like I asked, you *will* get me hurt." I kissed his lips. "I did what you asked all weekend, now let me have my two cents."

"Okay, but before you go." He reached over and kissed

me so well, I almost forgot what it was I was supposed to do.

He let me go. I stumbled a little bit and pulled myself together.

"Wait." He caught my hand. "But you don't have a gun."

"A good hunter doesn't need one."

50

Saturday. It was too dark to see the time on my watch.
Somewhere between the 5th and 6th hole, Château Élan,
Braselton, Georgia

I ran through the golf course without shoes on. I heard shouts in the distance, but didn't hear anyone near me. It felt like the time Maxim and I were treading upstream in that bass boat toward the juke joint. I felt like a sitting duck.

My dress was light, so I decided to step out of it and took off the pearls and shiny costume jewelry. I had on a black slip and black undies underneath. I needed to look like a shadow.

As I tiptoed through the manicured lawn, I began to hear familiar voices. The moon's ray dipped into a manmade pond around some bushes. The silhouette of Francine Dixon pointing her gun at someone came into a moonlit view. I plodded toward her and her next victim.

When I reached her, she had Gabe on his knees. Maxim was sprawled on the ground alongside him. Unlike the last time I'd seen him in that position, this time I thought he was dead.

"You don't have to do this, Josette," Gabe said.

Josette? I asked myself. So Francine wasn't this trick's name?

"Don't call me that. You don't have the right to call me that anymore."

"I wanted out, Josette. I thought you did, too."

"I did until you fell in love with that reporter. You were supposed to kill her."

I gasped.

Josette spun around. "Angel, get over here before I kill Bella's father."

I didn't move.

"Get over here before I kill your friend Charlene."

What?!

I stepped out of the shadows. Charlie was kneeling in front of Gabe. She still had the clothes on she'd worn when I left her yesterday. Francine had to have come to my home.

"Trick, you've messed up now," I said.

"And you left me for this ghetto chick, Gabriel." She smirked. "This is why you had to die."

"But I didn't, and I didn't dime you out when the feds asked me who all the players were. Why do you think that?"

"Because you thought you knew who came to kill you," I said. "But there was another shooter in that parking garage. She had a penchant for wearing stilettos in the worst places."

"I learned my lesson. I'm wearing sensible shoes to-night." She chuckled.

"You know, I haven't liked you since the first day I laid eyes on you," I said. "Everybody thought I was being un-fair, but I was right all along. You're one evil broad."

"That's the best you got?" She scoffed, while walking closer. "You're so great with words. I thought you could come up with something better than that, but then again, I did switch your drink with a brew your Uncle Pete was familiar with."

"You witch." My heart skipped a beat; I stumbled back a little. "You poisoned me with contaminated chacha?"

She smiled. "I did, and I should have done it a long time ago. It would have saved the body count. Your friend and former lover showing up were like cherries on top."

I was so stunned I couldn't move. "Are you saying you killed all these people because of me?"

"No, I'm saying I had most of them killed because of you, but your uncle—that snitch—and your baby daddy here—what a waste of a good mind; you should have been grateful. And as for your friend here . . . she's never around when you need her." She walked around to me.

"And what about Salvador?"

She pointed her gun at me. My vision was too blurry to see what she had in her chamber. "I haven't hurt him. He knows nothing of this."

"I'm pretty sure he does now. When I think back on the day you and your buddy ambushed me and Gabe in the parking garage just before ROTB, you weren't a great shot. But that was over six years ago, so I assumed you had gotten better. You haven't." I snickered. "That's why you've resorted to poison. Because you totally missed all your kill zones."

She placed the barrel near my temple. "Do you think I need glasses to make this shot?"

"Why do you talk so much?" I heard my voice slur. "Go ahead and do it. It beats the alternative, listening to your stuck-up voice."

"I thought that after all this time you would want to know why I've done what I've done."

"Nope. You can save that for *Matlock* or *Moonlighting* or one of those detective television shows, because I don't care why. All I need to know is you will be going to hell tonight."

She stepped back. "Sorry to burst your bubble, but I won't be going anywhere. The only person that knows who I am is Gabriel Hwang, you, and your crew. And you are all about to die. I may have a little fun with Justus, but he will be mine, too."

I grinned. "You think you're slick, but this isn't that kind of show."

She kept her gun pointed at my face. "What is that supposed to mean? This isn't that kind of show? You're not running this. I run this—"

Swoosh.

Her eyes widened. She looked down and saw my dagger hit her in the chest.

Swoosh.

Another one hit her. Her gun slipped out of her hand. It hit the ground with a thud and didn't go off.

My third dagger sliced the air with the same *swoosh* sound.

She dropped to her knees and coughed.

I stepped forward and kicked her gun to the far right of us.

She looked up at me. She was breathing heavy. A trickle of blood oozed from the side of her lips.

I pulled another dagger from my back holster and stood over her. Her hands were still in midair but trembling. She was in shock.

"I don't like to be cut off when I'm talking. Now . . . where were we?" I turned to see the police sirens blinking near the inn. "I've run out of time, so I'll have to table this discussion."

I spun around and threw my uncle's last dagger into the

place that would stop her dead in her tracks. I didn't bother to listen to her body fold to the ground.

Saturday, 11:00 PM
Somewhere between the 5th and 6th hole, Château Élan,
Braselton, Georgia

"So you finally got the chance to use your knives?" Tiger said, as he wrapped his tuxedo jacket around my shoulders.

The police had Justus and Charlie sequestered for questioning. Gabe was talking with his handler at the FBI. Maxim was on a gurney in an EMS van, and Francine Josette Dixon was resting in a body bag in the Braselton Coroner's van. I sat at the Supper Club table giving my testimony to Marshal Sanchez, after Tiger had injected an antidote in my arm for that bad shine.

From what I heard, Dixon was the last member of this organized hired-hit-man ring. Gabe and Braden were hired to cook their books, but Gabe had turned FBI informant. He didn't die as Salvador and I thought we witnessed. Somehow he survived and entered the witness protection program (WITSEC).

He didn't know I was pregnant when he left, else they would have forced me to go with him. Dixon had been watching me all this time to see if Gabe had actually died.

"When rumors of him being in the city surfaced, Dixon got desperate. She blackmailed Ty to keep extra tabs on you. He had no clue she was that shady. She was using him and he didn't know how to get out of it without hurting his wife," Sanchez said.

"How was she involved in Sean's death?" I asked.

"She wasn't. She was just associated with it because of Ty."

"You have either two ways to live in this world: good or bad. When you make that choice, you gravitate to the one you serve," Tiger said. "The circle of organized crime in this state is small and she was spinning with it."

"Thanks for getting my message and bringing my knives to me," I said. "I knew that girl was crazy, but dang. She was choco loco."

He grinned. "Frisco used to say that."

"I feel like Frisco was working by my side tonight."

"He probably was, but you know, Angel Soft, you can always rely on me to be your heavy."

I scoffed. "Let's not go back down that road. My head is killing me."

"No, hear me out." He sat beside me. "I know I've left you hanging the last couple of years. The business was growing and I didn't know how to manage it all, but I got it under control now, thanks to your sister."

"Please, this is not the time to talk about Ava."

"I'm talking about Whitney."

"Really?" My head began to swim.

"Yeah, she's taking care of the office real good. I know you want her to go to law school, and I want her to go, too—"

"Tiger, stop." I panted. "I think I'm passing out."

51

Sunday morning
Home, Sugar Hill, Georgia

I dreamed of doors slamming, a shower running, children laughing, Bella running through my room, squealing, hugging me, and kissing my cheeks until they went numb. And then I felt a soft tapping on my forehead. *Thud. Thud. Thud.* The tapping continued until it jerked me into consciousness. *Splat.* I opened one eye, saw a nightmare, and closed it.

Thud. Another tap on my head.

"Mama!" I grabbed her hand and observed what was in it. She held a wooden spoon. She had been hitting me with a wooden sauce spoon from my kitchen. I tried not to growl, but I was sleepy and agitated now. "Were you hitting my head with a spoon while I slept?"

"How else was I going to wake you?" she asked, but it wasn't a question.

"Mom, I have had quite a night and I'm tired." I turned over and snuggled into my pillow. "What are you doing back here so fast anyway?"

Then she smacked me across my backside with her hand. "Get up!"

I jumped and followed her command.

"What is going on?!" I rubbed my butt and grabbed my duvet cover over my chest. I was cold.

"You have a lot of explaining to do," she hissed.

"For what?" I huffed. "And why are you here? You're supposed to be in the Islands until Tuesday? It's Sunday, The Lord's Day and . . . My Rest Day."

"Shush. Rest, my . . ." She took the spoon and popped me on my arm. It was the only body part that I hadn't covered. "You can't rest until you answer three things."

"Fine . . ." I groaned and threw my head back against the headboard.

"One. Early, I mean early last night, I received an interesting phone call from the concierge at Château Élan thanking me for bringing so much great PR to their resort, but regrettably rescinding our contract to host your wedding because of new remodeling to the Château, thanks to you, the U.S. Marshal's Office, and DeKalb County Police. What in hell, Angel?" She paused. "WHAT IN HELL!"

"Hold on, now. That's not fair. They can't put this on me. Francine Dixon is responsible for what went down and it's all over the news. I can prove it. Get a paper. She tried to kill me. In fact, she tried to kill me and Gabe years ago when I was pregnant. But it's all good. She's . . . gone."

"I saw the news online, so I know what happened." She smacked her lips and rolled her neck. "But how dare you let that woman almost shoot out the winery? You couldn't have killed her sooner? All that wine."

She shook her head and mean mugged me at the same time.

"Um . . . perhaps if I had added killing her to my daily planner, I could have done it. . . . ?" I shrugged. "My head hurts. I'm kind of woozy. I think your spoon beating has aggravated my old concussion."

"Which takes me to Number Two: Where is Gabriel Hwang?"

"How does that take you to . . . ?" I laid my head back against the headboard. "He's alive and he knows about Bella. In fact, if it wasn't for him . . . never mind. That is too long a story to tell right now. . . ." I sat up and rubbed my eyes. "Is that why you flew back here? Gabe?"

"No, dear. I flew back here because of Number Three." She pointed at me.

"You came back for me?"

"Yes, I came back to see if my baby was okay, but then when I practically had to break down your bedroom door to get in here, I'm shocked to find you in bed with that." She pointed at me again. "What is that?"

"What are you talking about?" I wanted to shout, but my head hurt so badly I just wanted to lay back down. "Tell me what you're talking about so I can go back to sleep. My head is killing me."

"Maybe your head hurts because you slept on that huge diamond wedding band on your finger."

"Wedding band? What are you talking about?"

"I know what I'm talking about. I can smell diamonds from miles away. Yes, young lady. You're hiding it under your duvet along with a wedding gown that I didn't pick out for you. I don't understand you, Evangeline Grace Crawford. Why do you have to be so difficult?"

"You're talking too fast. My head is swimming. Okay." I took a deep breath. "What are you talking about? What ring? What gown? I don't have a—"

I pulled my left hand from under my bedcovers and lifted my hand toward my face. I gasped. *Holy Cow.* Sure as a Georgia summer day was long, there was a white gold and diamond tall wedding band with diamond crosses etched all around. It was stunning and it was on my hand.

And then I looked down. I was in bed wearing a blush pink wedding gown. The color looked so pretty on my skin. The corset was filled with beading and blush roses and the skirt was tulle and more roses and more roses and fluffy.

"Wow." I ran my hands up and down the dress.

"Woooh . . ." Whitney must have come inside my room while I was fawning over my bridal gown, because I hadn't noticed her. "Did you get married? Gurrl!"

Mama popped her in the back of the head with the spoon. "That was my question, but I do have another."

"What now?" I gulped and looked up at them.

Their attention was no longer on me but on my bathroom door. I heard water running and a man's voice singing.

"Who's in the bathroom?" Whitney whispered.

"The groom, I guess," I said as I played around with the tulle in my skirt.

Ker lurk. This time the wooden spoon popped me on the top of my head. *Ow.* I looked up.

Mom glared and threw her hands on her waist. "What do you mean, 'you guess'? You don't know who the groom is?"

"There was a lot of wine. I don't know . . . My head hurts."

"Eww, you're a bad bride." Whitney giggled.

"Do you think this is funny?" Mom hissed, then turned to me. "Are you aware of the mess you've made? How dare you elope and do this to me?"

"I'm not sure if I did." I threw my hands up. "I can't remember what happened. Must be because of that bad shine last night."

"Foolish girl." Mom pursed her lips.

The bathroom door jiggled.

Mom gasped and stepped back. She bumped into Whitney, who did her best to keep from pushing our mother back.

Whitney ran over to my side of the bed. "I like a good mystery, so let me get a better look."

I clutched Whitney's back and hid behind it. "Let's find out who the groom is together. Shall we?"

Meet Angel Crawford for the first time in

A Good Excuse to Be Bad

In stores now!

Turn the page for an excerpt from
A Good Excuse to Be Bad. . . .

1

Wednesday, 11:00 PM
Club Night Candy, Underground Atlanta, Georgia

I f I weren't so screwed up, I would've sold my soul a long
time ago for a handsome man who made me feel pretty or
who could at least treat me to a millionaire's martini. Instead, I lingered over a watered-down sparkling apple and
felt sorry about what I was about to do to the blue-eyed
bartender standing in front of me. Although I shouldn't;
after all, I am a bail recovery agent. It's my job to get my
skip, no matter the cost. Yet, I had been wondering lately,
what was this job costing me?

For the past six weeks, Dustin, the owner of Night
Candy and my Judas for this case, had tended the main bar
on Wednesday nights. His usual bartender was out on ma-
ternity leave. According to Big Tiger, she would return tomorrow, so I had to make my move tonight.

Yet, I wished Big Tiger would have told me how cute and
how nice Dustin was. I might have changed my tactic or
worn a disguise, so that I could flirt with him again for a
different, more pleasant outcome. See, good guys don't like
to be strong-armed. It's not sexy, even if it is for a good reason. Such is life . . .

Dustin poured me another mocktail. Although I detested the drink's bittersweet taste and smell, I smiled and thanked him anyway. It was time to spark a different, darker conversation. The fact that his eyes twinkled brighter than the fake lights dangling above his station made it a little hard for me to end the good time I was having with him.

"If you need anything, let me know." He stared at me for a while, then left to assist another person sitting at the far end of the bar.

I blushed before he walked away.

Get it together. I shook it off and reminded myself that I was on a deadline. I wanted his help, not his hotness and definitely not another free, fizzled, sugar water. It was time to do what I was paid to do.

When he returned to my station to wipe my area again, I caught his hand.

He looked down at my hand on his, glanced at my full glass, and grinned. "Obviously you don't need another refill."

I giggled. "No, I don't, but I do need something from you."

"I was hoping you would say that." He smiled and took my hand, then held it closer to his chest. "Because I've wanted to know more about you ever since you walked into my club."

"Great." I couldn't help but giggle back. "Does that mean I can ask you a personal question?"

He nodded. "Ask me anything, sweetie."

I leaned forward and whispered in his ear. "Do you have a problem with me taking someone out of here?"

"Of course not. You can take me out. My patrons don't mind, long as the tap stays open." He chuckled.

"No, Blue Eyes. I'm not talking about you. I'm talking

about dragging someone out of your club. Very ladylike, of course, but I wanted to get your approval before I did it."

He stepped back, looked around, then returned to me. "I don't think I understood you, sweetie. You want to do what in my club?"

"Take someone out."

He contorted his grin into a weird jacked-up W. "And what does that mean?"

"It means that you have someone in the club that I want, and I'll shut this club down if I don't get whom I came for. I don't want to cause a scene, so I'm asking for your cooperation."

He scoffed. "Is this some kind of joke?"

"No, it's a shakedown, Dustin Gregory Taylor, and surprisingly, you're the one who sent me. So I need you to play along with me right now. Okay? Sorry for the inconvenience."

"Sorry?" He stumbled back and let go of my hand. "Who are you? How do you know my name?"

"You're causing a scene, Dustin, and that's not good for business. Why don't you come back over here and I'll tell you . . . quietly."

He looked around the bar. The club was jumping so hard only a few people around us noticed his confused facial expression and his almost backstroke into the glass beer mug tower that stood behind him. He ran his hand through his hair, then walked back to me.

He murmured, "Who told you about me?"

"We have a mutual friend." I pulled out my cell phone, scrolled to a saved picture, and showed it to him. "I'm sure you know the man in this mug shot. It's your cousin Cade. Correct?"

His brow wrinkled; then he sighed. "What has he done now?"

"What he always does, Dusty, robs banks and skips bail. But do you want to know the worst thing he's done?"

Dustin just looked at me. He didn't respond.

"Well, I'll tell you anyway. He convinced your mom to put a second mortgage on the family house, in order to pay his bail the last time he got caught. Guess what? He got caught three months ago and then he missed his court date, which means—"

Dustin yanked the towel off his shoulder. "Say what?"

"Your mom's home is in jeopardy if I don't find him tonight. My boss Big Tiger Jones of BT Trusted Bail Bonds is ready to turn your childhood home into his Smyrna office, if you know what I mean."

"Son of a . . ." He turned around in a full 360. His towel twirled with him. "This isn't fair."

I nodded. "Life can be that way sometimes."

"I had no clue he had gotten back into trouble. He didn't say anything to me, and my mom . . . No wonder she hasn't been sleeping well lately." He rung the towel in his hands, then snapped it against the bar. "I don't believe this."

"Believe me, I understand how frustrating it is to watch your family make horrible mistakes and you or someone you love pay the price for their burden." I thought about my sister Ava. "Dustin, I have to take Cade downtown tonight. We both know that he's here in Night Candy right now and has been sleeping in your back office since his ex-girlfriend Lola kicked him out of her house. So tell me how you want this to go down, nice or easy?"

"Neither." He folded his arms over his chest. "You can't do this, not here. It'll ruin me."

I sighed. "I know, ergo this conversation."

Last year after a stream of violence and crime, the Atlanta Mayor's Office and the Atlanta Police Department issued a new ordinance against crime. Any businesses that appeared to facilitate criminal activity would be shut down. Night Candy already had two strikes against it: for a burglary gone bad that ended in the brutal murder of Atlanta socialite and real-estate heiress Selena Turner, and then there was that cat brawl between two NFL ballers' wives that was televised on a nationally syndicated reality TV show. The club definitely didn't need a showdown between a habitual bank robber and me. I'd tear this place up and anyone who stood between me and Big Tiger's money. I'm that bad, if I need to be.

"Maybe it won't." I touched his hand with hopes that I could calm him down. The last thing I needed was Cade to notice Dusty's agitation. "But you must do as I say."

Dustin leaned toward me. His starry eyes now looked like the eye of a hurricane. I shuddered. Man, he was hot.

"Listen to me," he said. "It's not you I'm concerned about. Cade has made it clear to everyone that he'll never go back to jail. He will fight. Lady, he'll burn my club down with all of us inside before he goes back in."

I patted his shoulders. "I believe you, and that's why Big Tiger sent me. See? Look at me."

"I've been looking at you all night."

"Exactly. This froufrou that I have on is a disguise."

"Didn't look like a disguise to me."

"That's my point, Dustin. I can sweet talk Cade out the back where Big Tiger's waiting for him in the alley. No one will suspect a thing, not even the plainclothes APD dudes hanging around near the champagne fountain."

He looked past me toward the fountain, then lowered his head. "I didn't see them there."

"That's because your attention was on me, just like Cade's will be once he sees me." I grinned. "All I need you to do is to introduce me to him. I'll take it from there."

"Makes sense, but there's a problem." He ruffled his hair

again. "Cade's in the cabanas upstairs, but I can't leave the bar. I'll let Ed, the VIP security guard, know you're coming. He'll parade you around for me. What's your name?"

"Angel."

"Angel, that name fits you." He looked at me and then over me. His eyes danced a little; then he frowned. "You're very pretty and too sweet looking to be so hard. Are you really a bounty hunter?"

I slid off the stool, smoothed down my hair and the coral silk chiffon mini cocktail dress my little sister Whitney picked out for me, then turned in the direction of the upstairs cabanas. "Watch and find out."

Night Candy sat in the heart of downtown Atlanta— underneath it, to be more exact—on Kenny's Alley, the nightclub district inside Underground Atlanta. Real-estate moguls, music executives, and Atlanta local celebrities frequented the club whenever they were in town. They also hosted popular mainstay events there. The upscale spot had become so über trendy that unless you were on the VIP list, getting inside was harder than finding a deadbeat dad owing child support. But getting admitted was worth the effort.

On the inside, Night Candy was its name: dark, indulgent, and smooth. Chocolate and plum colors dripped all over the lounge. Velvet and leather wrapped around the bar like cordial cherries. It even smelled like a fresh-opened Russell Stover's box. Dustin looked and smelled even better. I wished we'd met under different circumstances.

The club had three levels with VIP at the top and the best live music I'd heard in a long time: vintage soul, reminiscent of Motown girl groups with a dose of hip-hop and go-go sprinkled on top. My hips sashayed up the stairs to the music until I stopped.

I checked my watch and huffed. In three hours the judge could revoke Cade's bail. There was no time for errors. Cade had to go down now.

I texted Big Tiger. He had assured me he would be outside waiting for us. Trouble was, Big Tiger's promises had 50/50 odds. I promised myself to hire a male tagalong next time, preferably one as big as this Ed guy standing in front of me.

Whoa. I reached the stairs he guarded. Ed was a massive, bronzed bald-headed giant. He had brawn and swagger. My little sister Whitney would eat him up. Dustin must have given him the green light, because by the time I reached the top of the staircase, he was smiling and holding out his hand to help me inside the VIP lounge.

As he gave me a personal tour of what I called a Godiva version of a party room, I spotted Cade and exhaled. The Taylor men definitely had great genes. I didn't have to take a second look at his Fulton County Corrections Office booking photo to know it was him. He was drop-dead handsome—bald and dark, a bad combination for me. I'm a recovering bad-boy-holic. I hoped he wouldn't give me too much trouble, but the thought of a good crawl with this guy was enough to send me to church first thing Sunday morning.

I melted into a milk chocolate lounge chair across from his cabana and waited for his jaw to drop at the sight of me. And boy, did it. He was talking to a barely clad and quite lanky teenybopper when he saw me through the sheer curtain covering the cabana. I grinned and slid my dress up too high for a woman my age to ever do without feeling like some dumb tramp. I wished I could say I was embarrassed acting that way, but I couldn't. I liked having a good excuse to be bad sometimes.

The sad thing about all of this was that the young

woman holding on to Cade didn't notice him licking his lips at me. After five minutes of his gross act, she stood up and walked toward me. My chest froze. Maybe she had seen him and was now coming over to warn me to back off or to claw my eyes out.

Yeah, right, like I would let that happen. Homegirl better think twice about dealing with me. But I didn't want to hurt her. I didn't get all shiny and done up to scrap with some girl over a fugitive. Besides, I promised Dustin I wouldn't show out up in here. So I gripped the chair as she approached and relaxed when she breezed past. I watched her enter the ladies' room, then patted my cheeks with my palms. I was getting too old for this crap.

As soon as the child left his side, Cade slinked his way over to where I sat. I looked below at the bar where Dustin watched me. I waved my fingers at him until he dropped the martini he was making. *Man, he was cute.*

While I daydreamed of a date with Dustin, Cade stood over me. "So you know my cousin?"

I turned toward him. "Is that your way of introducing yourself to me, or are you jealous?"

He smiled and reached for my hand. "My apologies." He kissed my hand. "I'm Cadence Taylor, but everyone calls me Cade. Don't tell my cousin, but I think you're stunning."

"No, I'm not." I giggled. "I'm Angel."

"I can see that." He sat beside me. "Like a guardian angel . . . no, a cherub."

"More like an archangel."

He clapped and laughed. "Not you. You don't look like the fighting type. You have sweetness written all over you. You're definitely Dusty's type."

Oh, great. Now you tell me. I moved closer toward him. "And you have 'Bad Boy' written all over you."

He grinned. "You don't have to be afraid of me. I'm a good guy when I need to be."

I smiled back. "Can you promise to be good, if I ask you for a favor?"

He nodded. "Anything for you, Angel."

"I'm tired. I'm ready to go home. Can you escort me to my car? I was supposed to wait for Dustin, but I don't have the stamina for this club life."

"Of course, you don't, because you're a good girl." He stood up and reached for my hand. "Surprisingly, I'm not a clubber either. How about you leave your car and I take you for a quiet night drive through the city, then over to the Cupcakery for some dessert. By the time we get back, Dusty will be closing up this place."

"I don't know. I don't think Dustin would like that so much. Sounds too much like a date."

"Yeah, I guess so." He scratched his head like his cousin, another Taylor trait.

"Besides, your girlfriend would be upset if you left her here."

"What girlfriend?"

I pointed toward the ladies' room. "Her."

"Oh, her. We're not together."

I came closer and whispered in his ear. "Neither are Dustin and me."

He smiled and his eyes outshined the VIP lounge.

"Why don't you escort me to my car and follow me home instead, just to make sure I get there safe?"

He placed his hand at the small of my back. "I can do that."

Because Cade almost carried me out of Night Candy, I couldn't text Big Tiger to let him know that I was coming outside. All I could do was hope he was where he said he would be.

We stepped outside. No Big Tiger. I hit the hands-free Talk button on my phone earpiece and voice-activated Big Tiger's phone number to dial. I got nothing. My heart began to race. Where was he?

"Is something wrong?" Cade asked. His hands were all over me.

I removed his hands, but said nothing. I had no words.

Sometimes bail bondsmen needed women locators to lure a defendant out of their hiding spot. I didn't mind doing it. Honestly, I needed the money, but we had a deal. I brought them out; he rode them in. So why was I out here alone? Well, not entirely alone . . . with Octopus Cade.

Cade watched me. "Are you having second thoughts?"

"I have a confession to make." I scrambled for something to say while fiddling for my handcuffs. They were trapped somewhere under the chiffon.

"So do I." He pulled me toward him. "I can't keep my hands off you."

I wanted to cuff him, but I couldn't, because he had wrapped his hands around my waist.

"Not here, not like this." I removed his hold on me again, but held on to one of his hands.

He smiled until he felt—I assumed—my cold handcuffs clank against his wrists. "What the—"

"You've violated your bail agreement, Mr. Taylor," I said. Still no Big Tiger in sight. "So you'll have to come with me."

He chuckled as he dangled my handcuffs—the ones I thought had locked him to me—over his head for me to see. A piece of my dress had wedged between the clamp. They were broken. My heart hit the floor.

"Unless these handcuffs are chaining me to your bed, I'm not going anywhere with you, sweetie."

Then, quicker than I anticipated, he head-butted me. I saw stars and fell to the ground. A pain so bad crossed my forehead, it reminded me of labor pains. I couldn't scream. I had to breathe through it to ease the pain.

The head-butting must have stung Cade, too, because he stumbled before he could get his footing. I caught one of his legs and clutched it. I closed my eyes and groaned as he dragged me down the alley. Through the excruciating bumps and scrapes I received holding on to Cade, past the onlookers who didn't care to help this poor damsel in distress, I asked myself, "Why wouldn't I let go?"

My forehead and my skinned knees throbbed now. I'm pretty sure Whitney's dress looked like wet trash. To make matters worse, I was angry with myself for putting myself in this position. I couldn't afford to be so cavalier anymore. I knew that before I took this stupid assignment. I knew it while I sat at the bar. I knew it the day I became a mother, but I did it anyway. What's wrong with me? I couldn't leave my daughter alone without a parent. Now I had to hurt this fool to get back to my baby in one piece.

Cade stopped and cursed. My heart beat so fast and loud, I prayed it would calm down so I could prepare for his next move.

"Angel, sweetie, I think we need to have a little talk."

He pulled me up by my hair, my store-bought hair. I wore a combed-in hairpiece because I didn't have time to go to a hair salon and I didn't want to damage my hair. However, Cade's tugging made the plastic teeth dig deeper into my scalp. I screamed to keep from fainting.

"Shut up!" He slapped me. "You stupid—"

Before he could say another word, I grounded my feet then threw a round kick so high and hard with my left leg that I heard his jaw crack against my stilettos. He hit the ground, unconscious. While he was knocked out, I turned him over and handcuffed him again, but from the back this time and with the chiffon visibly gone.

I dialed Big Tiger. "Where are you?"

"Where did I tell you I was gon' be?" Big Tiger's voice seemed crystal clear. "Right here."

Someone tapped my shoulder. I jumped.

"It's a good thing I showed up when I did. You could have killed the man. I'da lost my money and then I would have had to take care of your raggedy bond." Big Tiger laughed, then helped me hoist Cade up. "Why didn't you wait instead of messing up your sister's dress? How many dresses have you slaughtered now?"

I looked at him and growled. "Say that again. I dare you."

"And your face, Angel Soft." He squinted. "I think we'd better call 911 after we put homeboy in my truck."

I walked toward Big Tiger with the intent to give him a right hook across his jaw. When I lunged, I think I fainted. I don't know what happened next and I almost didn't care until the EMS worker asked me whom I should call to let them know I was being taken to the emergency room.

"Call my sisters. Tell them where I am and make sure Ava comes to get me."

Then I faded back to black and it felt good. In my dreams, Dustin was on his knees proposing to me with some chocolates and a pink diamond.

His voice was so clear. "Angel, will you . . . be healed in the name of God."

God?